More Praise for The Unknown Knowns

"Rotter's perceptive and humorous story goes beyond the obvious sendup to explore the private and at times desperate ways his characters strive to secure their own homeland, from the borders of their bedrooms to the cargo of their dreams, showing how the logic of personal rhetoric is never far removed from the political. . . . Rotter's imagination is formidable and fresh."
—Joseph Salvatore, *The New York Times Book Review*

"Pokes serious fun at the paranoia that has stalked America since 9/11." —*Elle* ("Trust Us" pick)

"Rotter nails both the lingo of bureaucratic self-justification and the fantasy-inflected imagery of psychosexual arrested development in which our public discourse is so thoroughly marinated, offering a satiric funhouse mirror image of modern American reality."
—Amanda Heller, *The Boston Globe*

"Ambitious . . . Unlike his protagonist, Rotter maintains control of his imagination, delivering a fast-paced, inventive book that tests the waters of fiction and fantasy and emerges victorious."
—Adrienne Day, *Time Out New York*

"Riotous yet highly controlled . . . Rotter [has] imaginative verve and an eye for absurdity—personal, literary and political."
—Kerry Fried, *Newsday*

"Immediately, we know we are in Paranoiaville; take a left at Surreal and go down into Dada. And it feels good, yes, it does, to laugh. . . . '[Has] our collective disinterest in and ignorance about a lost aquatic civilization with an unapologetic feminist worldview finally come back to bite us?' You tell me. When you stop laughing."
—Susan Salter Reynolds, *Los Angeles Times*

THE UNKNOWN KNOWNS

A Novel

JEFFREY ROTTER

SCRIBNER

New York   London   Toronto   Sydney

SCRIBNER

A Division of Simon & Schuster, Inc.
1230 Avenue of the Americas
New York, NY 10020

First Scribner trade paperback edition March 2010

SCRIBNER and design are registered trademarks of The Gale Group, Inc.,
used under license by Simon & Schuster, Inc., the publisher of this work.

For information about special discounts for bulk purchases,
please contact Simon & Schuster Special Sales at 1-866-506-1949
or business@simonandschuster.com.

The Simon & Schuster Speakers Bureau can bring authors to your live event.
For more information or to book an event contact the Simon & Schuster Speakers
Bureau at 1-866-248-3049 or visit our website at www.simonspeakers.com.

Designed by Kyoko Watanabe

Manufactured in the United States of America

1   3   5   7   9   10   8   6   4   2

Library of Congress Control Number: 2008030705

ISBN 978-1-4165-8702-6
ISBN 978-1-4165-8703-3 (pbk)
ISBN 978-1-4165-9546-5 (ebook)

For more information, please visit www.jeffreyrotter.com

For Margaret and Felix

"There are known knowns. There are things we know that we know. There are known unknowns. That is to say, there are things that we now know we don't know. But there are also unknown unknowns. There are things we do not know we don't know."

—*Donald Rumsfeld, February 12, 2002*

ONE

The obvious way to describe water is with adjectives. People like to say water is murky or dappled or turbulent or calm. They call it brackish, crystalline, emerald, white. Deep, shallow, filmy, or unfathomable. But all those adjectives don't even come close to describing water like it really is. They just float across the surface, like dead leaves or algae.

You could also try describing water with action verbs. You could say it rushes, or pours, or drips. You could also say it seeps, for instance. Water can boil or it can freeze or it can steam. But it doesn't matter how many verbs you throw at the water; they don't stick either. Trying to describe water by what it does is kind of like telling a story by throwing a book at your wife.

Another way people sometimes describe water is in context. I'll give you an example: a man walks by making water noises. His tube socks are drenched and they're going *squish, squish, squish*. With every step he takes: *squish, squish*. But when you ask the guy if he wants a dry pair—you have the socks right there in your hand; you even offer them to him—he shakes his head no. And that's when you hear it: you hear the fluid slosh inside his skull like milk in a coconut.

Here's another example of describing water in context. A little kid is pulled out of a swimming pool. His skin is red and raw. He's crying without making a sound. Something bad has been done to the water.

Or here's an even better example of water in context: two women go over a waterfall in a big bucket. The water is so crazy all around them that no one can hear them screaming, not even the women themselves. An ambulance backs up to the edge of the water. The lights are insistent, swirling. They paint the mountain red, and to look at them makes you feel like you don't have enough pockets to put your hands in.

There are probably other examples that I'm sure you could come up with. But here's the one I keep coming back to, the one that's relevant to my present circumstance. A guy jumps into a swimming pool, pointing his toes to mitigate the splash. Water knifes up inside his swim trunks, it pinches his nipples. He blows bubbles through his nose to prevent the water from entering his skull. The water floods his thinning hair and his body hangs limp in the pool light. The body hangs limp while the guy thinks about water.

That guy is me. I am the guy in the water thinking about water.

TWO

More context. My name is Jim Rath. I was born in Columbia, South Carolina, where I grew to my current, completely uninspiring height of five foot six. Five years ago, for reasons that were obscure at the time, even to me, I moved to Colorado Springs. I am currently age thirty-eight, though that number seems to be changing rapidly and time hasn't been especially friendly to me. I'm hairy-armed and cowering, a guy you'd expect to see squatting by a campfire just a few weeks before the beginning of history. People say I have a high forehead, but I know what that means. I'm losing my hair. No great loss; I was never all that handsome or brave anyway. And my balding caveman looks never matter much when I am standing underwater.

It was after hours in the hotel pool at a Colorado Springs

Hilton. The month was August but the water felt more like March or April. I descended, eyes closed behind my scuba mask, until I felt the grout and the grit of the tile floor against the balls of my feet. The pockets of my Jams were lined with lead fishing weights to keep me from floating away. I drew down the intake of the snorkel so it would barely breach the water. My presence would be difficult if not impossible to detect from above. Then I opened my eyes and described what I saw through the lens of my diving mask, writing everything down in a waterproof notepad.

My goal was a thorough understanding of water. But not on a chemical level. Not in any way that you could test. That wasn't of any interest to me. I had more consequential interests. I wanted to know why the water is always calling to us, what it wants to tell us. Where do we belong in relation to it? I asked. What is the water hiding down there? I was in the pool to ask the hard probing questions that no one else would ask. Because I figured out some time ago that the truest and most singular way to know the water is by getting right in it. By reaching in with bare hands and pulling out a couple of its slippery monsters.

For six months in 2006 I spent every free night I had at the Colorado Springs Hilton hotel, standing for hours at a time on the swimming-pool floor, my head totally submerged, just gazing into the water. I was fortunate enough at that juncture in my life to have a lot of free nights, so I was at the Hilton about six or seven times a week. At first all I saw looking into the water was water. But as time passed and my senses got more acute, I started to see other stuff. Crazy stuff. Edifying stuff.

There is—and this sentence is the threshold of plausibility that I will ask you to cross if you dare to read the rest of my story—a lost civilization in the water.

THE UNKNOWN KNOWNS

I'll say that again, and invert the sentence, so you can get used to the idea: in the water there's a lost civilization.

And what I've seen over the past twelve months has me totally convinced that it's been down there for thousands and thousands of years just waiting for us to discover it. I have a name for it, which I made up myself, but it fits. Nautika.

Though I arrived at this discovery almost a year ago, and all kinds of negative circumstances have intervened since then, my eyes still ache with the marvels I beheld down there in the Hilton pool and in hotel pools across the state of Colorado. I've been diagnosed with a chlorine condition, and I still take drops. But I'd trade both my eyes to see it all again. I'd trade my wife (again). I'd trade my happiness (again). And (again) I'd trade my freedom. Again, again. Even though the ankle bracelet doesn't fit like they said. You don't "get used to it like a new pair of dress shoes."

I was standing on the bottom of the Hilton pool. I looked up to see the surface rippling overhead, responding to the whims of the central cooling unit like a kind of weather. Up through the varying strata of water I studied the domed roof of the hotel solarium, its brown steel ribbing and frosted glass expanding against the moonlight like the room itself was taking a deep breath.

We're in the habit of calling it the surface of the water, but couldn't it just as easily be the boundary of the air? Because it all depends on your perspective, where you're coming from. And either you cross the air-water boundary in the spirit of humanity and good faith or else maybe you should just stay in your lawn chair with your beer and tell your wife how pretty the ocean is.

I consulted my watch. It was a Helvner, waterproof and pressure-resistant to a depth of five hundred meters. Only three thousand of these babies are made each year by special appointment of the Saudi navy. You won't believe what they retail for. I'm lucky to have a generous uncle with connections in the Mideast naval community and cash to burn. Of course I don't have the Helvner anymore. That was one of the first things I had to sacrifice.

I made a note of the time in my waterproof notebook: 10:49 p.m. Then I focused my eyes on a light burning at the far end of the pool. I thought simple thoughts; I thought about hydrogen bonding and refraction, basic properties of water. And slowly, so slowly it seemed to happen in reverse, I entered the semiamphibi-ous state of advanced consciousness known to the Nautikons as *ooeee.* This is not the place to divulge the secrets of *ooeee,* but suf-fice it to say it's a regimen of circular inner breathing designed to stimulate the latent man-gills. And in my case I also use a snorkel.

It is in this altered state of awareness that I receive certain "reports" from the annals of Nautika. They come to me like radio waves but thicker, with colors and bodily sensations attached. I have visions, smeared and echoey, but visions nonetheless. I get the narrative and absorb the granules of sociological detail that are critical to my knowledge of our lost aquatic ancestry.

Yes, our lost aquatic ancestry. You think I can't smell your sus-picion? Oh, I can smell it, all right—the fruited stench of unbe-lief, even through the supposedly impenetrable membrane of the page. You have your reservations. The scrutiny in the eyebrow area? I'm painfully familiar with it. Jilly did that too, the director at the Center for Gender and Power. She was afraid of my ideas. So was my wife. You think I'm crazy too.

Jim is a damaged person, you think. His reason has been cracked by emotional pressures exerted from his social milieu and from his inner makeup dating back to a codependent childhood with a single mom. That's probably what you're thinking, or words to that effect. You're figuring this guy's life went sour so his mind retreated somewhere less stressful. Maybe he has a chemical deficiency or a surplus, or both. Maybe his wife contributed to this imbalance through negligence. It happens.

Believe me, I understand your doubts. I'd have them too if I weren't me. But I am me, as evidenced by my being held accountable for actions widely perceived as mine. And besides, if you think this is hard to swallow, just wait; the curve of credibility doesn't get any gentler from here on out.

There are questions that demand answers. Sure there are. Why was a guy named Jim Rath spending hour upon precious hour in a hotel pool in a city called Colorado Springs? What motivated him? I wouldn't blame anyone for thinking my behavior was out there, or even antisocial. I wouldn't even blame you for concluding, circumstantially, that I did all those terrible things they say I did. My wife talked to CNN. So did some regular lady from my hometown who I'd never met, about intubation, paralysis, how I'd never understand what that felt like. They all say I'll be judged. And they're right: I am being judged. But believe it or not, Jim Rath's motives were pure, and his heart, the private heart imprisoned within his public heart, it is fully innocent.

I'm a curator by training, with enough credits for a master's and three years of on-the-job experience building exhibits at the Colorado Springs Center for Gender and Power. I've always sought truth in dioramas, in glass-walled habitats and pinprick galaxies. At the Center for Gender and Power, I tried to inject each of my costumed scenes with something more than theater. I wanted them to pulse and sweat and live, to seize the viewer by the collar and say, I am the world!

If you don't believe me, you should have seen my *Twelve*

Scenes from the Life of Margaret Sanger. I gave the mother of modern birth control more than period costume—I gave her a period, complete with a meticulously reproduced menstrual rag. Jilly the director wasn't impressed, and maybe this episode led indirectly to my dismissal a week later, but I'm the kind of guy who says you have to immerse yourself in it—or what's the point?

What many people fail to realize is that curating isn't just about arranging stuffed penguins around a Plexiglas ice floe or turning Styrofoam balls of varying diameters into a solar system. It's also about research and meditation, and it's about thought experiments. A museum is a world that you can see every inch of in an afternoon; so that world has to be real and simple and true from the minute you walk through the turnstile to the minute you reenter the blinding sunshine of the disordered general world with the little metal pin still clipped to your lapel.

In the summer of 2006 I was planning a new museum. My own museum. It had to do with water, so I wanted to learn everything I could about water from the inside out. The museum I had in mind was going to be based on the Aquatic Ape Theory of Evolution expounded by the noted visionary and scholar Elaine Morgan. If you're not familiar with it, look it up right now. It's all completely well founded and empirically documented. David Attenborough did a special on PBS. This isn't fringe science I'm talking about, not by any stretch, no matter what the pith-helmeted old Richard Leakey cabal tries to tell you.

Every middle-schooler knows about the Fossil Gap. The missing footage in the filmstrip of human evolution, the bit that would explain how we came down from the trees and stood upright on the savanna to take a look around, and how we grew noses with downward-pointing nostrils and used them to look down on each other. If we could only fill in that gap, we'd understand ourselves. But there aren't any fossils to tell us that part of our story. Why would millions of years' worth of fossils suddenly disappear from the Olduvai Gorge? Because we're digging in the wrong place. We'd need frogmen to find those missing fossils. Elaine Morgan tells us that during the Fossil Gap humankind went aquatic, took a three-million-year sabbatical in the sea. And it was underwater where we made the leap from fuzzy little golems to self-knowing humans with posture and tools.

All three mammalian subclasses—the monotremes, the marsupials, and the placentals—have sent what they call volunteers back into the water, where they gradually reevolved into aquatic species. Long ago some rodent went swimming and turned into a beaver. A horse got wet and gave us the hippo. A bear went scuba diving—and *hello!*—look who's a walrus.

Then there's Steller's sea cow, the bovine of the deep that was hunted to extinction in the 1700s. A *sea* cow. A *cow* of the sea. Here's how I see that happening on the white retractable screen of my genetic imagination. Picture a single cow: she's sick of macho bulls, sick of horseflies, sick of bedding down every night in her own excrement. So one afternoon she takes a look at the ocean and says to herself: "Well, that's an option."

This would be on the Kamchatka peninsula. At sunset. The tundra burns red and the cormorants cry for their supper. She walks to the edge of the paddock and across a stretch of dark sand to contemplate the vast Bering Sea. It's starting to appeal to her. No flies, no bulls, clean, maternal.

She dips one hoof in the surf and feels a weird sensation course up her shank. It's the spark of natural selection, and it gives her chills, right down to the udders. Two hooves in the water and she stops to practice holding her breath. Next she's up to her knees in the green froth. The sun tosses its last honeyed arc across the water and the fire enters her intelligence. She takes a few more steps, lowing to herself. The shore is steeper here, and with each step the sea claims more and more and more of her hairy hide. The forelegs wither into flippers. Her back legs fuse together to form a broad paddle. As the fur falls away, her body goes sleek and green. She arches her back and with a flick of her tail plunges into the briny cold Bering. Her skull telescopes into her shoulders; her belly balloons; and her big cow eyes grow even bigger, astonished at becoming the next new thing on earth.

The same thing happened with people.

My museum was going to do for the aquatic ape what the natural history museum in New York City did for Steller's sea cow.

I don't want to get bogged down in theory or bore you with all the evidence, but it's my conviction that this lost aquatic civilization was destroyed in a volcanic eruption some 3,500 years ago. (More on this later.) The Museum of the Aquatic Ape would lay out the grand design and social history of our former seafaring cousins in a sequence of dioramas. The sculpted figurines would be built to scale with poignant details and fins and real emotions on the faces to register what we've lost. This, I thought, was the only way to get people to listen. Show them the drama. Convince them that it was real and felt and endured and forgotten. That's the power of a museum.

You couldn't strictly classify this as Science. It's more poetic than that. I saw it like a mental dovetailing of Margaret Atwood, Hélène Cixous, and—I don't know—Stan Lee, maybe. That should give you a feel for the density of gravitas I had in mind for this place. And despite what my wife said, it had nothing to do with Aquaman. The Museum was social critique, a protest; it was a counterweight to the blatantly masculinized Savanna Theory of human evolution; Louis Leakey would fume when he came through the high revolving door; it was the truth. But I don't want to go into all that right now. My wife's name is Jean.

Sorry for the long-winded explanation, but that's why I was spending all those hours underwater in a Hilton pool. I was designing a museum about water, so I had to immerse myself in it. And things were moving along at a good clip. They were. But then Jean smart-bombed the sacred bonds of our marriage, and then the Nautikon arrived on the scene, and the Feds got involved and—well, everything went to hell.

Yes, to hell. Which is where I am now, doing all this remembering. Every story gets told from somewhere, and my somewhere is here on the deck of the *Endurance,* my houseboat and my holding cell. But it hardly matters where I am. Wherever I go now— hell, the federal penitentiary, a secret prison in the Balkans—I'm in Nautika, even with the security cuff strapped to my ankle. They can't rendition you from your dreams. Even right now as I sit in my deck chair rubbing my foot to get the feeling back in my toes, I see it. Before me lies the chalkboard bay scribbled with whitecaps. Gusts of sleet wipe it clean, but not before I read the word that's being spelled out there for me: NAUTIKA.

THREE

But I'm getting way ahead of myself. Slow it down, Jim. Deep breaths. Let's go all the way back to the Hilton. To me, standing on the floor of the pool, looking into the water.

In the amphibious state of *ooeee,* time does not pass with its usual rigor. The Helvner told me that it was after midnight (12:06). Meaning that I'd been under for more than an hour (1:17). I made a note of this and surfaced. My hair felt brittle and my eyes ached from the chlorine. I gathered my things and slipped under cover of darkness to my waiting Corolla.

The drive home from the hotel that night was an exercise in mounting dread. Inside our suburban Colorado Springs town house, my wife waited for me—or maybe she didn't. I was already beginning to suspect that she wanted out of our marriage. This suspicion would be borne out, and painfully so, on the night when she actually left me. Jean disapproved of my ambitions, the research in the pool, the museum; the mere mention of them plunged her into a sullen silence. She married me on the supposition that I would be a balanced helpmeet, that I would pull my weight. Oh, sure, she knew I was whimsical, a little flighty even. But she was drawn to my boyishness, my comics collection, the scale models that I'd had shipped out from my mother's attic in South Carolina.

The first year we were together I was still holding down the gallery job at the Center for Gender and Power. And even when Jilly asked me to clear out my desk, I handled the disgrace like an emotionally mature person. This was October 2004, when I was still reeling from my *Margaret Sanger* coup. I'd pushed the conventions of sociopolitical diorama design to the brink of acceptance. (Or maybe a millimeter beyond that brink, if you ask Jilly.) Anyway, I got fired. Jean had just accepted my proposal of marriage that spring, and I didn't want any bad blood in the professional sphere of my life to hemorrhage into the personal one. So I put on a brave face.

"I'm just going to dust myself off," I remember telling Jean the night I was laid off. This was after three years at the Center, so there was a lot of dusting to be done. The silica of shame was thick on the knees of my downfall.

"That's the spirit," she'd said. And it was.

The next morning I made a few calls and got a job with a literacy group that paid well and allowed me to travel. If you've never seen a bookmobile, it's a vehicle stocked with books that are doled out free of charge to underserved schoolchildren. Mine was a Chevy van decorated with a huge bespectacled worm. For months I rose diligently at 6:00 a.m. every school day to make my rounds of the local libraries. I sat Indian-style on the primary-colored carpets to read Clifford en español.

A couple months later Jean and I were married, and I moved into her place. She owned a town house in the kind of complex where everyone wants to have dinner parties all the time and no one takes your designated parking space. I'll never forget the night after our wedding, when I backed the Corolla up to the town house door. I was so excited I accidentally popped the hood and then the gas cap before finally finding the ejector lever for the trunk. The car was packed with my meager possessions, most of which were tied up in garbage bags and pillowcases.

I didn't get out of the car right away; this was a moment to savor. I remember thinking that if I savored it long enough Jean might rush outside to help me carry in my stuff. But she didn't, and after fifteen minutes the car started getting cold, so I gave up waiting. I had to knead my backside to get the blood flowing again. I'd expected this to be a big moment, but instead my leg fell asleep.

"That all you brought?" Jean said. I was standing at the threshold of married life with only a microwave oven in my arms. She was wearing a terry bathrobe and a big stocking cap. I wanted to kiss her, but the oven would have gotten in the way.

"There's more stuff in the trunk."

She gave a weird smile and stepped aside to let me through. I set the microwave on the kitchen bar and turned around to face my new bride. I still don't know where she got the costume, but there she was—big, physically edifying Jean—wearing a leotard adorned with a stylized gold eagle. On her head she wore a golden tiara, and on her hip a golden lariat. On her wrists she flashed a pair of silver cuffs.

"Diana Prince?" I whispered.

"Steve Trevor," said Jean—said Wonder Woman, my wife—with a wink. On the sofa between us lay a U.S. Army dress uniform, with a natty peaked cap and patent leather shoes. I wasted no time getting in costume. Then Jean lassoed me with the Lariat of Truth and dragged me into the bedroom. We made love in character once that night. And then we made love out of character, or rather in the character of ourselves, twice.

Nearly two years passed. There were more playful sex scenarios and there was plenty of emotional growth, though in retrospect probably not enough. But in those heady first months of marriage we were into each other to a degree that suggested longevity. As an evolutionary strategy, love works too well. We should know what it's really after, where it leads.

By the beginning of last year the first blush of romance had peeled away and the rough glue-smeared underlayer of misery had become plainly visible.

When I arrived home from the hotel that night, I could see the yellow curb stenciled with our condo number. I wish I could say this was a welcome sight, but frankly it filled me with apprehension. I parked, hauled up the hand brake, and listened to the engine tick as it cooled. To my freaked-out ears it sounded like some sort of urgent telegraph message. The message was telling me to restart the car and drive away. Do us all a favor, Jim: go. Disappear into some dull yellow obscurity where your ideas can't hurt anyone you love.

I walked to my doorstep and inserted the key in the town house door but waited a minute before turning it. I had good reason to hesitate. For many nights I'd come home to find Jean in a state of emotional nonpresence. What I mean is that she'd thrown up an invisible shield of isolation around herself. An empathy partition. You could walk all the way around it feeling for an opening or a loose panel, but there was no way in. She looked painfully pretty inside it, and completely unmarried.

At last I turned the key. The sound of the bolt scraping in its chamber had all the finality of a cocked rifle. The door swung open and I stepped across the brass jamb.

Jean sat on the couch, watching *Nova*. She didn't look up. It was as if I reflected a frequency of light that was beyond her perception, ultra-ultraviolet. I could see her splayed form molded by the glow of our single torch-style lamp. She looked like a person of import lying in state. She looked dead. She looked at the TV.

I closed the door softly. In these new condos there's no other way to close a door. You can't slam it no matter how hard you try, and I've tried, believe me. I hung my laser-pointer key chain on a hook, watching it bang softly against my wife's laser-pointer key chain. Banging and intertwining and deflecting. Like us.

Stepping in behind the couch, I spoke to the back of my wife's head, but she didn't turn to face me. So I circled the sofa and spoke to the front of her head. She shifted to the left and groaned to let me know I was blocking the TV. At my back I could hear galaxies being born. The soundtrack was synthesizers and wind chimes. In front of me, my own galaxy was dying, in utter silence. This went on for several minutes, me moving from the front to the back of the couch, until I finally got the picture. She clicked off the remote, sat up, and knotted the sash of her bathrobe.

Our marital trouble boiled down to a difference of opinion. I contended that the world deserved a Museum of the Aquatic Ape, deserved to know the alternate truth of human ancestry. Jean contended that I needed to get a job. But I'd had jobs. I drove that bookmobile for a whole year before I hit the train. I challenge anyone to drive a commercial vehicle in a big red dog costume without incident. Besides, I wasn't the first guy to be propelled toward great things by failure (take Gandhi, for example, or Don Quixote). And I'm definitely not the first visionary-like personality with a disapproving spouse.

Her voice reached my ears like an incantation from beyond the grave, all echoey and slo-mo. I thought, naturally, of Doctor Strange, the shaman of Marvel Comics. How he sat lotus-style on that pentagram rug in his Manhattan town house, summoning genies with Sanskrit spells.

"Are you even listening?" This was Jean's voice, suddenly become clear, earthly. I realized that she'd been talking to me for some time. "I said your mother called." She inserted an ugly pause. *"Again."*

There was resentment on that front. Jean was convinced that I'm unrealistically attached to my mother. She called her Betty, after Betty Friedan, although her name is in fact Gerry. Gerry Rath, Ph.D. Jean made fun of her drawstring pants and her cropped hair, her ceramic vagina art.

I tried squeezing into the few available inches at the foot of the sofa. Jean's foot recoiled at the touch of my thigh and I heard her groan. In fact she has a nice way of groaning. It's the same sound she made during our lovemaking. Back when we still made love. For Jean irritation and amorousness have the same repertoire of noises. That was one of the things that turned me on about her initially.

When I landed the job with the literacy group, we decided to go out and celebrate. The Corolla was in the shop, so I borrowed the bookmobile. When I pulled up in front of her apartment complex, she groaned at the scandalous nature of what I was driving. I winked. She climbed in the sliding side door.

It was Jean who got the idea to read "bedtime stories" in the back of the bookmobile (although I was the one who took the heat for it from my superiors). And this wasn't exactly Berenstain Bears or *Make Way for Ducklings*. The material was far more advanced.

She groaned when I told her about what happens after hours in Busytown, when the Lowly Worm comes out of his apple. She groaned and groaned until the bookmobile was filled with the sound of her groaning.

I mark that night as a watershed in my feelings for Jean. Those feelings have not abated, no matter what she's done to me, or I to myself.

"Are you even listening to me? I said Betty called. For like the *fifth* time."

"I made a lot of headway tonight," I replied, raising my eyebrows in an expression of positivity.

"Did you see Corey?" She asked this without any real interest. Corey was the night clerk at the Hilton. He was a nice guy who was weirdly jazzed about what life had handed him, despite what it had in fact handed him. We're talking about a man who wore a neck brace and did the over-the-back slam-dunk gesture at every perceived victory. Our relationship involves comics. It's a bond, so he gives me special access to the hotel facilities after hours. Jean always disliked Corey, or disliked the me that she saw through the lens of Corey.

"I got some cool ideas about weaponry," I said, placing my hand on her ankle—a mistake. "Normal weapons like lasers would dissipate in the water, so they used these sonic cannons—

with like a burst of superfocused sound. They were pretty cool weapons." I withdrew my hand and mimed a shoulder-mounted rifle, like a bazooka or something.

"She said do you want her to send some vest to you. You left a vest there that you made in fifth grade."

"And also there are cultural echoes with like dolphin language and whale calls," I said. "Which are supersonic too."

"A vest she said you made out of yarn or something. I can't believe you made a vest." She still wasn't looking at me. "Do you want to know what I think the subtext of that phone call is?"

"Come on, Jean. Everything doesn't have a subtext," I said. Jean has a degree in psychology, which has been a help/hindrance in terms of her own personal growth. "The thing about supersonic rifles is they could frighten and confuse an enemy without actually killing him."

"The subtext of the phone call is this: Look at my creative son, he's so creative. You don't deserve my son, Jean, you little bitch, because you don't value how creative he is. He made a vest out of yarn and you can't foster his creative vision."

I sat forward. "She wouldn't say the b word."

"And do you know what the *sub*-subtext is? Or the *sub*-sub-subtext?"

"No."

"Then I'll tell you." Here she Frisbeed a throw pillow across the room. "Your mother is a very lonely and depressed person."

I tried to put my hand on Jean's ankle again but discovered that it was still a mistake. She sounded a meaningful sigh and picked up her water glass.

"Will you turn off that light on your way out?" she said.

"On my way out where?"

"Out to the bedroom."

Jean had slept on the couch off and on for the past three weeks. The couch was close to the front door. And the front door was the door that she would very soon walk through to abandon our marriage.

I got into bed still wearing my swim trunks. Once I was comfortable, I propped the three-ring binder on my knees and wrote the following:

Nautikon weaponry: shoulder-mounted sonic rifles, "startle" grenades, and hypersonic scatter guns for dispersing schools of marauding bull sharks. There was no war within Nautika because of women running the government, so the weapons were strictly for protection and could only be wielded by the Dolphin-women cavalry—who were outcasts and sworn to self-immolation after battle!! See-thru glass breastplates?

I woke up the next morning to a distant sense of toasting bread. I heard it before I smelled it, raisin swirl, discharging noisily out of the toaster. Then came the unmistakable sound of a butter knife rasping testily across a dry surface.

"Jean?" I said. No response. I paused a few seconds and called again: "Jean?" I heard the chuckling of her laser-pointer key chain. I heard the front door close, that horrific vacuum-seal sound. Then the town house was quiet except for my tentative breathing.

That morning I spent writing, or really just taking notes and making pencil sketches in my binder. For a while I fell asleep on the couch. When I woke up it was Jean's imprint on the corduroy upholstery that I felt, not my own. Her residual body heat was trapped somewhere deep in the cushions, and I tried with mind magnetism to extract it, draw it into myself. I know everyone can understand this, because we've all been in love before. But it didn't work, so I was forced to lie there feeling her warmth from an upholstered distance.

I slept again and this time I dreamed about being trapped under an endless sheet of polar ice. Above me I could see the sun, weak and blobby like the beam of a flashlight through the wall of a pup tent. I looked for a hole or some slushy area compromised by algae, but there was no escape.

When I woke up the third time it was well after noon. My hair was still ratty with chlorine, so I showered and even took the time to use a cream rinse. I made an egg sandwich and stared at the stainless-steel door of our dishwasher while I ate. By the time I realized that there was egg yolk in my hair, it was already dry. While I was sponging my sideburns it occurred to me that the day was slipping away. I had to get something done. So I drove out to the storage plaza, stopping at the Hot Mart on the way for a coffee and a chocolaty Paycheck bar.

Stor-Mor is just past the airport, several acres of identical orange-and-white corrugated buildings inside a high security fence. When I signed my contract two years earlier, they gave me a four-digit pin number for the front gate, but I forgot it. And anyway you can punch in any four digits and the hydraulic gate opens. I located my unit, easing the Corolla close to the entrance. The combination to my padlock was 19L, 25R, 3L. I nailed it on the first try. (The agents would famously use a bolt cutter; maybe you saw the footage.) The garage door shrieked as I clean-jerked it open, then I stood back to let the hard Colorado daylight color my secret library.

The storage unit was my only selfish space on earth. Until

they got that warrant and hauled everything in for state's evidence, no one else had ever been allowed inside. Not even Corey at the hotel had clearance to see it, and certainly not Jean. She would soon prove that she couldn't be trusted around mint-condition comics.

I slipped on my white gloves and stepped inside. At the center of the room stood a lopsided globe of Earth-Two, the Golden Age planet of DC Comics. This was a science fair project of mine, aged twelve, that took some two weeks to complete. Looking back, I see it as quite possibly my first curatorial effort, the precursor to the Museum of the Aquatic Ape. I did a Mercator projection and some careful research to map the many nations and kingdoms and then pasted all this onto a papier-mâché ball.

Jean never got to see any of this. She would have laughed. I invite her to laugh now as loudly as she wants. Let everyone laugh at my private world. Who cares? I have no secrets anymore. The newspapers have made sure of that, and the subcommittee is telling the world all it wants to know about Jim Rath, prisoner, pariah, domestic terrorist.

The walls of the storage unit were arrayed floor to ceiling with acid-free archival boxes. These I had alphabetized clockwise around the perimeter of the room using gummed labels and a Sharpie.

In the extreme upper left corner you would have found my second most valuable item on earth, *Action Comics* No. 99 (the one with Trick-Shot Shultz using Superman's forehead as a golf tee; F; $445). In the same box I kept the premiere issue of *Atoman* (featuring Wild Bill Hickok; VG; $280). Then there was *The Beyond* No. 17 ("You have called us forth by playing the Lyre of Doom! We are ready to do your evil bidding, master!"; NM!!!; $330).

Nearby, I kept one of the most trenchant meditations on male insecurity ever. This was *The Cat* No. 4 ("All my life, humans have hurt me—hounded me! Today, all mankind will fall—beneath the hooves of the Man-Bull!"; VG; only worth $5, but to me it's priceless).

Dead ahead, midway up the shelves, was a complete series of *Mr. District Attorney,* including the prescient issue No. 5 ("Exposing the cruelest racket in the world—'The Counterfeit Medicine Mob!'"; G; $60). Next to that was *Nyoka the Jungle Girl* No. 27 (NM; $280). Skip a few boxes, and you'd find *Plastic Man* No. 39 (VG; $136). "Who dares follow Plastic Man down the stairway to madness?" I can't tell you how many times I answered that question in the affirmative.

I had a real oddity from 1952. The virulently anti-McCarthyite issue of *Shock SuspenStories* (Jingoistic he-man says: "Give it to him, the dirty Red!"; Modern woman says: "Stop it! Please! What you're doing is wrong! Act like Americans!"; VG; $205). My collection also included several well-preserved issues of *Rulah, Jungle Goddess.* Why so many comics about feral women? Feel free to write your own report on this topic and e-mail it to the Pentagon.

I'll wrap up our tour on the bottom shelf, where you'd find one of my most prized possessions shielded from insidious forces and mildew in a doubled plastic sleeve. *Wonder Woman* No. 26 ("The Golden Women and the White Star!"; G; $260). If this had been Superman, the price would be double. But that's the Neanderthal world of comics collecting for you! You should see the meatheads who do the appraising.

I tugged a length of kite string to snap on the overhead bulb and then pulled down the garage door behind me. My task was secret—I was looking for the so-called lost issue of *Namora* (No. 4, 1948). Suppressed by the Comics Council, halted by the publisher, this was one of only five copies extant on our planet, or any other planet that I know of. Now, thanks to your government trying to protect our vital interests, there are only four. Taking out insurgents one rare, collectible comic at a time!

Namora, if you don't know, was the cousin of Prince Namor, the Sub-Mariner. Like Namor, she was fathered by a land dweller but raised in Atlantis, where she joined the ruling elite. In the late forties they handed Namora her own series, but it was discontinued under suspicious circumstances after only three issues.

I removed the apocryphal issue No. 4 from its plastic sleeve and laid it out on my felt desktop, using long surgical tweezers to turn the pages. It looked so frail, the images so quaint, with their one-piece bathing suits and USO hairdos. Who would ever consider this a threat to American values? What could be so dangerous about a half-aquatic heroine with shapely legs and somewhat libertarian ideals? Historians will tell you she was gagged for her overt feminist themes, and for the "unequivocal depictions of Sapphic romance." And it's true, issue No. 4 describes a feminist coup in her undersea birthplace, Maritanus. Under the mutinous leadership of Namora herself, all the women depart to establish their own colony deep in the Sea of Japan. There they form a psychic alliance with the Amazons to battle a school of marauding bull sharks. At the end we see one cell depicting subaquatic homosocial hand-holding. Big deal.

It was my mother who acquired this relic for my collection. The occasion was my eighth birthday, and it probably cost her plenty. On an assistant professor's salary this was a huge sacrifice, one that I have never forgotten.

I'd come all the way out here to Stor-Mor because I couldn't remember an important detail from this issue. How did Namora and her rebel band get from Maritanus to the Sea of Japan? I found the answer on page 24, a caravan of blue whales with saddles strapped to their humps, those little huts you see on the backs of camels in movies about Cleopatra. This was something I could definitely use in a diorama.

We're talking now about my physical storage unit. But of course I had another unit. It was padlocked in the section of the brain where we keep our hopes. Based on certain pressures I feel when going there, I have determined that it resides somewhere in the rear left of the skull. This is where I built my conceptual dioramas and printed the imaginary white placards to hot-glue on the walls beside them. This was the Museum of the Aquatic Ape of the Mind, behind its own shrieking garage door, corrugated orange and white, no secret password to enter, no archival boxes for the agents to raid, no voice-mail messages for some congressman to broadcast in front of a whole chamber of dignitaries.

I sat down and felt the pressure of tears mounting in my sockets, felt the heaviness in the rear left of my skull, and with these sensations came a wave of sadness.

By the time I got home, Jean was already back from the office. She works in organization management for a corporate development firm. When you're dealing with Complexity Theory and critical thinking all day, it can get pretty stressful. You'd be surprised how much resistance there is when you offer alternatives to command-and-control leadership methods. So I couldn't blame Jean if she brought her work home with her sometimes.

I lingered at the door, car keys and laser-pointer springing from hand to hand. From there I could see her on all fours in the full bath, rummaging through the cabinet under the sink.

"I'm back!" I shouted cheerfully but maybe not loud enough.

"Where did you put my goddamn razor?" said Jean. "Have you been using it again?"

"I went out to do some archival research," I said. "For the Museum."

"Why can't you shave your armpits with your own razor?" she said. And then to herself: "What's *wrong* with him?" Her head was under the sink. I could tell by the muffled quality of her voice.

"So . . . did you eat yet?" I fired the laser in the direction of the bathroom, drawing the shape of a heart on her substantial behind. "Hon?"

"If you don't stop with that thing, I'm going to have my brother break your fingers."

"Okay! I was thinking burritos."

I'd learned from experience that the best way to manage Jean's bad weather was with a steady outpouring of sunshine. Stay positive, Jim. Stay up. Let her know she's safe. Of course that tactic failed miserably in the end; nothing could keep the storm front of heartbreak at bay forever.

Even as I sit here on the deck of the *Endurance,* on this dismal, drippy night, I feel the muscle reflex at the corners of my mouth that signals happiness. My lawyer congratulates me when I smile. "Keep it up, Jimmy," he says. "It helps." This is the Fat Man, my court-appointed counsel, with his steady intake of Diet Pepsi. I am a cheerful person by nature, but the more I think about where that's gotten me, the more I want to repudiate optimism in all its forms. I can't think of a lot of compelling reasons to smile. But look here: at the corners of my mouth. They point in the direction of optimism. Keep smiling, I say. Keep shining.

My wife and I spent the rest of that evening in separate states of engagement. Jean watched a depressing show about child prostitution on public television and ate a microwave burrito. I ate a microwave burrito standing at the kitchen island, watching Jean.

"When do you plan to stop staring at me?" she said finally.

"Jean, is this something we should talk about?" I said. I wasn't staring. "Talking might be a good idea. If it's the Museum that's bothering you, I can put that aside for a while." This was all said in the spirit of diplomacy; but I couldn't put the Museum aside—not for a while, not for a day. I was trying to be conciliatory, to the point of sugarcoating destiny, never a good idea.

Jean put the remainder of her burrito on the coffee table, perilously close to my autographed copy of Elaine Morgan's *The Descent of Woman*. I worried about bean seepage but didn't say anything. She considered me with paper-dry eyes.

"I don't even know what museum you're talking about, Jim. I don't even know—"

"The Museum of the Aquatic Ape," I volunteered.

"—what this museum is. It doesn't exist in the reality of our life. The whole Aquaman thing, I mean it was cute for a while, but honestly."

I surprised her by smiling. "This is good," I said.

"Look, Jim." She stood and moved close beside me. "This inner life of yours, I always liked that."

"We're talking. It's a development."

"I used to get a real kick out of your inner life. It was one of the things I liked about you."

"Liked." My smile vanished when I realized we were in the past tense.

"Yes," she said. "Now I just want things to be real."

"Liked?"

"You can go out to Stor-Mor and play with your models, but it's got to be a hobby. Do you understand? I'm not just talking for me, because the next woman you meet—"

"Next woman?" At this stage I think I was yelling.

"—the next woman is going to say the same thing. Jim, you don't even know how to swim."

"I'm going to stand here until you take that back."

"About swimming?"

"The other thing. The next woman. Which is pure fantasy. I'm not going to sit down or move or blink until you take it back."

She turned off the TV, bundled up the remains of her dinner, and dropped it in the kitchen trash.

"I'm serious," I said, trying not to move my lips, trying not to move anything. "I want to be adult about this, but I'm not moving." She set the timer on the coffeemaker for 7:00 a.m. and went to the bedroom, closing the door behind her. "Not moving until you take it back!"

Jean returned forty-five minutes later, just as I suspected she would. She found me, true to my word, standing completely motionless in the dim kitchenette.

"You have to move sometime, jerk." She pushed my shoulder and gave me a laughing look, as if we were complicit in some kind of comedy skit. I recognized what she was doing. She was giving me the opportunity to soften my stance, to acquiesce. But this was not an offer I could permit myself to take.

"I'm sorry I said you play with models. How's that?" She poked me under the arm, a vulnerable spot. "Truce?"

I refused her extended hand and with it her offer of détente. To accept would have been a breach of my stated position, and then the whole thing would have crumbled.

"I'm sorry I said you stole my razor."

I gave her a hurt look, trying not to move the muscles of my face, which is impossible. The hurt look requires a squinching of the eyebrows and the slight protrusion of the lower lip.

"Ha!" She poked with both hands now, index-fingering both my underarms. "You moved. Game over, Jim!"

I tried not to use my lips when I said, "It's not the razor. It's that you don't believe in me." I felt like the most depressing ventriloquist on earth. Try saying the word *believe* without moving your mouth. "You don't believe in me anymore." Next came the pleasant sting of tears, not from sadness but from keeping my eyes open too long. I wondered if even this tiny reflex action would count as moving.

"I do *deleeth*," said Jean, mocking me. I held my position. She saw the tears in my eyes.

"No—come on," she said, putting her face so close to mine that I could see the inconsistencies in her lip gloss application. "I believe in Jim."

She put an arm around my rigid shoulders, now aching and starting to cramp. "I believe in the old Jim. I like the nerdy comics guy Jim. Bookmobile Jim. Sea Monkey Jim. But there has to be a part of your life that's not that. I'm not saying you're obsessed.

Okay, you're obsessed. But maybe that's *my* problem. Maybe you need somebody who—"

"I don't need somebody who." My lips were still not moving, so the word *somebody* came out sounding like *sundoddy*. A tear had found its way into the trough that goes from the nostril to the corner of your mouth. Whatever that's called. I couldn't think of the name of it, but it tickled anyway. Still, I held fast to my position.

"Well," she said, releasing my shoulders. I saw the diplomacy dry up. The window had closed. She was done. "Maybe that's my point."

By nine o'clock that night I had allowed my knees to buckle. Soon I was kneeling on the linoleum, my forehead resting against cool stainless steel. I was actively revising the rules, or adding new corollaries to the old rules. I thought that allowing gravity to do its work wasn't, technically speaking, moving. Not in an active sense, not with malice aforethought and all. Out of the corner of one eye I could see the minutes ticking by on my Helvner.

Maybe, I remember thinking, *maybe this* is *getting ridiculous. Maybe you should just leave, Jim. Go to the Hilton. Let Jean think about things while you're gone.* I was tired of playing the martyr. If she wanted me—the actual Jim, Sea Monkey Jim—she could make the next move. Why should *I* always have to make the next move?

I recall that being my reasoning at the time, which in retrospect seems kind of flawed.

When I stood up, my knees clicked. The sound was like a death sentence, a clicky death sentence. I didn't recall my knees making noises before. I was thirty-eight years old in the worst way possible.

FOUR

Rep. Neil Frost: Son, I'm sure your lawyers have briefed you on why we wanted you here.

Agent Les Diaz: Yes, Congressman. I've been briefed.

Rep. Frost: We just want you to answer as honestly, clearly, and completely as you can.

Diaz: I make it my policy never to do otherwise.

Rep. Frost: Good for you, son. You comfortable? Want some water? Get some water in here for Agent Diaz.

Diaz: That won't be necessary.

FIVE

It was 9:45 by the dashboard clock when I eased out of the condo parking lot. My shoulders still felt crampy from standing still so long. Through the windshield I took one last look at our curtains to see if Jean was watching me leave. She was not. So I honked, flashed my brights, and waited a minute. Still nothing.

My first stop was the Hot Mart, for my customary Paycheck bar. At 10:15 I reached the Hilton hotel and pulled the hand brake on the Corolla without depressing the little thumb button at the end. I didn't care if it made that ratchety noise. I felt reckless and fatalistic. Like I'd played the Lyre of Doom and was now ready to face whatever interdimensional hydra I'd summoned forth.

The sliding glass doors of the Hilton lobby slid open and I accepted their whispered invitation. Corey gave me a what's-up signal but I was too bummed to respond in kind.

"You don't look so good," he said. I neither denied this nor confirmed it. Corey could see in me whatever he wanted to see.

He informed me that the pool was being "serviced," a word that aroused my suspicions. I was told to "cool it" for an hour or so. I took a seat in the lobby to wait. The sofa suite at the hotel is Colonial-style, decorated with some kind of brocade showing military life in the period reflected in the design of the furniture. It was, I always thought, like embroidering a midcentury modern love seat with a picture of the atomic bomb. My eyebrows, I realized, had been arched for some time. I returned them to their default position and settled back into the imperialist upholstery.

With my three-ring binder on my knee I began to organize my thoughts for the evening's session. This was not easy, of course, given my delicate state. Whenever I fought with Jean it didn't just make me upset, it had an impact on my sense of being. I was always surprised that I still commanded a presence at all, that I occupied space and moved through it. That in my opinion is the most creepy symptom of regret, the sense that you are dislocated from existence. It took Corey's "what's up" to remind me that I *was*. If this sounds dramatic, it's not nearly as dramatic as it felt at the time. I was attached to Jean with ontological tentacles. Jim and Jean. Jean and Jim.

I moved my eyes back and forth, and the dim museum of my brain showed me one familiar tableau after another. The hotel desk, where the poseable figure of Corey sat drawing pictures on a cocktail napkin. The pool area, where patio furniture crouched menacing and spidery in the dark around an impassive black lake. Back to Corey again, whose realistic details had shifted in the short interval like actual organic matter, flesh and breath. To the left of the desk I saw the bank of elevators. The lights above the doors suggested the rise and fall of real passengers through actual floors. By scanning the room in this manner, seeing it as a series of discrete dioramas, I was verifying my own subjectivity in the face of the Jean situation.

It was nearly 10:45 by the time the maintenance man cleared out and Corey gave me the green light to enter the pool area. The pool is housed in an extension off one side of the hotel. And though it might be an enticement to a weary traveler on the beltway, it's kind of a rip-off when you actually get inside. The patio furniture looks wrought-iron but it's really powder-coated aluminum. The tiled floor is of Spanish derivation, polished like they're begging for a lawsuit. But look closer and you can see the flamenco characters are SpongeBob and his starfish friend. The water laps with genuine fervor against the sides of the pool, but the air is redolent of feet and bleach.

After hours they keep the pool area dark, but the mercury-vapor lamps shine in from the parking lot to project a mirror of the pool on the glass walls. A lesser intellect might be fooled by this, might not know where the water ends and the solid world begins, but I have no trouble with illusions. I know them too well.

I stole to the edge of the water, avoiding eye contact with the surveillance camera, per Corey's instructions. Where the tiles give way to a glazed blue lip I slid in, toes pointed, until I was submerged up to my collarbone. I strapped on my scuba mask, an old-fashioned Cousteau job made of natural rubber. It's got plenty of face suction and the Plexiglas is so thick it might even be bulletproof. Though I wouldn't want to test this hypothesis.

I pinched my nose and blew out to attain a more amphibious pressure in the ear canal. Then I slipped the nozzle of the snorkel between my lips and wetted it with my tongue. On better nights, the snorkel had the rubbery flavor of adventure, and often I hung there sucking on the nozzle and dreaming of past explorers of note—Sir Ernest Shackleton, Ponce de León, and Mungo Park. But that night the nozzle tasted like nothing but imminent failure.

The lead shot in my pockets dragged my body to the bottom, and I stood there for some time trying to enter the semiamphibious state of *ooeee,* but it was no good. I couldn't focus. When I tried the circular breathing, I could feel myself start to hyperventilate. I tried to summon up Nautika, the wondrous domed city, Queen Ô enthroned in Her grand alabaster ovum. But all I could think about was the noise. You know what I'm talking about, that weird noise in hotel pools, like if you glued a contact mike to a housefly and broadcast it over a transistor radio. It's sexy and nagging and reminds me of Jean.

Anyway, the *ooeee* was a no-go. Eventually I gave up, surfaced, and toweled off. On the way out I gave Corey a silent valediction. He responded with the two-handed big breasts signal and pointed toward the elevator. I heard the doors slide shut without looking at what I presumed was an ample-bosomed woman riding up to her room. On an ordinary night I would have definitely looked, but this was not an ordinary night.

In the parking lot I stood for a while gazing up at the sky. Which is really something you can't gaze *at* but *into,* because it doesn't end. How far can we look when we're looking into infinity? There must be a limit to human sight. I thought I should look that up. Then it occurred to me, standing there gazing into the night sky, that gazing into the night sky was something losers did and I got even more depressed.

So it was with heavy heart that I dropped into the driver's seat of my Corolla. I switched the key to the Electrical position and the dashboard glowed like an aquarium. If there was a button on the dash that I could press and send the car through a wormhole into a parallel universe without Jims, I would have gladly pressed that button. But there is no such button. Instead I started the car. And I drove out of the parking lot into a different kind of parallel universe, one that was so sucky it hurts to describe it.

Fifteen minutes later, I was in the doorway of our town house. Almost at once I felt something, or the lack of something, emanating from within. It was, I would soon discover, the negative energy of loneliness, and it filled the vessel of my being with all the intensity of very bad sinus pressure. Every light in the apartment was burning, but I knew in an instant, I knew, my feet not even across the threshold, that my home had been drained of love. I rushed to the bedroom. The bra drawer stood bare.

I said it aloud: "That's it; she's left me." But was I convinced of this? Not yet. I was just trying out the expression on my tongue, readying the organ of speech for the impact on the organ of misery. Then I found Jean's "good-bye note," and I wasn't practicing anymore. It was true; she'd left me.

I call it a note, but there wasn't any note to speak of, not in the verbal sense. No tearstained condolence card or "screw you" lipsticked on the bathroom mirror. She didn't scribble anything on the back of a utility-bill envelope like "I know this will be difficult for you, Jim," or "Someday I hope we can talk, Jim," or "These years together, Jim, have meant so much to me, but . . ."

But.

On the kitchen island I found my cherished copy of *Sub-Mariner* No. 6. A paring knife pinned it to the countertop. Which must have taken excessive force because the surface is a slab of solid butcher block and our knives aren't exactly Henckels. I needed to give my hands something to do, so I rubbed them together. Then I used them to rub my face. Then I wiped my nose on the collar of my shirt. Then I scrubbed the collar with a damp paper towel.

I tossed the paper towel across the room, where it landed on the sofa. "Damn her!" I shouted, or wish I'd shouted. Why take this out on Prince Namor? (NM!; $125!; "The Sub-Mariner Fights the Periscope Peril!") Why take our marital trouble there, to the comic-book front? Jean considered my comics rivals for her affections, but why? I guess I'll never know. True, I often ran to them for consolation and what you might call succor when my wife's arms would have done the job. But, honestly, I was never selfish with my inner life. Never. I invited her in. I opened the door to my inner life and made the sweeping gesture. Please, Jean, after you!

But instead of stepping inside to see her husband's marvelous passions up close, what did she do? She joined a book club. They met three nights a week that summer. What kind of book club meets that often? And that's where she met the cabinetmaker. I think he played rugby. When I saw the Sub-Mariner comic pinned to the countertop, I thought immediately of this guy. I didn't even know his name, had never laid eyes on him, but I could picture him all right. He was in the scrum, or whatever they call that stupid sublimated homosexual orgy. His ass in the air and his large hands callused by years gripping an auger or a jigsaw. Now they're gripping the toned hamstrings of an opponent. He's so equal to the moment, this guy! So—I don't know—engaged with life. The buttocks tell you all you need to know. Very, very, very firm—too firm for flesh inside those mud-spattered nylon shorts. I gave this a lot of thought and nearly cried.

As a boy I had never been afraid to weep. Mother told me that only men and the emotionally paralyzed can't cry, so I tried to show her that her little boy was neither. I bawled my eyes out as often as possible. I wept at every stubbed toe and every imagined slight. And whenever I cried Mom took me to the Kress for a candy bar. (Yes, the Paycheck—sweet, chocolaty nexus of emotion!) Which may explain my rapid weight gain in elementary school, the tearful calls home from the principal's office, and the names they called me. In playground terminology I was a textbook "crybaby" and also a "fatty." Or, when facing the most ruthless foes, a "fatty crybaby fatty-fatty." Later, I was just a "fag."

But when I grew up, I stopped crying. I lost weight. It's not that I wasn't sad. It was like the tear machine rusted up. Maybe something had jammed in my lacrimal ducts. Maybe I was becoming the thing my mother feared most for me, either an emotional paralytic or a man.

So there I was standing at the kitchen island, rocking the paring knife back and forth to save poor Prince Namor (even though I knew this issue would never be Near Mint again, knowing it was Good at best and would command no more than $45 from only the most pitying or nearsighted collector). And there I was trying to cry, but the crying wouldn't come. I was a maudlin, tearless knife extractor. I wanted so bad to punish Jean with my hot tears. But I couldn't cry and she'd never be there to see it if I did. Besides, what kind of a dicky move was that, punishing her with hot tears? I was such a dick.

Left with little recourse, I went to a bar. And it was there that the real trouble started, the trouble you know about, the trouble that made the news and landed me here with an ankle bracelet. It was on that very night that I first laid eyes on the Nautikon. My life's only pursuit and my life's final disappointment. He was drinking alone at a corner booth in a hotel bar. But now I'm getting way ahead of myself.

When I walked into the lobby, Corey looked up stiffly. His head popped out of his neck brace, turtlelike, and he regarded me with a kind of glazed-over alarm. His eyes were bagged but his hands were awake. They scuttled across the desk at the sound of the sliding glass doors. I could see that he was covering something up with a brochure, and when I got closer I understood why. He'd passed his shift making dozens of drawings of Red Sonja in all kinds of demeaning positions.

"What are you doing back, Mega-Brow?" he said. It was a nickname.

I winced but tried to shape-shift the expression into a smile. "*Sub-Mariner* No. 6," I said.

"The one with MacArthur?"

"No, the issue after, Chor-Boy." This was another nickname, spoken here with malice.

"Dude, you have that?"

"*Had*. She destroyed it." This wasn't entirely true. I'd finished the job, feeding it into a shredder and then strewing the remains across our marital bed. It was an act.

"Man, you have *got* to leave that wench," said Corey, my friend.

"Yeah."

The hotel bar is just past the front desk, through a pair of high green doors that never seem to close. The place is called Rambles! (The exclamation point is not my own; it's actually on the sign.) Rambles! remains crowded until well after midnight principally because they offer complimentary popcorn. You can order one beer and enjoy a bottomless basket. The decor is some kind of bizarre Manifest Destiny motif. Murals of the Northwest Passage adorn two walls. And the banquettes are made out of barrel staves and wagon wheels, if you can picture something so homespun and moronic. I picked an empty one close to the door, ordered a beer for the sake of the popcorn, and sat there examining my own escalating sense of doom.

At the bar sat three unattached women, a vacant stool beside each one for spacing purposes. The bartender was an ex-Marine whose nose I had always suspected of being false. He'd worked as an explosives expert in Gulf I, which probably explains a lot. It was difficult in the dim light of Rambles! to work out the man's true age, but he always nursed a miniature can of cranberry juice, a sure sign of urinary-tract trouble.

The music on the public address was rock and roll of some indeterminate era, with extended saxophone solos that were wildly out of phase with the decor. From where I sat I could just barely hear the bartender telling dirty jokes as he moved from one woman to the next, the pitch of his voice rising sharply when he met the punch lines.

I heard him say: "That's not my penis!" He blurted out the first syllable of *penis* like he'd popped a cork out of his mouth. When the women giggled, he wrinkled his fake nose, and his eyes actually twinkled. I laughed too, but with bitterness, a knife against the throat of everyone's happiness. They all turned to look.

I had been sharpened to a point by desolation. So lonely I was a danger to society. A pariah, a leper, quarantined by my own unsuitable stupidness. Jean had been the conduit between me and the rest of you. Would it be too cheesy to call our marriage my lifeline? Probably. But when she severed that lifeline I was set adrift, an astronaut. The earth receded beneath me and with it all the appurtenances of our small love. A pair of burritos, the afghan on our love-worn sofa, ankles entwined, soft kisses on the brow as I fell asleep, the TV talking to us about the nature of humanity and the humanity of nature—everything drifted out of reach as I hurtled off into space.

But my loneliness ran even deeper than that. It felt as if I were being torn from the very scrim of reality, like a Colorform sticker peeled off the plane of being. I was too weak to adhere to reality. And I had no one to blame but myself.

A little later, the bartender delivered another punch line— "I said Sasquatch, not *Gas*-quatch!"—and I laughed again, still bitter but less pointed, more resigned. I was getting tired.

Then I heard someone else join in on the laughter. The sound was manly and honking. It made your gut curl up, like when the Fat Man blows his nose. I had to squint to determine its source, a figure seated in a dim banquette by the wait station. He sat low in the booth, and when he laughed again I could see his teeth flash blue in the compound bar light. I watched the man for a while, noticing how he kept stealing glances at the server's boobs. Her name was either Donnie or Kareese, though it was hard to tell which because she wore two name tags, one on each breast. Maybe she'd named them. I've heard of that sort of thing happening. She was lining popcorn baskets with slips of wax paper. Every time she reached up to add another prepped basket to the stack, her knit shirt pulled taut across her bustline.

The lights flickered and flared, and I turned to see the bartender toying with a rheostat. The effect was cheap and dramatic, like the light show in a low-budget rainforest diorama. Suddenly the overheads flared and it was as if a spotlight had been cast on the corner banquette. The laughing man was rendered in stark detail. The bright light revealed him to be a handsomer guy than I'd previously thought. He was sexy but in a desolate way, like a brakeman or a drifter. His hair was brown and he had the kind of upper lip you normally associate with a mustache, even though there was no mustache in sight. His face came to a point at the chin end and was flat at the top. The eyes were wide-set, fishlike. The man's mode of dress was what they now call business casual: teal turtleneck, blue sports coat, putty slacks, shoes.

Kareese sure seemed to like his look. The man's drinks arrived with clockwork regularity, each one in a clean new glass. To me she was less attentive, though I required very little. Just more napkins. Which she never brought.

Seated, his posture was rigid and chesty, suggesting that we were dealing with a tall man, but when he stood to go to the men's room I saw that his long torso and powerful shoulders were just a ruse to conceal a pair of stubby legs. You might even call them underdeveloped. The guy waddled. But he kept his chin up, proud, almost like a sea lion balancing a cocktail on his nose. When he came to the pair of low steps leading to the restrooms, he hesitated.

I examined his bulging pockets and determined that he was carrying breath mints or a complicated portable phone. Or both.

But what really caught my eye was his curious tic with the turtleneck. He kept tugging the collar up over his chin as if he were trying to conceal his throat. And there was something else suspicious about him: even in the fake gaslight of Rambles! his skin gave off a distinctly bluish cast.

I wasn't thinking about the Museum. I wasn't thinking about much of anything. My wife had just left me; I needed to be alone with my beer and my memories. But something about this stranger redirected my focus onto Nautika. I looked at his bluish complexion and thought about how much he was drinking. I studied the turtleneck and considered what he might be hiding under that high knit collar. Were they hickeys, or were they man-gills?

"Okay, slow it down, Jim," I told myself, speaking softly into my beer. "Slow. It. Down."

I was losing my grip, or so I thought at the time. When your wife leaves you, I told myself, it rips the seams out of the fabric of your reason. Man-gills! As if. Blue skin! God, I felt like a jerk. Jean was right, I thought. I was obsessed, I didn't let people in.

I tried to concentrate on my beer, but a face kept appearing in its bronze surface. The man had plucked some kind of harp string in my consciousness, he'd played a suspended chord on the Lyre of Doom and it would continue to vibrate until this very day.

Even tonight, so many months later, so many miles away, as moonlight registers on the bay, I can still relive that weird sensation. I was not going crazy. I was feeling something, like when you think you're going to sweat but the sweat won't come out of your pores.

I needed to focus on something else. So I pulled the three-ring binder out of my shoulder bag. It was a little hard to see, but I started expanding my notes on Nautikon weaponry and doing sketches of dolphinwomen. The glass breastplates were translucent red, which made their blue breasts look kind of purple.

My shoulder bag was army surplus, Vietnam-era, an heirloom from my dad. It was decorated with a dozen or more feminist buttons, souvenirs of my mother's expanded consciousness, and by extension my own. I had started collecting them in elementary school. This was in the 1970s, when buttons had something to say. Like THE PERSONAL IS POLITICAL. Or WHY BE A WIFE? I had one that was just a cameo of Betty Friedan in three-quarter profile. The notebook was a relic too, from the 1970s of my childhood. It was a denim-covered model, with a dungaree-style back pocket stitched on the outside where I could keep my Uniballs.

Why am I giving you all this boring detail about my boring possessions? Because I want you to see from the outset that I was just an ordinary citizen, doing things we all do day to day in this country. I didn't ask for this burden. Didn't ask to be the first terrestrial man in modern memory to come face-to-face with a genuine Nautikon. You might have reacted the same way I did. And then it would be you sitting in this deck chair, rubbing your ankle to get the feeling back in your toes. You and not me. And how would that feel?

But I'm getting ahead of myself again. That night in Rambles! I wasn't ready to believe what I was seeing. By all appearances this was just another business guy in a hotel bar. One of literally thousands across the nation.

We sat for a while like this, everyone listening to the music and the jokes and enjoying the bar atmosphere. Then I heard the man in the corner banquette crack his knuckles. He was standing again. I thought he was headed back to the bathroom, which would be his third trip of the night. Instead he started walking directly toward me. He had a big heroic-looking head and he was swinging it back and forth like some kind of assassin drone surveying the barroom for its next kill. I thought, and I was just toying with the idea, that if this guy really was a Nautikon, he might be seeing our world for the first time. What a trip that would be. It was such an intense thought that I had to put it out of my mind. That's when he caught my eye (or maybe I caught his) and my hands started scrambling across the table looking for something to manipulate. He was just a few feet away, he was looking at me. But then he stopped short and hung a left toward the bathroom. I exhaled.

I waited a couple minutes and then (why? why?) I slipped in behind him.

What I saw in the men's room blew my mind.

It was a two-sink arrangement, with those spring-loaded knobs to discourage waste. The Nautikon had pulled the plunger and filled one of the basins, which must have taken a great deal of diligence. While I took up a concealed position behind the wall-mounted air dryer, he rolled down his turtleneck like a gym sock. Around his throat he wore a gold chain. I thought about what kind of amulet of Neptune might be dangling on his hairless chest. That is, if he was a Nautikon. Which I didn't think he was. Not yet. The room was so quiet you could hear water giggling down the overflow drain.

Then he plunged his face right into the basin and held it underwater for a long time. I used my imagination to picture the man-gills pulsing in the tap water, inhaling. Again, I was just playing with the idea that this guy might be a Nautikon. (Of course he wasn't; that would be delusional. Or would it?) Then the guy reared back and slapped his cheeks, spraying droplets across the mirror. He actually made a roaring sound. It was animalistic and primal. It bounced off the tiled walls, a beast trapped in a toilet tank. He held still for a long second, pursing his lips in the mirror and examining his teeth. That's when they were revealed to me. Along the left side of his throat, just under the miraculously stubble-free jawline, I saw two parallel slits. They flopped open once, twice, and then fell flush against his neck, disappearing in the folds of his mighty throat. Holy crap, I thought. Holy crap. I wanted to watch him forever, repeat this scene five hundred times. But my window was closing fast. The Nautikon had started toweling off, and if I'd stood there another second, he would have busted me for sure.

By the time he returned to his booth, I was already back in mine, hunched over the three-ring binder, astonished at the words my Uni-ball was forming on the page. Astonished and faintly queasy. Maybe it wasn't so crazy, this idea that he was aquatic, that he was gilled, that he was a sea ape. I have to admit that I'd completely forgotten about Jean. Forgotten that just three hours earlier my own marriage had imploded and decayed.

These days my mornings are spent in hearings. My evenings drag by on the deck of the *Endurance,* where I stare out at the bay like it's going to explain everything. At night the deep shipping channel way out there is haunted by supertankers. Their red eyes signal to each other in the fog. They're exchanging rumors; they know things. Sometimes I like to ask them: "Supertankers, tell me, am I way off base here with this Nautika stuff?" I speak these words aloud. "Is there a valid reason they're treating me like a terrorist? Is this what it feels like to have convictions in a world that's grown so suspicious of conviction?"

Conviction. Such a funny two-faced word. The minute I started having them, they wanted to give me one.

The supertankers don't answer, of course. How could they? But sometimes I'm convinced that they're trying. They're using a code. If you wait until the wake of the tanker reaches the marina and then count the number of times *Endurance* rocks on her hull, it can tell you a lot about what's going on out there. If the *Endurance* rocks a certain number of times, we're dealing with a supertanker of staggering tonnage. Just a few rocks and it's empty, going out to pick up more merchandise. It's the way the world works. Right now I'm counting three, four, five, six. I hear a buoy drumming against the *Endurance*'s hull. Seven, eight, nine. The ropes strain against the dock. Ten, eleven. And then the marina slackens and the night restores the calm.

Back in my booth at Rambles! I watched in amazement as the apparently aquatic businessman finished his fourth drink. It was approaching 1:45 a.m. One of the ladies at the bar got up to leave, prompting the others to follow suit. That left me, Kareese, the bartender, and the other guy, whom I hadn't fully identified yet as whom I would soon identify him as. If there wasn't hard rock music pumping mercilessly out of the speaker system, we might have been in the grips of an awkward silence. I looked at the other eyes and they in turn marked my expression, my dress, my undrunk beer. Each of us was a mystery to the others, if not a mystery to ourselves.

There were seventeen bubbles remaining in my nearly stagnant beer. I ticked them off in my three-ring binder as they burst. Seventeen, sixteen, fifteen. When the last bubble was gone and optimal flatness was attained, I decided that would be my cue to leave. But the stranger got up before that could happen. I paid my tab and slipped out after him, looking back once to see the four surviving bubbles clinging to the rim of the glass. In the lobby I hid behind a fern while he mounted the elevator. After the doors closed, I watched the lights climb to the third floor.

"Give me something on three," I told Corey.

"Jim," he said, not looking up from Red Sonja. By now he'd done a whole stack of napkins. "Go home."

"I'm serious, Corey. Jean left me. I can't go home." I realized there was a disconnect between what I was saying to Corey and what was happening to my face. I was smiling.

"Dude," said Corey. He'd always been a sympathetic friend. "I could have told you that would happen. What're you grinning at?"

I shook my head. What *was* I grinning at?

Corey slid the key card to room 319 across the desk with a wink and a scowl.

"When room service comes in the morning," he said, "do me a favor, Jim, and jump out the window."

He was talking, but I was barely listening. All I could think about was wow. The Museum would really be a different matter now. Jean would definitely have to come back. People would begin to recognize my contribution and my insights. If I was right. If what I had seen was real. And it definitely was; or it definitely wasn't. Wow, I thought, registering the gravitas of my situation. Wow. My hands were hard to control when I slipped the key card into my breast pocket.

"Jump out the window," I repeated. "Right, Corey."

Upstairs in room 319 I unloaded the contents of my shoulder bag on the desk. Binder, Uni-ball, candy wrappers, comb.

Entering a hotel room is like walking into a civilized world that was there before human occupation. It gives you the sensation that a habitat has been prepared in advance of our arrival, fully formed. I stood for a moment to absorb the quiet tableau: largely mauve and peach. I took note of the recessed lighting, the decorative wallpaper border that's a survey of neoclassical stonework, the brass lamps that are too brassy for brass. A cascade of dry air spilled down in one corner.

There were so many telling details. A metal stem with a rubber bulb stuck out of the wall, level with the kickplate, anticipating someone opening the door in rage or sexual haste. The bedspread, with its botanical or geological or fauvist pattern, waited there for a sleeper or a lovemaker or a traveling insomniac. The DO NOT DISTURB placard flapped gently in the central air, ready to be deployed. The red light on the bottom right-hand corner of the telephone flashed some uncollected message from the yet unpeopled outside world.

I sat on the bed and called home in the event that my marriage wasn't over anymore.

On the answering machine I left the following message:

I know you're gone, and you'll never actually hear this. But I hope you'll reconsider, because your husband might seem like a loser now, but that phase is coming to a close. I have some suspicions, and if they check out, the Museum is going to be even more awesome than I told you it would be. This is Jim—call me at the Hilton, room 319—bye. And I miss you. This is Jim.

Yesterday in the hearing, they made me listen to that message again. Not just me, they played it in front of all these reporters and dignitaries. It should have been embarrassing, but really it wasn't embarrassing at all. My lawyer laid his broad advocating hand on my shoulder, anticipating a breakdown, but all I did was smile.

When I hung up the phone I could hear a muffled voice coming from the room next door, 321. I recognized it—the slightly honking tone from Rambles!—and I couldn't believe my luck. The strange man who might be a herald from some nautical race but was also possibly just a traveling businessman with a neck condition, he was staying in the suite right next door.

"Talk about a high-pressure front!" I heard him say, to someone else in the room. "Movin' in from the *east,* baby!"

I pressed one ear to the wallpaper. The TV could be heard cackling in the background, and it dawned on me that he was shouting at a meteorologist.

"How'd you like to *do* my pollen count, sweetheart?" he said. And then: "My lake levels are rising too—*rising!*"

It was weird. The guy was personifying the weather itself, a trait, I knew, of animistic societies. What is the connection? I thought, and then wrote it down. This question was underlined four times in my notebook. I sat at the Colonial secretary, so relentlessly waxed that I could see my own reflection in the grain.

"For the sake," I wrote,

of conjecture, let's just say that this guy is in fact an emissary from some doomed aquatic civilization [and no, I wasn't convinced of this yet]. It might stand to reason that he would have a more intimate relationship with the weather. Maybe the people we land-dwellers disparage as "meteorologists" are revered figures in Nautikon culture, priestesses even, in some kind of thunder cult.

He might be looking at the weather lady like we look at televangelists or saints.

The very locus of reason shifted in my brain; that's how blown away I was.

I tiptoed around the ruins of my core beliefs for some time, marveling at the new possibilities, until the TV in the room next door was abruptly switched off. Silence followed. And though I should have gone to bed, I stood again to press my ear to the wall, and stayed like that for a couple of hours. As a conductor I used one of the complimentary water glasses, and I found that by not removing the paper sanitary cap, I could filter out the low-frequency hum of the central cooling unit. But all I heard was snoring—bold, stentorian snoring, but snoring nonetheless. Did he snore through his gills? I wondered. Do fish snore? This was something I'd have to look up. Finally I got a cramp in the side of my neck and went to bed.

So as not to arouse the suspicions of the cleaning crew, I slept on top of the blankets. The waxy duvet was a welcome bed companion after so many nights alone while the cold nonpresence of my estranged wife took the couch. Sleep did not detain me for long, though.

Morning came like sharks. And though the heavy pinch-pleated drapery didn't let in much daylight, I was up and about just after sunrise. After using my palms to erase my impression on the mattress, I took stock of the previous night. Yes, I thought, I *had* gotten carried away. I *was* seeing things. There are no such thing as man-gills.

My hair was a mess in the mirror. I pushed my fingers through it to find that it was also a mess in reality. Then it came back to me in a rush: Jean, the absence of Jean, the death of happiness. It was as if all the air had been sucked out of room 319, out of the entire Hilton, out of Colorado itself. If I'd dared to open the drapes, I would have seen scores of people kneeling on the sidewalks, clutching their throats, eyes popping out. I fought for breath. Jean was gone. Jean, gone. Jim, alone. I blacked out but only for a second.

There's no such thing as a Nautikon, I thought, swishing complimentary mouthwash in my cheeks in a crazy effort to revive myself. My forehead fell against the bathroom mirror so that my eyes could study themselves at close range. I had to confirm my own subjectivity, but this degree of self-regard only sent me into a feedback loop of identity and nothingness.

Then I spoke out loud, and the sound of my voice disrupted the loop: "There's no such thing as a Nautikon. No such thing as a Nautikon." The word came out smelling like spearmint.

When I think of how in denial I was that morning, I have to laugh. If I'd trusted my genetic intuition instead of some hypermasculine concept of "reason," I wouldn't have tortured myself so. There *was* such a thing as a Nautikon. He was booked in the room next door. If I pressed my ear to the wall, I could hear him snoring. Gill-snoring.

I consulted the weather on television, keeping the volume so low that I had to sit very close to the screen. Who knows why I did this. Maybe I wanted to see what he was watching the night before. Maybe I thought it would explain something. But the lady on the Weather Channel didn't look like a priestess in a weather cult. She was young and blond, her voice tuned like a pitch pipe. Her eyes were caked in thick shadow so it looked like she was staring at you from behind a painting. Then my suspicions were aroused all over again. She was wearing some kind of high Edwardian collar, which was weird for a broadcaster, or for anyone other than an Edwardian (which she wasn't). It was unbuttoned to the sternum, a white-berried shrub that you parted and saw something naughty going on under the neighbors' pergola. But what was she hiding under that high collar?

Malindra was the name she gave at the top of the five-day forecast. There was, she said, a diminished chance of thundershowers. A high-pressure front would bring sun and breeze. It was the routine weather monologue, the hands caressing a vibrating magic map. But not all was right with Malindra. She turned slightly to the left, cupping a low-pressure front over the Mid-Atlantic, and her jaw gave off that now-familiar blue glow. Doubting my own eyes, I messed with the color function on the remote. Malindra's complexion phased from pale blue to lizard green to juicy magenta. I smeared the whites of her eyes by pumping up the contrast. Then, when she turned to throw back to the anchor, it was there again and bluer than ever: her blueness. Her Nautikon blueness.

"Thanks, Malindra," said the anchor as a hurricane graphic appeared over his right shoulder. "We'll check back with you on the hour." He too was more blue than you might have expected.

I shouldered my bag, clicked off the TV, and went downstairs to the lobby. Technically I was a freeloader, so I wasn't sure if the Hilton's complimentary breakfast applied to me. But Corey was just getting off the graveyard shift. He was sleep-deprived and maybe a little suggestible, so all I had to do was rub my stomach and he gave me the go-ahead to hit the breakfast bar.

It wasn't long before the man from room 321 showed up. He chose a table by the glass wall that looked out on the pool. After putting his head in his hands for several minutes, he finally met the waiter's eye. This was a surly kid, probably from the technical college. He handed the man an empty plate, then gave him a coffee and a rude gesture in the direction of the all-you-could-eat steam table. No words were exchanged.

As for my plate, it was already piled high with scrambled eggs and two pink boomerangs of melon. I was on coffee number four and was feeling a degree of intestinal distress. The men's room was beckoning, but no matter how loudly my bowels beseeched me, I couldn't tear myself away from the suspiciously aquatic-looking humanoid three tables away. I took several large bites of cantaloupe, reasoning that the fruit molecules might stanch the flow.

I don't want to get on a soapbox, but I'm a vegetarian. I have concerns about genetic leakage in meat products. It's a published fact that beef eaters are ten times more likely to develop bovine attributes. Look around you at the steak house and you'll see what I mean. Eating pork products makes you several times more susceptible to airborne pig parasites, particularly if you live downwind of a pig farm. Sure, you might call me a hypocrite. Jim, you're eating eggs, you could argue; will that turn you into a chicken? And it's a fair question. I guess it's one of my inherent paradoxes. If any guy gets chicken attributes, it will be me. I eat eggs by the gross.

One day we'll be able to resequence our DNA and choose whatever genetic traits we want from a drop-down menu. Some claim this will result in mutant warfare. I disagree. In my opinion it'll diversify humanity to the point where "species" is no longer a valid way to classify. In the future we won't be assigned to certain so-called Body Tribes at birth. That's another museum I'd like to do: the Post-Taxonomy Museum of Anthropology.

The man returned from the breakfast bar, his plate groaning under a mound of sausage patties. It was then that I noticed something else peculiar about him: he wasn't wearing the turtleneck anymore. That morning it was a pair of red Jams and a white T-shirt adorned with a Hawaiian-type dancer and the words SPRING MIXER 2001—HULA LET THE DOGS OUT? This confirmed it for me: he was just some dude. Why would an emissary from the domed city of Nautika dress like a frat boy? Even worse, I couldn't see any sign of the man-gills. For a second I considered the possibility that he was wearing neck concealer. Then I put it out of my head.

The other complication was that he was breathing our air. How to account for that? I wondered. Maybe he's a hybrid, I thought, like Prince Namor—with an air-breathing mother and an aquatic dad. I shoveled in a few more forkfuls of scrambled eggs and tried to concentrate. Then I noticed that his gaze had drifted to the pool. His eyes were gauzy. He was pining. But for what?

Fair Nautika? With its soaring glass spires framed in coral? Its cavalries of dolphins outfitted with seaweed tack, mounted by broad-chested Nautikon warrior women? Queen Ô, Mother of All, wise and unsullied by man-rage? Nautika is widely known as a matrilineal society, which means women dominate the political and economic spheres of influence. They wear loose-fitting see-through robes of pearly fabric and crowns made of live sea anemones. They don't have wars or stubbornness or rape.

Suddenly I snapped back to reality. The Nautikon (let's just call him that; that's what he is if you hadn't guessed) was on his feet and walking into the pool area. Without breaking stride, he removed his T-shirt to reveal an impossible chevron of a chest. I sensed the other diners gasping, especially the women. The man-gill is a breathtaking adaptation, I thought, as I moved to a table closer to the glass partition, where I could get a better view. He entered the pool with a knifelike motion. No wake, no splash. This guy was flawless.

I remember once I went to an aquarium where you could walk through a glass tunnel while sharks swam overhead in a massive tank. But what I witnessed in that Hilton pool was even more awesome than sharks. I was watching a real Nautikon ply the deep. I knew at that moment; he was everything I imagined him to be. I counted so many Mississippis before the guy surfaced again that I lost track. When he went under for a second time, I made my move.

Leaving a generous tip on the table, I slipped into the pool area. My favorite chaise longue was already occupied by a shirt-less man in a jean jacket. He was reading the free newspaper that came with his room. I sneered at him and found an empty chair on the opposite side of the pool, where I opened the binder on a pebbled glass tabletop and started taking notes.

When the Nautikon surfaced at my feet, I was so freaked out that I almost chucked my pen into the Jacuzzi. In his hand he carried some kind of waterproof calculator. I call it a calculator, but I'm sure the technology was way beyond my terrestrial compre-hension. There was no reason for me to panic. He took no notice of hairy little Jim Rath. For several minutes he hung on the edge of the pool, tapping his advanced aqua-calculator with a tiny sty-lus. Then he did something really confusing: he took out a plas-tic sample cup—eerily similar to the pee cup at the doctor's office—filled it with water, and sealed it. Then he flew up out of the pool to stand right in front of me. I think he might have dripped on my shoe.

My god, the guy was magnificent, and I don't mean that in a gay way, although he would probably be magnificent in a gay way too. His body was virtually poreless and as sleek as the skin of an action figure. On his muscular back you'd have been hard-pressed to find a blemish or a freckle. The legs were short all right, but they were sturdy. The feet were flat and, yes, even flipper-like. His brown hair fell in wet cords across his scalp, in a pattern that was unconventional for hair. He appeared to be wearing a wig or a weave. But here's the weirdest part: where the guy's nipples should have been, he had nothing, as in no nipples. I hardly need to point out that this is a widely accepted hallmark of the highly evolved mammalian male.

I could have gazed upon his magnificence all morning long, but more pressing concerns soon intervened. A beacon of urgency shone from my bowel region, and this time it would not be denied. While the Nautikon toweled off at a nearby table, I hurried to my room to unburden myself in private.

When my duty had been fulfilled, I covered any traces of my presence with an aromatic spray I found in the closet and then I made a second call to Jean. She didn't answer our home phone or her office phone, so I tried her cellular.

"Jean," I told the voice mail, trying to temper my excitement with a note of remorse:

> *Remember how I told you there may be genetic vestiges of aquatic "apes" among us even today? Well, I'm not saying I have proof of this, but there is a circumstance going on here at the Hilton that I'm not at liberty to discuss but suffice it to say I saw a guy with*

all the hallmarks of what I've been talking about. He has the hall-marks.

Here I paused to allow my words to sink in. Then I said:

I know my research has been a hardship on you. You have trou-ble believing what I have come to believe—but that's okay. Dis-trust is a precondition of terrestrial consciousness. We're evolved that way, Jean. It's natural. And there's no reason for you to apol-ogize for it.

As I sit here all these months later watching spring infest the Atlantic, and knowing that the coming months will bring the swans and trailing cygnets to feed at my doorstep through slushy wads of houseboat bilge, I'm feeling weirdly Zen about Jean. I can sit in the courtroom all morning listening to my voice-mail messages, fielding questions about my sexual inconsistencies and my comics, with the unswerving conviction that I was right. I wasn't fair, maybe; I wasn't nice; I wasn't selfless or yielding; but I was right. It wasn't the Nautikon that destroyed our marriage. It was the human factor, i.e., Jean. Like most terrestrial humans, she has a deep-seated urge to believe that we're alone on earth. It's the pre-Galilean mind-set, and it tore our love apart.

I continued talking to the voice mail: "I hope one day to prove everything to you," I said.

Can I prove it to myself? No. Not yet. Maybe not ever. But absolute proof can't be like a precondition for doing stuff. We would have never fallen in love if it was. You may not believe me now, Jean, but a love like ours can and does survive all kinds of

*uncertainty. We hate plenty of things that we know don't exist, so
why can't we love something we don't completely believe in? We
can. I'm living proof of that. I may not be reachable at this number much longer, but I'll be in touch periodically to update you on
my progress. This is Jim. Bye.*

I consulted the Helvner. The hour was 9:18 a.m. There was no
time to waste. Checkout was at 10:00. If I turned my back for a
second, the Nautikon could slip out of my grasp forever. A grad-
ual acceptance of his true identity was taking hold, starting with
my hands, which felt busy, unusually busy. It progressed inward
to touch the hairs of my forearms, my nipples, my heart. And I'm
speaking here of the muscle not the metaphor. It was like easing
yourself into cold water, who he was. I just had to go in deeper, I
thought. Deeper, and he would be there.

The elevator was superslow, so I took the stairs. But there was
no exit on the ground floor. Another flight down I opened the
door to find myself in the parking garage. From some remote corner came the compound echo pattern of dripping water. My heart
juddered when I heard a car engine engage. I peered through the
colonnade of cement pylons to see fluttering brake lights. The
white Ford had suspicious plates that didn't indicate any state of
origin; the alphanumeric code exceeded the six-character maxi-
mum. A car of importance, a mystery car. But the head bobbing
over the steering wheel? It was unmistakable.

Seconds later I leapt behind the wheel of my Corolla. I saw
the Ford charge up the ramp from the garage and heard it whinny
as it hit the street. I followed, trying to maintain a discreet distance, but the Nautikon was driving erratically and I was kind of
excited. He nearly missed the on-ramp, and so did I. We squealed

across the yellow vee, and I smelled hot tread. When we were both safely on the interstate, I fell in behind a panel van.

A whole anxious hour passed before we arrived in Denver. It might only be seventy-five miles from my home, but the Mile-High City is terra incognita, another dimension of civic possibility. Call me provincial. I've only lived in two places my whole life—Columbia, South Carolina, and Colorado Springs. Wherever I wind up next will definitely be for the long haul, the prosecutor has promised as much. He has acne scars that you never see in the newspaper photos. With the sentencing some five months away, all I can do is let my peers decide, or maybe a military tribunal.

SIX

Rep. Neil Frost: You know, we've requested this special hearing for a special reason. To see if we can't improve the field efforts and interoperability of the myriad agencies concerned with the homeland effort. But our microconcern here is the widely discussed and litigated Oaken Bucket incident.

Mr. Diaz, many of us know what's widely known—the details of the case from what we've read in the papers and from the court documents—but I wonder if you could give us your first-person account. Now, I'd like you to dial it all the way back to the beginning. Tell us how you first met Mr. Rath.

Agent Les Diaz: If I may, Congressman, I'd like to rewind it back even further, to way before I was recruited by Central. I was a young gun on detail at TTIC. It's 2003, this was in ███████, Maryland,

and I was compiling lab data for toxicity on fruit juices and baby formula—routine rookie stuff. But my record was exemplary, if you don't mind me bragging. I'd put in for a transfer and was being considered at that time for fieldwork. It was just a matter of what degree or what value of assets I was going to oversee, contingent on my track record. I think it was in January of '04 when I got the call from Dick Dodd at the Water Terror Emergency Readiness Team—

Rep. Frost: This is WATERT?

Diaz: Correct. WATERT.

Rep. Frost: And are you still technically with the CIA, or are you now with the TTIC?

Diaz: That's privileged. But, yes, I'm a CIA employee. Least that's what it says on my paycheck. I'm just on detail assignment with NCTC.

Rep. Frost: So you went from TTIC to NCTC?

Diaz: They absorbed TTIC. Dodd, at that time, was holding a spot for me in humint analysis, with a desk in the Northern Virginia office. I was eventually bumped over to the Rec Division, where there was a hole in the field team.

Rep. Frost: I see. Why precisely were you acquisitioned by WATERT? And why was an agent with your skill set, security clearance, and years of government service assigned to pool inspection?

Diaz: First of all, it wasn't just pools. Our sphere isn't single-faceted. It's more like what you'd call multifaceted. The Rec Division, for which I was tasked with leadership, protects a whole spectrum of water features. With WATERT we incubated teams in each of the significant bands of activity, and each team was then populated by operators. My proprietary band of activity is recreational. And, let's get one thing straight, it's as critical a set of assets as you get in the water-treatment or fire-prevention bands.

But why me? I assume it's because of my lab training and background—my dad owned a pool cleaning business. So the match was serendipitous to a large degree. While the rest of WATERT was tasked with hardening our pump stations and reservoirs against terrorist porosity, my mandate was the more family-orientated water resources. Your waterslides, wave pools, Jacuzzis, et al. Which is nothing to sneeze at. Those are the assets that come closest to our kids. That's where Islamofascists could inflict the most collateral damage in the fun department. My credo is bring justice to the enemy so you don't have to dick around bringing the enemy to justice—and that includes the enemies of our swimming pools.

But hell, I don't think I have to justify our activities to you, Congressman. There are a lot of creeps out there, and recreational waters have too long been a potential point of entry for extremists. This isn't some fantasy. It's the real deal. And it's some scary stuff. We're out there taking the pulse and scripting *Die Hard* scenarios to test the emergency response plan. And, Congressman, if the ERP doesn't float, buddy, you dry-dock it and start over. Same as you would in Karachi or at JFK.

We're dealing with percentages and micropercentages of probabilities. Somebody so much as reads the Koran in a hot tub, we've got clearance to act.

Vulnerability begins and ends with the private-sector mind-set. Most swimming pool areas, and even your waterslide facilities, you understand, still operate on the old Cold War model, with an architecture wide open to threats. But this ain't Harry Truman's water park anymore, Congressman. There's a certain amount of ingrained trust of the private sector, or what we used to call the public, that we don't have the luxury of indulging anymore.

Rep. Frost: You'll have to pardon my rudeness, but aren't you blaming the victim to a degree here? It can't be the kid on the water-flume who's guilty when some jihadist blows a fuse.

Diaz: No. Allow me to calibrate you on that point, Congressman, because it's darn important. There's a sense—as you suggest—among your radical containment types, that we as a nation have invited this threat. That we said, "Come on in, Muslim extremists, the water's fine!" We never said that. The struggle we're in, the consequences are too severe to return to that old mentality of "Blame America First." We start blaming ourselves, who do we throw in jail? Who do we rendition? Us. And where we rendition ourselves, I have no goddamn idea.

So, no. I don't blame America first. Or even second. On the list of culpability, America's way down near the bottom. But do we put the burden on the people to understand what they're facing? Should we punish our own population by strapping them down with the onus of national security? Heck, no.

This is a set of challenges that are way different than our public understands. Sure, we're a democracy. And, sure, our decision making needs to be rooted in the public. But rooted in and answerable to? Totally different. We're dealing with enemies that can turn inside our decision circles, so keeping the public in the loop of those decision circles? Well, that would not be wise. It's people like you and me, but mostly people like me, who need to rely on our inner gyroscopes and make those tough calls, without jeopardizing the program or the public with too much insight, or oversight.

With WATERT, our mission, going forward, is to develop and embed vicinity technology that lets us screen people using techniques that don't impede the throughput, i.e., getting the swimmer, or the waterslider, whatever the case may be, in the drink with the minimum of intrusion. Why spoil their good time? We leave that to the terrorists.

What am I talking about in the good old lingua franca? Radar. Radar and radiation-scanning systems just like they're implementing for containerized cargo at ports of entry. These could easily, easily be leveraged for pool safety. I also wrote up a plan, that Dick Dodd still has on his desk, for smart ID cards where we collect biometrics from every foreign visitor and check them against our U.S. visit entry-exit system before they can enter any of our recreational waters, including Jacuzzis.

So essentially in a nutshell we're in the consequence management business, the known knowns *and* the unknown unknowns. And heaven knows somebody needs to be riding this pony, now more than ever. Because there's a certain degree of public awareness that has dropped in terms of these matters. That to me is depressing.

And if you don't believe the water's in jeopardy, don't take it from this old soldier. We've got ample humint to back it up. Al Qaeda's number-three man himself, Abu Zubaydah, told us that Khalid Sheikh Mohammed has some nasty plans for our water systems. [*laughs*] And all we had to do was ███████ the crazy creep to get him to talk. Which is, I suppose, what you'd call irony.

Rep. Frost: Irony? How do you mean, Agent?

Diaz: Well, we ██████████. He tells us their plans to attack our water. Irony. Sometimes all it takes to protect all our precious water is a few more quarts of the stuff. But you know, this war on terror is jam-packed with ironies like that. Too bad you have to redact most of them, because I bet the public would get a kick out of it.

Rep. Frost: Yes, one day maybe we'll write a book. If you don't mind, let's get back to something we don't have to redact. It's 2006. You just joined WATERT.

Diaz: Right. Starting in March of that year I was deployed on a tour of chain hotels to report on the vulnerability of their water features. This includes ice sculptures, by the way, which is tricky business in terms of evidential residue. Ice melts. But that's just the sort of on-the-ground headache we're dealing with out there.

I started with what would have been an eight-month tour of some 180 hotels and business suites across the Lower 48 that we'd identified as potential targets. We had an El Niño spring in the East, and that made for slow going. I prefer for reasons that are strictly my own not to drive in the presence of lightning.

Rep. Frost: That's prudent thinking, son.

Diaz: Thank you. But despite the weather I was making pretty good progress. By June I had cleared all the Radissons, Hiltons, and Hyatt Regencies between the Big Pond and the Big Muddy. By and large they've all got airtight filtration systems and properly vetted pool maintenance staff.

I wish I could say the same for our chain hotels in what you might call the Big Sky Conference. I ran into a little trouble in St. Louis with some seriously compromised pool boys, many of Syrian descent, and an alarming number without proper working papers. But that's all in my report.

The Plains States were a snooze, primarily because there aren't any hotels. I did visit one waterslide facility in ███████, North Dakota, that aroused my suspicions. The owner was a Shia convert if you can believe that. Full-bore Scotch-Irish jerk like me, he'd marched in a couple St. Paddy's parades. Then one day he cracks open the Koran and everything goes straight to Allah. Anyway, that wasn't what raised my hackles. Thing is, he was also ex–Navy SEAL, and he had a shed full of fertilizer that he was hard-pressed to explain. The man is in custody now, and his water park is under federal management—like they all ought to be, if I may voice my opinion on the matter.

My subsequent recommendation to WATERT command was that in future all waterslide facilities be federally mandated to install Z barricades to hamper truck bombs. Or failing that, landscaped berms around the perimeter. All you'd have to do is calculate the approach slope . . .

Rep. Frost: Yes, berms. Well, we all commend you on your good work, Agent. Nobody's not commending you. But I'd like to stay on track if I could; let's fast-forward to the quote unquote Rath case.

Diaz: Absolutely. This would have been in Colorado Springs. It was middle of August—August sixteenth—by the time I checked in to the ███████ Hilton. I'd been detained part of the afternoon under an overpass outside Pueblo. It was severe lightning, so by the time

I got to the hotel the hour had grown late. The clerk on duty, a Mr. ███████████, offered me a suite on the second floor with two doubles. I had reserved a king, but it was late, so I didn't argue. It's a dynamic situation out there, as in the opposite of static, so you have to roll with whatever bedding configuration is handed to you. But when I got upstairs, I discovered that it was also a smoking room. Now, I have sensitivities to tobacco, and air impurities play hell with my lab gear.

So I rode back down the elevator dragging my rolling suitcase, with my laptop bag around my shoulder, and the clerk tells me he's got a junior suite on three with a double. No smoking. "I'll take it," I said. He had to send in the cleaning crew to work it over before I could move in, so I asked him where a guy could get a Comfortable Screw while he waited. Fellow begs my pardon. And I say: "The cocktail drink? Everybody knows what a Comfortable Screw is."

"I'm not everybody," he tells me. That was for sure. The guy was one sad sack, if you don't mind my saying. He's got on a neck brace, ink stains on his fingers and lips, and he's doing these drawings of cavewomen or something on napkins. But even with all those shortcomings I sensed a high degree of dignity. "I'm a Roman Catholic, sir," he says.

Well, so am I. But where in the Apostles' Creed does it say thou can't get a Comfortable Screw after a hard day's work? I explain that what I want is one part Southern Comfort peach and three parts OJ, a Comfortable Screw, and I want four of them, and then I want my forty-plus winks on a Sealy Posturepedic without any smoke damage. He points me in the direction of the bar.

The place was called ████████! Nice ambience, had all these authentic Wild West touches and complimentary popcorn. I ditched my bags behind the front desk and grabbed some pine as close to the waitress station as I could. I hope the female congressladies present will not mind my saying this, but I have a constitutional weakness for the female contours. It's like an allergy—or like whatever's the opposite of an allergy. And it's not unusual for a cocktail waitress to sit up and take notice when I enter her server zone. But, hell, I'm not on trial for that, right?

Rep. Frost: No. You're not on trial for anything.

Diaz: You're the boss, Congressman. Well, I ordered my drink, but I started feeling, you know, self-conscious about my breath. I was wearing a turtleneck—my preferred shirt of choice, weather permitting. So I pulled the turtleneck up over my mouth like a—well, like a turtle, I guess. I exhaled into the fabric and then inhaled through my nose to evaluate the odor. Sure enough, it was rank. Four months of gorditas and rest-area coffee will do that to you.

Before the waitress came back—I recall her going by the name Caprice or Coreen or something—I'd popped three Altoids. As you might well imagine, wintergreen and peach liquor is not a winning taste combination. They interact negatively on the palate. So I hit the head to rinse out my mouth. It was then that I noticed Mr. Rath.

Rep. Frost: Describe your primary impressions of Mr. Rath for the commission, if you will.

Diaz: Gladly. He was seated alone at a booth right close to the door. Seemed to be in some kind of distress, although it was dark. I didn't want to stare, but I did notice that he was a small-boned man, kind of slight in the shoulders like a girl. His face was round and conveyed a pielike quality. His hair was a mess, kind of a straw color and a straw consistency, almost exactly like straw. I'd never seen anything like it. And he had one high forehead. Jesus, you've never seen such a high forehead. Well, now you have, in the mug shot. The hairline started I'd say four or five inches above the eyebrows. At first I thought he wore glasses, but when I got to study him more closely in the light of day I realized I'd been mistaken. It was something about his eyes, how they looked magnified, like they were out of scale with the rest of his face.

Mr. Rath on that first night was wearing a green dress shirt and polyester slacks. He made the sort of style statement you might associate with an old Penney's catalog. You see guys in rock bands dressed like that, and pedophiles. His neck was fat and his cheeks were real sunburned. Type of guy who spends a lot of time out of doors but doesn't get much exercise.

Rep. Frost: Sounds like you got a good look at him.

Diaz: It's in our training, the profile. But yeah, I got a good look at him. And he got an eyeful of me too. And I think he liked what he saw, if you know what I mean. I'm standing at the bathroom sink a couple seconds later, washing the bad taste out of my mouth, when I feel this shift in the air pressure. Somebody had opened the door. When you're an agent, you get trained to sense these kinds of shifts. So I act natural, but I'm glancing up at the mirror and I see the guy, see Rath, standing behind the hand dryer like he's hiding from me. I think, Jesus—this never happened when my wife was alive. It's not really germane, but I was having trouble with let's say sexual perceptions. Having a wife sends out a certain signal, you know, of your preferences. I toweled off, and by the time I turned around, Rath was gone.

On the way back to my table, I see him sitting at his booth. Now he's got a notebook open in front of him. It's one of those three-ring binders like we had in grade school, and he's drawing pictures and taking crazy notes, almost tearing the paper he's writing so hard. I'm like, what's he writing, a love letter?

The bar is in this sunken pit area, so you have to walk down three steps to get to your booth. I got so wrapped up looking at this guy that I tripped and landed on my knees on the carpet. You know, no harm done, but I hear the girls at the bar start laughing. Then the bartender joins in. Great big guy; I figure him for ex-Marine—and that hunch checked out later. Then Rath, he starts laughing too. The little pie-face goon actually starts busting on me. It's like they're all in on the joke, you know, which is at my expense.

I dust myself off and take a seat, and Caprice comes over with a free one.

"Sorry about the steps," she says, sweet as crumb cake. "Happens every night."

She's like a dead ringer for a weather lady we had back in Maryland, and I tell her as much. Caprice takes the compliment and I get back to my beverage. This one would be number four, and like I'd promised the man at the front desk, four drinks and it's bedtime.

When I got back to my room, nothing was on but Spanish TV and weather, so I checked the forecast. I remember it was a load off when they called for a high-pressure front coming from the east. That meant a break from the lightning. I could do my tests in the morning and maybe get the heck out of this creepy place. The next city on my list was Denver, which I was looking forward to. They have a Radisson there with some really creative water features.

Rep. Frost: Quick question before we move on, Agent Diaz. Were you ever made to feel as if your assignment—that is, swimming pool inspections—was of a lesser tier of value to the department?

Diaz: Yeah, but I don't hear anybody joking about it now.

SEVEN

t's 6:35 a.m. and I'm seated on the tiled banks of the Lazy River. It rolls through the Radisson Hotel solarium in Denver, Colorado, a snaking cement trough of chlorinated pool water. True to its trademarked name, it's languid and more or less river-like. Just below the waterline, the tiles are embossed with blue zigzags that make me think of the Berber pottery my mom brought back from her sabbatical in Algeria. The water pitcher had one of those hands with the eyeball inside it, and all around the base were jagged lines. I looked all this stuff up. The zigzags are signs for water that date back to the Neolithic. Even multi-national hospitality chains can't escape the iconography of the ancients.

The Lazy River issues from an obscure source under the cocktail bar. I follow it downstream with my eyes, to watch it pass through a gap in the wall and out onto the patio where it feeds the big kidney-shaped pool. It's mid-August in Denver, and the interlocking red brickwork of the patio glares like radiation inside a pomegranate.

I'm starting to think I'll always be here, sitting in one deck chair or another, beside one hotel pool or another. But just like Heraclitus said, you can never step into the same Lazy River twice. I have engaged this day, the second morning after Jean left me, as if the whole world had overnight reinvented itself, repositioned itself and reordered its priorities. Even my iced hibiscus tea is a weak attempt at personal transformation. Yesterday it would have been coffee or grape soda.

I reach for the cool beaker on the tiles beside my chair, tracing the sweaty lip with my thumb while I think of other lips, sweaty and cool with passion. I remember those nights with Jean, the dalliances in the bookmobile and elsewhere. For some reason I'm having irregular pulse issues, maybe even a heart murmur. The three-ring binder is opened on my chest like one of those shiny foil tanning devices, and a film of perspiration has formed between the denim and my ribs. My heart beats fast, fast, and then everything goes slow and the light gets smeared. Then the pattern begins again. Fast, fast, smeared.

The Nautikon checked in yesterday around noon. I gave him thirty minutes to clear the registration process and exit the lobby before I entered. It had been a long drive from Colorado Springs. I was operating on very little sleep, but I was ready for anything.

"I'm here to surprise a college buddy of mine," I told the clerk, a young woman of about eighteen. I was improvising, which is something I probably shouldn't ever do. "He's a barrel-chested guy with rich, glossy brown hair. You couldn't forget him. He probably checked in an hour ago."

She looked at me, that guileless girl clerk. I searched her eyes for signs of life, then I searched her hair. Hair can tell you a lot about a person's moral compass. Hers was pointed in all different directions, the compass and the hair. She hadn't taken the time to comb it before coming to work that morning.

The clerk poked at the computer keyboard like she was picking lice from my scalp.

"You mean Les Diaz?" she said without looking up. I laughed.

"If he says so!"

"Room 517."

"What have you got next door? I want to surprise my old pal 'Mr. Diaz.'"

Hating me with her eyes, she handed me a key card in a small envelope.

When I tiptoed past room 517, I could see the stainless-steel carapace of room service already at his door. I eased in my key card and entered room 519 on the heels of my feet, pausing just inside the door to remove my shoes. Stealth seemed critical to whatever it was I was doing. I urinated with caution, striking the porcelain bowl just above the waterline so I wouldn't make a splash. I didn't dare to flush. Then I padded into the other room and pressed one ear against the skinny wall that separated our twin destinies.

I heard his door open, close. The muffled suctioning sound reminded me, for a second, of our town house in Colorado Springs. I thought of the desolation I'd felt when I entered our airless, love-free home two nights earlier.

From the adjacent room came the clang of the room-service

tray to shock me back to reality. I could hear the Nautikon eating and toying with the TV remote. Soft salsa music gave way to an unbeatable offer on dog necklaces, and then weather.

"—another *bea*-utiful day in the Mile-High City." The voice belonged to a man, clotted and gooey, like it issued from his groin. He sounded just like the Snowman, which is my code name for that Representative Frost from Indiana or Delaware who's leading the hearings. "Westerly breezes," said the weatherman. "High fluffy clouds. My advice to you? Get out there and fire up the Weber, it's going to be a—" Click.

The swaying salsa music returned. I heard timbales and some trembling woman's voice crying for *corazones* and promising *mucho azúcar*.

I pressed my ear harder against the flocked wallpaper until the design was branded on my cheek. (Rocky Mountain columbines; the state flower; it's against the law to pick more than twenty-five in one day.) I listened for several minutes to the music, the chewing, and the sonorous nose breathing of the Nautikon. It was decidedly unaquatic conduct. I thought, He's toying with me. He's messing with my expectations. But why would he do that? Because he knows that I know, but perhaps without even knowing it himself. Sound weird? People know stuff all the time without ever knowing that they know it.

While my mind was on other matters, evening fell. The sun dropped behind the mountains and the room was filled with a bummed-out blue light. Exhausted, I fell onto the bed and rolled to the opposite side, dragging the starchy bedspread with me. I was a mummy or a blintz or a baby all swaddled up in blankets, but no matter what I imagined myself to be, I couldn't get any sleep. Jean, or the idea of Jean, the core essence of my wife, was sitting right on my chest. She accused me of paying no attention to her, but the truth is I used to lie there every night doing nothing but pay attention to her. I could study her sleeping face in the light of our clock radio for hours. Her eyes were almost as pretty shut as they were open. The lids had a greenish thing going on just below the surface, and on top of that was a peachy pink overlay. I watched them flutter along with her mixed-up dreams, trying to decode the pattern of fluttering, render it into images and ideas. I know Jean's dreams were bad ones. Sometimes while I watched her, she would let out a little whimper. I always stroked her hair and said, "Jim is here, sweetie." Jim is right here.

The wake-up call came at 6:15 the next morning. I felt like having a conversation, but the voice on the other end turned out to be mechanical. Not even a tape of a human voice. A synthetic woman person, scolding me. In the not-too-distant future, this will be the only kind of voice we trust. It will wake us up every morning and sing us to sleep at night. At least that's what I wrote in my notebook, which I'd kept at my bedside table.

From the deck of the *Endurance* I see a motherly lighthouse beam sweep across the bay, and it helps me a little to understand my own ideas. The lighthouse is another kind of mechanized wake-up call. Some drowsy captain sees it and thinks, Thank you, lighthouse. The rocky shoreline appears through the fog, he makes some corrections to his heading and feels right about what he has done and what he knows will happen.

I was beginning to know what would happen. This adventure would lead to some conclusion, to some meaningful place for my life to land. I hung up the phone and jumped out of bed, stretching first one way then the other to feel the loose skin on my sides tighten. Then I gargled the free mouthwash, took my prescription eyedrops, and smoothed my hair with tap water. Before I was even fully awake, I found myself standing at the breakfast bar just off the lobby. That's where I ordered the hibiscus tea and claimed my deck chair on the banks of the Lazy River. I checked the Helvner:

6:35 a.m.

The Radisson Hotel is booked solid with church groups in matching oversize T-shirts. But this early in the morning, even God's children are sleeping. Only a handful of vacationing families ply the Lazy River. A woman of about thirty floats past on a yellow inner tube. In her lap a little boy is clawing at the elastic top of her one-piece. I catch a glimpse of curving bosom, maybe even some nipple, and then look away thinking about candy bars.

I never floated down any lazy river in my mother's lap. I never as far as I can remember saw my mother in a bathing suit. She was way too serious-minded and safety-conscious for anything quite so reckless as an inner tube. The family phase of our lives was passed in the safe confines of faculty housing at the University of South Carolina. We were right next door to the graduate housing, but the faculty got bigger kitchenettes. Mom taught me not to discriminate against our non-Ph.D. neighbors. I could play Uno with anybody I pleased, she said, grad students or faculty. But the truth is we didn't get out much.

My dad died the night before his dissertation defense. Which means he died without a terminal degree. This was in 1974, when I was six. His topic was horseflies and something about mating. My father could have taught me everything I needed to know about horseflies, but after his death I had to pick up whatever I could down at the university pool. I was trying for my minnow badge, and the horseflies were bad that summer. You can't just swat them away like normal flies. I never made minnow, and since then I've had to improvise my own swimming methods.

My dad had a heart attack, which I guess you could say is a pretty unimaginative way to die. But he had a genetic defect, so it wasn't like he had much choice in the matter. Mom found him at our kitchen table the morning of his defense. He was dressed to meet his dissertation committee, one hand frozen at the amateur-ish knot of his necktie, the other hand somewhere else. He'd been up all night cramming, and the momentousness of the situation must have gotten to him. He was weak, like men always are. I was six, but maybe I said that already.

By now the Single Mom and her kid have slipped down the Lazy River. They're under the archway that leads out to the patio. Pretty soon they'll sail off into the fake estuary where the Lazy River meets the pool. And I'll be alone again, me and my hibiscus tea and my memories.

After Dad died, Mom and I got a lot closer. By society's puritanical standards, it might have been considered pathological how close we got. We slept in the same bed and gave each other pet names. In our little faculty-housing efficiency we built what you might call an ideational domestic space. She read to me from the *Whole Earth Catalog,* the *Moosewood Cookbook,* and *Free to Be . . . You and Me,* the book not the record. When I was fourteen I wrote a term paper on the myth of the vaginal orgasm. I could identify spelt and bee pollen years before spelt or bee pollen came into vogue. I was a junior member of NOW. I knew how to operate a tampon.

End of memory. A brown hairdo has appeared above the cocktail bar. I see the fierce forehead, the ranging eyes: the Nautikon rises! This morning he's dressed in Jams and a clay-colored

Windbreaker, collar turned up. When he comes around the side of the bar and enters the pool area, I can see that he's carrying a beer. I'm shocked. Honestly. Scandalized. The feeling approaches total disillusionment, but then it gradually diminishes into mere annoyance.

It seems reckless, coming here as an emissary of a lost race and then ordering beer, well before noon. But then I have to ask myself: What meaning can our terrestrial "clock" have to a Nautikon? Indeed, what is daylight to a guy who was raised in the hourless fathoms of the Mediterranean? Whatever negligible sun filtered all the way down to their domed city, it was too pale to spirit their diurnal goings-on. Unlike the tacky ball of fire that is at this moment pounding the glass walls of the Radisson solarium, their sun was a bright cluster of jellyfish. Their moon a silvery cloud of migrating cod. Beer at 7:00 a.m.? Who am I to judge? I drink my hibiscus tea and feel the back of my neck begin to burn.

What happens next causes me even more consternation. The Single Mom is leading her boy back inside the pool area, rollbouncing the inner tube beside her. The Nautikon takes up position at a nearby table and immediately starts to play eyebrow games with the woman. He's flirting with her, using the plucked circumflexes of his brows. I too feel the sway of their seduction. His, after all, are eyes that have watched the barnacled bellies of whales pass overhead. These are eyes that have seen ruin and crappiness on a colossal scale. They've delighted at swarms of phosphorescent shrimp and wept before an old crushed city that they once called home. The Nautikon has motherless eyes, and I think with some satisfaction of how they match my own fatherless ones. They're brown too.

But he's not exactly motherless at the moment. The Single Mom is practically ovulating under his gaze. He beckons with one finger, and she complies, taking the seat across from him. Meanwhile, the kid stakes out a position by the Lazy River, dangling his piglets in the water. We were all boys once. Or girls, depending.

The Nautikon turns his back to me so I can't read the sexy charms that are almost certainly convulsing across his face. But I can see the effect they're having. The Single Mom is laughing, showing a mouthful of teeth that are yellowed but straight. She tugs playfully at the hem of his Jams and gives him that straight yellow laugh. I have to hand it to him; he works fast, especially for an aquatic. This would never be tolerated in Nautika. A male approaching a female unbidden? That would be a brash transgression of ancient matrilineal law.

My heart resumes the weird pattern of beating fast and then faster and then slowing up until everything gets kind of smeared. It feels like falling in love, but mixed with the tiniest hint of inevitable loss. They're the imps who crank the gears of love: loneliness and betrayal.

He touches her hand and my hands grow cold.

My own mating ritual was less about animal magnetism and more about compounding ironies that eventually led to doing it. Jean met me when I still worked at the Center for Gender and Power. Her Catholic studies group, the Sisters of Ruth, paid a visit one day to check out our latest exhibition. Actually it was more like a fact-finding mission. Jean's parish priest had asked the group to evaluate the show, called *Faith Rape: The Myth of the Godhead and Sexual Violation,* to see if it contained any serious blasphemies.

They walked in, four women in their twenties, eight rolling eyes and a frenzy of smirks. I don't remember having a first impression of Jean, except that she was at least a head taller than her companions. The natural impulse was to identify her as their leader, but that was just the tallness. In fact their leader was a squat woman named Bess Howard, who had a loud voice and the ever-frowning face of a Carmelite nun.

The show had just opened the weekend before to withering reviews in the local alternative weekly. Mostly they focused on the Virgin Mary diorama, an exploration of the phrase *full of grace* through the critical lens of gender politics. You know: Is "immaculate conception" a euphemism for date rape on a cosmic scale? Is consensual sex possible when the guy in the equation is the creator of everything? Tough questions like that were posed and perhaps even answered.

Jilly wanted the "phallic manifestation of Yahweh" and the ambivalent terror and arousal of the victim Madonna to be conveyed with poignancy and resonance. But, she said: "Go easy on the comic book shit, Jim. No melodrama."

What I came up with was, I thought, pretty subtle.

Mary is viewed from behind, kneeling in her blue robe and head scarf, so you can't actually see her face. One hand is raised to block the celestial light that emanates from behind a scrim. It took me a long time to find the colored gel that said *miraculous* and, at the same time, *menacing*. In the end I picked yellow.

To represent the Creator, I built a shadow puppet that threw the silhouette of a lightning bolt on the scrim. Inside the bolt I added just the faintest outline of a penis, so vaguely dicklike that you might not notice it at first, but once you'd seen it you'd never look at lightning the same way again. Or that was my intention, anyway. The critic at the weekly likened it to the logo for a heavy metal band called Cock Storm. I looked it up, and I'm pretty sure the band doesn't even exist.

When Jean and her church group arrived, I was inside another diorama, "The Sex Life of Zeus." This was supposed to be my most ambitious display in the show. In one scene Zeus was going to pay a sexy visit to the imprisoned Danaë in the form of a shower of gold. In the other he would drop in on Leda in the form of a lusty swan, and the Greek god would have his way with her, swan-style. In dioramic parlance it was going to be a classic diptych.

I wanted to pull out all the stops. For the shower of gold I requisitioned one of those rain machines like they use in rainforest displays at the zoo. I planned to light the drops with a crazy golden light. For the Leda part I envisioned an animatronic swan that stood some seven feet tall. I wanted that long neck—whatever the swan equivalent of a gooseneck is—to writhe and strike at Leda's bosom.

I thought long and hard about how to portray a swan, or any kind of waterfowl, in a state of sexual arousal without it just looking stupid. Which must be a problem for the swans themselves too. I couldn't, for instance, risk giving the bird a penis, because people might laugh.

In the end the question of swan arousal was moot. Budgetary constraints meant that we couldn't get the rain machine or the huge animatronic swan. The Colorado Springs Center for Gender and Power was having funding troubles, so I had to make do with a stuffed bird rented from a taxidermy shop. And for the shower we put an intern up in the rafters to drop handfuls of gold glitter every couple of minutes. For cost purposes we combined the two myths, so that Zeus shows up in a shower of gold that turns into a swan and then does it with a woman who might be either Leda or Danaë. These were compromises that I didn't want to make. Still, when I stood back and saw the thing in action, it was pretty riveting. And unexpectedly sexual.

The problem that day, the day Jean came to the Center, was that our intern called in sick and I had to sub in the glitter position. About noon I saw the four women come around the corner of the gallery. They were talking about my Virgin Mary and one of them was saying, "Was that supposed to be a dick in the lightning?"

They all laughed, all except the tall one. Her eyes landed softly on the swan below me, and mine on her. From where I sat, she looked more beautiful than Danaë herself. The Olympian light shone on her upturned face like a golden apple. My hands were aching to do something, to expend the pent-up amorousness I was feeling. But they were full of glitter, and I didn't want to release it until all the women were gathered in front of the diorama.

Soon they stood directly beneath me, my future and sudden love along with her three unremarkable companions. I released a handful of gold and cued the sound effects: thunder; a mad fluttering of wings; and then the call of the mute swan, which isn't actually mute. It sounds like a crow with problems, or like an oboe clearing its throat. I released the second handful of glitter.

Bess Howard, the leader of the group, clawed at her eyes.

"Christ!" she screamed. "My eyes!"

"What *was* that stuff?"

"You okay, Bess?"

"Did that guy just *throw* something at us?"

"What guy?" I was dressed in burglar black to conceal myself from the visitors. I wore greasepaint.

"There's somebody up there."

One of the women pointed, and the Sisters of Ruth all looked up at me, Bess Howard blinking frantically. I tried to apologize but realized that the dynamic was all wrong. I was in a position of superiority, elevated above them. Any apology from this lofty perch would appear kind of condescending. So I slid off the rafter and started to lower myself to the floor, but I must have lost my grip. I was using an aluminum-based glitter that gets slippery when combined with palm sweat. Jilly wouldn't spring for polyester.

I didn't land directly on the swan. That would have been worse. I twisted my ankle and kind of fell forward with a yelp. When I did so, I tried to stabilize myself by grabbing the bird's neck. We both tumbled forward, me and the horny feathered manifestation of Zeus. His beak came off in my hand, and when I finally regained my footing, Zeus lay there in a pile of used glitter staring at me with those miserable swan eyes, beakless and emasculated.

Jean was the first one to speak. She said: "Is that what you call a swan dive?"

Everyone laughed. Even I had to admit it was pretty funny.

The next day Jean called the Center and asked for the "guy who fell on the swan." Jilly handed over the phone without looking at me. Jean asked me on our first date that very night. Before she hung up, she said, "And bring the glitter. I've got some ideas."

My eyes are filled with gold as I think about what happened later that evening, Leda and her ugly duckling. The "shower" of gold glitter, her naked body on mine. Zeus and Danaë. Then I hear the boy beside the Lazy River yell to his mother and I'm back in the present moment.

"Mommy! Mom-*my*!"

The Single Mom excuses herself by raking her nails across the Nautikon's shoulder. Hold that thought, her eyes say as she carries the child through the lobby to the bank of elevators. The Nautikon cradles his head in his interlocked fingers. The beer bottle glistens brown in the blue light of the pool. He sighs and shakes his head. "I don't know how you do it," he seems to be saying, except he's saying it to himself.

Then, in a single, preternaturally sexy movement, he strips off his shirt and stands up. He's walking in my direction, clutching his aqua calculator in one hand and flipping a menacing Maglite in the other. In six determined strides he reaches the bank opposite my table. With only the Lazy River demarcating our spheres of operation, I start casting around for a means of escape. A shame-activated cloaking device would be ideal under the circumstances. My heart pounds. Then, just when I think he might leap across the raging waters and accost me, he doesn't.

Turning right, the Nautikon follows the river upstream to its source. There a jumble of rocks, scree you might call it, conceals the pumps at the back of the cocktail bar. And although the rocks are probably just fiberglass sprayed with a concrete compound, the whole mise-en-scène is pretty convincing, even to a scrupulous diorama builder like myself. I make a mental note to take some measurements for the museum. He kneels to probe a frisée of plastic ferns with his Maglite, stopping now and then to diddle his aqua calculator. The whole act, now that I reflect on it, is deeply sexual in nature.

By now I'm thinking to myself, What could this guy be looking for? What could an aquatic being possibly expect to learn from our cheesy fake waterworks? Could our humble little museum mirages serve his mission of converting the bellicose land dweller to the peaceful feminine virtues of Nautika? Might our vain attempts to exceed nature through taxidermy and three-point perspective actually hold the key to repairing our damaged world? If that's true, I'm thinking, it would be very awesome.

Now the Nautikon's in the water. He swims the length of the river (several hundred meters, I'd guess) without surfacing for air even once. Holy Jesus, it's cool. I know that I should stay put in the deck chair, but I can't restrain myself, so I trail him along the bank. The guy's stroke is otherworldly. It's like a dolphin crossed with a sine wave, all fluid and loping and constant, and through the rippling water his blue sheen is amplified. In the water he comes alive, drawing forth the pure, feminine creature he's been concealing under that brutish disguise.

My pulse races and races, the room smears. Then I lose my footing.

In an instant I'm up to my neck in the surging river, trying to stay afloat in dress slacks and my trademark shirt—a look I like to call Harry Truman casual. The current is way stronger than I'd anticipated. I go under once, twice. I claw my way to the surface. A scene from swim class at the university pool flashes through my mind, followed by a still more terrible vision.

It's the Nautikon, and he's surfacing before me, just like that statue of Neptune's chariot coming out of the fountain at Versailles. At last I regain my footing. (The Lazy River, it turns out, is only three feet deep.) His eyes are flashing with intent, but not for me. He looks past me, through me, beyond me. But for a split second I see reflected in his brown eyes all of my faults. They must be enormous, I think, to contain all of Jim Rath's suckiness. I see my stunted monkey body in duplicate, two flailing specks drowning in his irises. He throws back his head, and droplets of water spray out behind him in slow motion. I see his teeth and I smell his breath. Anchovies and brine and beer and old secrets. Then he ducks under again and I'm left alone with my shivering body.

I drag myself onto the tiled shore and lie there for a while like a castaway. If you're familiar with *Kamandi the Last Boy on Earth* (No. 11; November 1973; VG $45), you have a sense of the gravitas of this situation. My feeling is utter loneliness. Desolation the day after the day after the apocalypse. Please bear in mind that my wife has left me. Please consider this. And also consider that the reason she left me is embodied by the guy in the Lazy River, and consider also that I just made a total jerk of myself in front of him. Consider all that stuff going forward, and maybe you'll begin to understand what I've done. Or what they say I've done.

On the elevator I try to ignore the puddle forming at my feet. I slink down the hall, listening to my sneakers go *squish, squish, squish, squish*. Only when I get to my room do I realize there aren't any dry clothes to change into. Fortunately the Radisson gift shop is stocked with souvenir apparel. I sink forty-nine dollars into a Colorado Rockies jersey, a pair of running shorts with the slogan MILE-HIGH branded across the backside, and a couple pairs of athletic tube socks. They come in a two-pack. After a quick change of clothes in the men's room, I hurry back to the pool, where (no!) the Single Mom is back for more action.

She's draped in a sarong, her plump legs crossed, flapping a sandal against her heel. Either it's an ear infection or the sound of the flapping is actually hurting my head. She arches her back to improve the bosom presentation, and right on cue, along comes the Nautikon, balancing two frosty glasses on the palm of one hand. The little boy? He's conveniently out of the picture.

The Single Mom shows those nicotine teeth. The Nautikon wags his head, delivers a boyish grin, and joins her at the table.

"June," he says. "It's awesome you're doing this. Give the rug rat a little time-out. Let him watch *Dora the Explorer*. Cut loose, girrrrl!" He musses her hair.

"Oh, Officer," she says. "Are you flirting with me? You know a single mother has a lot of responsibility." (Officer?) Suddenly her eyelashes start batting and you think they'll never stop.

"Comfortable Screw?" he says, sliding one of the drinks under her suspiciously perky nose.

"Believe me—it's been a while."

"What say we make up for lost time?" he says.

Have you ever felt utterly bummed? It's like regular disappointment except worse: you have a bucket full of admiration; you're drawing it too swiftly up the well; you're almost at the top when suddenly the bottom falls out, and all that welling-up water of love just drops. I guess I took it personally. But why not? When a man of virtue—maybe the first and last man of virtue—stumbles, even if he's just ordering a cocktail with a sexually degrading name for a plainly desperate surface woman . . . when he stumbles we all fall to our knees.

And if I was heartbroken, imagine what the maiden monarch of Nautika (the wise Queen Ô) would have said about this brazen act of macho jerkiness! The Council of Twelve would have censured him quite harshly if they'd known what he was up to. I mean, correct me if I'm wrong, but this guy was sent here on a sacred assignment to spread estro-wisdom to the surface world. And I would do my best to see to it that he succeeded.

Then—I'm not making this up—they look right at me. Using his hand as a cloaking device, the Nautikon whispers something to June. She laughs. It's a pitying sound. I cringe and the humiliation makes itself felt in the pit of my chest, where the bad feelings cluster. I have to put this incident out of my mind, I think; the Museum of the Aquatic Ape is at stake here. This isn't about my pride. Spreading the great message of Nautika—that's way bigger than my own petty insecurities.

The remainder of the morning I spent in my room with the drinking glass pressed against the wall. It was hardly necessary; you could hear the Nautikon's heavy breathing all the way down at the ice machine. He sounded like a walrus. June was a porpoise, cooing and calm. Not like the bedroom groaner Jean, my erstwhile wife and sex partner.

I'm the sexually noisy type. I hyperventilate. I pant. I even have some kind of high-pitched whistling sound that I can't control. They're sounds that you'd be better off forgetting when the act is over. But Jean's groan of annoyance/lust was so understated and ear-tickling that, long after she'd stopped, you thought you were still hearing it. Even the next day, at Stor-Mor or in the Hilton pool.

In the early weeks of our marriage, sex was a priority. She and I left the futon as seldom as possible, and then only to order pizza or for Jean to go to mass. She had to go to confession now and then to tell Jesus what we'd done. Before she left, though, she always saw things through sexually. The blood shifted under the surface of her face, and right at the very end the groaning escalated into a sharp chirp. That's how you knew it was over.

I would lie there on the mattress, still catching my breath, while she worked the waistband of her skirt over that broad superhot behind, pocketed her rosary beads, and walked out the door to make up with her ex-boyfriend, God.

I listened for close to an hour as the Nautikon went on treating his terrestrial bed partner to his aquatic love technique. Every time the headboard struck the wall my heart fractured a little more. My brain was still aboil with admiration: he was doing a good job. But it was funny, I remember thinking, how pleasure on one side of a divide can effect such sadness on the other. It was like Newton's Third Law, but for love. Equal and opposite reactions.

Finally the bed juddered against the wall and the two of them said "oh" in unison. It was lunchtime, and I fully expected them to call for room service, but a few minutes later I heard the long trill of a woman's zipper followed by the curt yelp of a man's zipper, and then the door to room 517 flew open. June gave a sleepy, satisfied giggle. I listened for the *ping* of the elevator, counted to ten, and then followed them downstairs.

When I arrived in the dining area, they were taking their seats at a corner table. The boy was with them, dressed in yellow from head to toe. He clutched a stuffed toy banana with startled plastic eyes and a determined grimace. It was a hybrid expression that you couldn't sort out. The boy's face, on the other hand, was easy to read. It was puffy from crying and his hair was matted down on one side. His Chuck Taylors were yellow too.

To cheer him up the Nautikon showed him a fun trick. He took a big sip of ice water and sang some weird, enchanting tune while he gargled. The effect was like a whale song, or like pressing your ear to a pipe and hearing your neighbor's radio. The boy was not impressed, but I was. I scooted nearer, as if entranced by the Sirens themselves. For the first time in days I was totally calm. I thought of the robed Spermata, serenading the Queen in Her twin birthing chambers from their ornate chancel. Their nutrient song was a catalyst to Her gestation. Their harmonies delighted, quickened, and completed the oogenetic processes.

There was a two-top free just within hearing range, so I sat down and fell in love again. I forgave the Nautikon all his transgressions. He ordered something called the Rocky Burger, but I just smiled. God, he was nice.

"Medium well, honey," he said, looking at the waitress's open collar.

I stopped her on the way back to the kitchen and whispered. "I'll have the Rocky Burger, medium well."

My food arrived on a chipped oval plate, a patty of low-grade bison meat with grilled jalapeños and a big spooge of Monterey Jack. I lifted the lid on the kaiser roll to watch the elastic cheese sinews stretch and snap before settling into small taupe clots on the charred surface of the meat. Even its native garb of iceberg lettuce and frilled toothpicks couldn't make it appetizing. I pushed away the plate, trying to enjoy the sensation of hunger. I felt like an anchorite in a food court.

But the emptiness in my stomach was soon filled with bile, of the medieval humors variety. I started to resent the Nautikon all over again. I swore at that moment that if I could travel to the distant past for an audience with Queen Ô, I wouldn't hold anything back. I'd tell her everything. I wrote this threat in the three-ring binder, underlining the words no fewer than five times. Even tonight I can see the greasy outline that was left on the page: Monterey Jack.

The Nautikon paid the check with a credit card. It hadn't even occurred to me before, but how was he paying for all this? He couldn't exactly bankroll the mission in *Eea,* the shark-bone currency of Nautika. He charged his lunch, he drove a rental car. Was some terrestrial concern underwriting his odyssey? If so, who? And why? Even tonight on the deck of the *Endurance* the conspiratorial possibilities give me chills. I tighten the afghan around my shoulders and look out across the bay. I guess I'll never piece it all together.

More than a day had passed since I'd practiced my experiments in human gill latency, and I was feeling a serious yearning for the pool. Moreover I was getting deeply stressed out. I decided a few hours underwater were just the thing. After lunch I went down to the parking garage to fetch my swimsuit and snorkel from the Corolla. I had to clear away a landfill of comics and grape-soda cans in the backseat to make room to change. My naked thighs slid over the vinyl upholstery on a film of sweat, which was not really that unpleasant, as sensations go.

My swim trunks were still around my knees when I heard the Nautikon approach. He was whistling an aimless tune. I recognized it at once—the "gargling song" from the restaurant. The notes pinballed through the low concrete garage, bounding from pillar to pillar until his music penetrated the very echo chamber of my head. There I felt it flood the halls of the Museum. I saw the aquatic apes in their dioramas, waxy and dead, come suddenly to life. Little sea children sat in a circle playing at Urchin-Jack.

They held hands in pairs, according to custom, singing their Urchin-Jack song: "Two by two, we are new, three and three, in the sea." Inside her historically accurate weaving room, I saw a Nautikon Councilwoman quicken her pace on the loom of estro-wisdom. While his song filled the Museum, the tapestry took shape, pearly white and seaweed green, a study of the Queen in Her opalescent ova, birthing the endless stream of Nautikon nymphs. The harsh lovely light from Her loins. The laughter of the newborns. The choir in its graven chancel. The whistling intensified. I sat paralyzed, my thumbs looped under the waistband of the swimsuit. The trunks stretched tight between my quivering knees.

Suddenly I heard a loud metallic crunch, and the whistling was replaced by a man's booming voice.

"Whoa, sorry, bro!" It was the Nautikon. The door of his Ford had banged into the side of my Corolla, and he was standing right beside me. He looked inside my car and I felt his eyes land on my midsection. "*Really* sorry!"

I wriggled into my trunks, racking my brain for some kind of explanation. Improvising, I grabbed a half-empty grape soda and a rumpled *Thor* comic. I pretended to read, and took a long, ill-advised pull from the warm can. The taste was like dust bunnies in cooking sherry. I gagged, puked a little, but managed to hold it in and even swallow. Not that it mattered. The whole routine was wasted on the Nautikon, who by now was rooting around in the trunk of his car. I watched him in my rearview mirror as he retrieved a green plastic box the size of an egg crate. The effort on his face was considerable.

When he'd finally left, I crept out of the backseat and climbed the stairwell to the lobby. He was nowhere in sight, which was frankly kind of a relief. I was more anxious than ever, so I didn't waste any time getting to the pool.

I sat on the smooth lip, dropped in, and clung to the edge for a minute, wetting my mask. I sucked on the snorkel and opened my waterproof notepad. The Helvner told me it was 2:35 p.m. I descended and began to dream about Nautika.

EIGHT

I t is the age of Hercules and the hour of Moses, in the year modern scholars will call 1509 B.C. Decades will pass before Zeus washes clean the sins of the Pelasgians with his mighty Deluge, a century will elapse before the throne of Crete is mounted by King Minos.

This is the thousandth year in the reign of Queen Ô of Nautika. And it is most decidedly Her last.

Gaze for a moment upon Her undersea city—the vast dome of red coral, its minarets of milky glass. See the gentle blue Nautikons flee as the hot blood of the earth spills upon the seabed. See the blood coagulate into ghoulish figures that writhe on the sand. Hear their screams as they boil the sea to vapor.

These demons are mere messengers, the heralds of the hell to come.

The Great Kataklysm is upon us.

By day's end the city of Nautika will sleep beneath a thousand furlongs of cold young stone. Her dome, her spires, her temples, and her marketplace—her children of the sea in their bright thousands—will be buried, fossilized, consigned to the lost chapter of an unread history. What was once an acropolis, a utopia, and a motherland will be a museum without entrance or exit.

But this dread tale begins not in Nautika but countless furlongs above, on the island called Sicily, the land given by Zeus to Persephone, the unwilling bride of Dis, on their wedding day.

On the outskirts of the village known as Sica stands a tumbledown cottage with packed-mud walls and an irregular roof of matted reeds. Inside, arrayed on long shelves, are crude iron instruments and terra-cotta jars filled with unctuous powders and potions. In one corner a small furnace burns despite the hot Mediterranean morning. The air reeks of sulfur and burnt sugar.

The laboratory's lone occupant is an aged alchemist in a ragged tunic. He stands transfixed before an object on his workbench. As if borne by some invisible hand, a small pink nautilus travels across the wood surface. The man's wizened face turns resolute. Something has been decided.

On this morning the very pillars of the earth are atremble. The giants anciently imprisoned in the hollows of Mount Etna struggle against their irons. Such is their fury that Hercules himself could not restrain them.

The alchemist is the one called Aricos, scholar and wise man.

His appearance bears the scars of wisdom hard won. The gray hair is scattered and spare, the shoulders twist rheumatic, and his eyes glow as if from pits of permanent concern. Aricos has paid mightily for what his mind contains.

The nautilus continues its trajectory across the workbench until it comes to rest against an earthenware water pitcher. The seashell's merest touch causes the pitcher to glow like a blown-upon ember. The Phoenician moon goddess Tanit appears on the broad handle. A Berber hamsa—the hand of protection—pulsates on the full belly of the jar. Aricos takes up the little shell, and the pitcher resumes its dull earthy appearance.

Suddenly an excited knock sounds on the laboratory door, wrenching the old man out of his grim reverie.

"Papa, Papa, come out and celebrate!" A woman's voice rings clear and joyful through the laboratory. "Today is my Arrival Day, and you have promised me a great gift!"

Aricos contorts his face into a smile. With palsied hand he opens the door to reveal a young woman. Her name is Labiaxa, and she is beautiful despite—or because of—her unlikely arrangement of features.

The other girls of the village shun her, mock her deformities. Labiaxa's feet are grotesquely large and flared, advantageous when she swims the nearby cove but objects of mockery when she bares her feet at the bathhouse. To hide the disgraceful webbing between her fingers, she keeps her hands behind her back. But there is no concealing the moon-shaped slashes on either side of her throat. They gape open when she is out of breath or ill at ease. The others call her Fish Girl. Her father tries to comfort her. He praises often Labiaxa's flawless skin, tinged as it is with the blue of the Mediterranean. The other girls of Sica are dark as terra-cotta and rough with blemishes, he says. Her body shines like the buffed inner walls of the nautilus.

But her father cannot prevent the village youth from insulting his Labiaxa, from hurling stones and hurtful words. No matter. Otherness has made her strong, youthful choler tempered her. Labiaxa has grown these eighteen years into her own woman, willful and brave.

But the secret she will learn on this, her Arrival Day, will shake the girl to her core—much as the earth, which just this moment belches and bucks, throws Labiaxa into her father's arms.

He guides his daughter to a long bench of pearwood. They sit gazing into one another's eyes, his earthly and unsmiling, hers limpid as a sun shaft in the bosom of the deep.

"This shaking!" She buries her face in her father's chest. "It frightens me so! That the world should quake on my Arrival Day—is this not a grave portent?"

With every tremor the mud walls shake loose clouds of red dust. Aricos collapses in a fit of coughing. His daughter strikes him gently on the back.

"Yes," he says when the coughing subsides. "There is much to fear. I'm afraid your Arrival Day may also be a day of departure."

"What ever could you mean, Papa? Who is departing?" She looks up into his wet eyes, her bluish cheeks streaked with white. "No!" she shouts. "I will never leave you! This day may make me a woman, but I will always remain your little girl!"

"I'm afraid you must leave me, my daughter," says the old man. He fingers the pink nautilus and his eyes wander eastward toward the shore. "And when you go, everything you have ever known about yourself will vanish as well."

He removes his skullcap and worries it in his hands. She is used to her alchemist father speaking in riddles, but this is something else entirely. Forcing laughter through gritted teeth, he continues:

"Today is a great day for you! A worrisome day for the world, but great for you! And now, Daughter . . . your gift! Long ago, when you were but an infant in arms, I made a solemn promise. Upon your Arrival I would reveal unto you a profound secret. A secret that would change your very destiny, and with it your past."

"My gift, Papa, is a secret? Tell me, oh, tell me now! I have been so looking forward to this day that I do not know if it is the earth that trembles, or my own heart!"

"I pray to Poseidon that this secret will make you happy, gentle Labiaxa, but I am afraid . . . Now, child, take an old man's hands in yours."

She does as her father instructs. And it is with grave hesitation that he begins to relate an uncanny narrative from his youth.

"When I was in my fourth decade," he begins, "I worked as a navigator on a royal trireme. You may not believe this looking at your crooked old papa now, but I was handsome then and strong."

"Oh, Papa . . ."

He closes his eyes and the story spills forth, interrupted only now and again by a rude ejaculation from the angry earth.

The day was mild. The sun generous. The sea glassy. The royal trireme was on its return voyage from Thebes. The journey had been long, but now Mount Etna was no more than twenty furlongs away. The crew could see the cliff houses of Sica in the distance, and the sight of their homes made them quicken their strokes.

The master was calling out a hearty oar song when a shout came up from the stern. On the horizon there arose a fearsome rogue wave. It swept across the sea, a curtain of water half as high as the cliffs themselves. There was no chance of escape. There was no time—and no way—to ready the warship for this churlish agent of Poseidon.

In an instant the trireme was lifted like a reed, overturned, and dashed into a hundred pieces.

All hands were lost. All, of course, except Aricos.

His last waking memory was of tumbling headlong into the fathoms, down and down beyond the reach of the sun. The cold of the abyss stung his bones. Next came blindness. And then, mercifully: sleep.

"I remember waking in a room whose dimensions and materials defied my understanding," says Aricos, opening his eyes. "I was forced to conclude that I had arrived in some antechamber to the underworld, the salon of my death. Oh, what a curious room it was, Daughter! The walls, they might have been blown from milky glass. But this was no earthly glass. For the room, though roughly spherical, was in a state of constant change. The walls breathed and moved. In the center of the concave floor lapped a small pool of water."

He scans the reed ceiling of the laboratory as if to conjure memory upon it.

"I lay on a low bed upholstered with the leather of some unknown but infinitely supple creature. Though the bed offered no covering, my body was warm, perhaps with fever. I sat up at once, my brain pounding and my ears singing, the better to survey my surroundings. The pool was clear, faintly touched with blue light—like an opal held up to a candle. I thought I heard, somewhere far below me, the singing of a chorus. The words were indistinct but somehow . . . threatening.

"I stood to peer into the pool. In its depths I discerned a pulsating red mass surrounded by a school of, I thought, small fish. They looked to be feeding upon the mass. And all the while, that menacing choir . . . Then a single voice emerged from the chorus. Ah—what a voice! Strange syllables bubbled up out of the pool to slither and echo around the glass walls, quite like a Sican flute played in a bathhouse. Instantly, as if my flaming skull had been touched by a Punic balm, all my bodily pain retreated."

Aricos touches his daughter's arm, another balm.

"That voice, dear daughter—it was your mother's."

Aricos lets these words expand between them until Labiaxa's face tightens with an unformed question.

"I don't understand," she says. "What are you telling me?"

"Patience, Daughter. Some mysteries may not be rushed."

Aricos presses his palms into the rough wood of the bench, as if holding back a menace rising up from the deep. His eyes thicken with sorrow's-brine, and he goes on:

"As I stood there, lost in the miracle of this limpid pool, the red mass vanished and the fish darted away. In an eruption of bubbles I watched a woman rise to the surface. She emerged, beads of blue raining over her naked body, and slipped onto the glass floor as graceful as a sea snake. Seeing Her, my heart . . . it tightened like a pearl."

The old man makes a fist.

"In his day your papa was considered a comely man! But before this most regal of creatures I felt like a monster. She was Athena, and I Polyphemus. She was a garden path no man should dare to walk. And I . . . I was a rude staff hacked from a yew tree.

I wanted to hide! To flee! But there was no escape! Another moment in the blinding rays of Her beauty and I would surely expire from shame!"

He touches his daughter's furrowed brow before continuing on.

"I will attempt to describe Her, though Her beauty, like the water itself, resists description. Words will only float across the surface of Her being, like so much flotsam. She was what wise men call the unknown made known. At one moment She appeared before me as a stately noblewoman, with all the bearing of an Aphrodite carved from agate. The next moment Her very anatomy would dissolve into a fountain of blue droplets. All around Her a corona of countless tentacles would writhe and dance.

"Perhaps it is best to describe Her human guise. She stood a hand taller than your papa. Her body was hairless, its mercury-smooth covering a pale blue. Along the crown of Her head ran a ridge, almost a fin. Her eyes were wide-set, nearly to the sides of Her tapered skull. When She spread Her arms in greeting, two fans of diaphanous skin spread between biceps and shapely torso. Her hands too were webbed, like a duck's feet but infinitely more graceful."

Aricos stops for a moment to consider his daughter's eyes.

"And Her eyes . . . As I peered into their black dilations they combined to form a single bead of red light, a drop of blood that saw me as I could never see myself . . ."

He presses his lips together.

"Ah, but what is the use in describing Her? . . . You will soon see the Queen for yourself, dear daughter! But I . . . I will never behold your mother again."

Labiaxa burns with questions—The Queen? My mother?—but she holds her tongue in deference to her heartsick papa. After a time, the old man regains his composure and continues on with his uncanny tale.

"She touched the walls that surrounded us," he says, laying a hand on the invisible wall of his imagining, "and the milk white glass turned suddenly clear. I saw at once that we were perched atop a tower inside a fragile bubble of air. All around us lay the endless sea. Spread out below, to the limits of my sight, I beheld a vast undersea city. And though we must have been many furlongs under the surface, the scene was gaily lit. Luminescent jellyfish floated past like papyrus lanterns on a lake, casting everything in a ghostly life-light.

"Our own tower was merely the tallest in a broad ring of glass minarets. There might have been a dozen or more, each one crowned with an onion dome that glowed with an urgent blue light. In the middle of this circle of buildings was a kind of lawn, bespattered with reds and blues, that seemed to my weary eyes to simmer like soup in a cauldron.

"But that was only the beginning of the marvels that met my astonished eyes that first day. The city was patrolled by an aquatic cavalry of woman warriors, dressed in shining crimson armor and mounted on dolphins. I remember a manta more fluid than a hawk and big as a chariot. On its back sat a circle of children diverting themselves with a ball and jacks.

"Farther below, on the sandy sea floor, a marketplace teemed with vendors. Ladies strode the broad avenues, their male companions trailing several paces behind like footmen. I remember a garden of blossoming sea foliage that ringed the city. It seemed to me that it was springtime in this strange land.

"Gazing up through the concave lens of our roof, I spied the red ceiling of the city itself. It soared over everything like a great fisher's net. Perhaps it was a huge reef—I saw flashing schools of fish swim around it—that had been carved into a massive dome.

"From where I stood I could see everything, dear daughter. Everything! But I understood . . . precisely nothing! My aquatic quarters lay atop the loftiest spire in the entire city, but my mind was earthbound.

"I was a sailor, remember, and thus well acquainted with fantastic tales of the sea. But I was a man of science too and by nature a skeptic. In these stories I heard nothing more than the delusions of lonely men, glittering lies and tricks of the mind strung out like baubles to sweeten our endless voyages. But if the sailors' tales were true, I had surely arrived in the mythical city called Nautika. And the lofty aspect of my hostess told me that I was now the guest—or perhaps prisoner—of its most highborn citizen."

The bench shakes beneath them. Labiaxa feels the tremors of the earth travel up her spine, climbing that column of sensation to fracture her consciousness. Her world is loosening, becoming less distinct, less certain.

"In Her womanly guise She drew close beside me and took to stroking my head, still cooing in Her melodious tongue. I fell back onto the bed as if drugged. She sat beside me. I fell asleep, and when I woke the sea maiden was still at my side. I slept; I woke; She remained. The length of my convalescence I can scarcely calculate. Nautika is far removed from the harsh signal of our sun. Passing hours are marked by incremental brightening and darkening of the surrounding sea. And time? It meant nothing to me there. For the longer I remained, the deeper I fell into the hourless realm of love."

Here Aricos stands. Taking Labiaxa's hands in his, he kneels before his daughter.

"We are not the same species, your mother and I," he says. "She belongs to an aquatic tribe; I was but a dry husk blown out to sea. And yet . . . and yet . . . we loved." He brushes the sorrow's-brine from his eyes. "We loved."

Labiaxa bends down to kiss his brow. Touching the moon-shaped incisions on her throat, her father says:

"And these, these are a bodily remembrance of that otherworldly love."

"What do you mean?"

"Gills," he says.

"So I'm not a freak? Not a monster? Do you mean to say I'm—?"

"Hear me, Daughter, and hear me well: our tales of merpeople and Nereids astride sea horses, they ring fabulous to our ears. But these tales are not fantasy. Your mother is Queen Ô of Nautika. You were born to us on this day eighteen years ago in that undersea city. Your mother wanted above all else to keep you there in her subaquatic queendom. But alas! You are a hybrid child, and in your infancy you were unfit to survive at such depths. The Queen, your mother, sent you back with me to live on the land. And she remained behind, in Her glittering temple beneath the waves."

He points toward the shore, and Labiaxa follows his gesture.

"Ah, Nautika! Sica! Water and air separate our two civilizations. But we are divided by a boundary still harder to cross. Gender. We Sicans live by the blunt laws of man. Cruel. War-making. Arrogant. But Nautika is a feminine world. It thrives on kindness and light, under the soft aegis of womankind. Thus they suffer no war, no greed, no poverty. Theirs is a kinder and vastly superior civilization."

Here Aricos embarks on a history that reaches back to the dim predawn of memory. In a primitive time, countless aeons past, our ancestors were driven by rival humanoids from the cradle of Africa to the northernmost reaches of the continent. This was the flight the Nautikons memorialize as the Great Estrodus. At journey's end, in what is now the land of the Berbers, they discovered a great inland sea connected to the Mediterranean by a network of rivers. Our protohuman forebears sought shelter in these waters. They took sustenance there, finding peace and a new way of life. Some returned to terra firma, but some, the wisest and most compassionate of this bold tribe, did not.

After many millennia their very bodies were transformed by proximity to the water. They adapted to the aquatic realm with gills, webbed appendages, streamlined bodies, a warming layer of subcutaneous fat, and voice boxes capable of hypersonic calls and echolocation. Never again would they breach the surface to sip the dry, cruel air that had caused them such hardship.

Over thousands of years the Nautikons built a sprawling undersea empire entirely cut off from their surface-dwelling cousins. Their domain spread across the floor of the Mediterranean, and as far east as the Black Sea. By the time of Aricos's telling, this singular city, the domed megalopolis called Nautika, was its final outpost.

Aricos rises stiffly from his knees and, dusting off his tunic, says: "But now, even that final outpost—" He attempts a smile. "But this is your Arrival Day, dear daughter! How can I bestow upon you such a burden as this at the most joyous moment of your womanhood?"

He replaces his skullcap.

"But Papa," shouts Labiaxa, "I don't understand. This is the best Arrival gift I could ever receive! You have given me a mother! At long last, a mother!"

"Yes, child. Yes. But, sadly, I must also take her away."

At these words the laboratory trembles violently. A ceramic mortar crashes to the floor.

When Labiaxa looks at her father again, he wears a glum expression. Throughout the morning, he explains, he has been consulting his instruments, and they have revealed to him portents of a most dire nature. Nearby Mount Etna is preparing to erupt. And when it does, Nautika will be lost forever.

"Not since the rape of Persephone have the fires of Etna been stoked to such fury. That was some thousand years ago, and it was a mother's rage that lit those fearsome flukes. But I see not Demeter's hand in this conflagration. This is surely the wrath of Dis himself! Today, the giants entombed thence have been roused to fiery violence once again. By dawn tomorrow your mother will be incinerated and entombed in stone, and alongside Her all the ancient wonders of Nautika."

Now comes the most difficult part of Aricos's story.

"Queen Ô saved my life," says the old man, looking older now. "And She gave me yours. In exchange the Queen asked only one concession. On your day of Arrival, what the Nautikons call *Eeeo,* you must be returned to Her. By then, She surmised, your gills should have been developed enough for you to live amongst her kind."

Labiaxa gasps. It is now plain what her father is asking of her.

"But why must I go?" she begs. "You know I can never leave you, Papa!"

"I'm afraid you have no choice. It seems the Queen has a secret fate planned for you. And nothing—whether it be earthly cataclysm or a father's love—may interfere with fate."

"Whatever can it be?"

"I dare not speak of it. I *cannot* speak of it, for it surpasses my understanding. My masculine tongue can scarcely shape the words. Know only that your mother needs you."

Her mind rebels. Her eyes dart about the laboratory, looking for some escape. But there is no way out. Labiaxa must return to the mother she never knew, to the home she never knew. To Nautika.

"I swore before all the gods," Aricos says, "that I would fulfill your mother's only wish. And now the hour of fulfillment is upon us." He cannot meet his daughter's beseeching eyes. "You must fly, child—fly to your motherworld!"

She clings to him, tears at his tunic. "But how, Papa? How will I find this place?"

"The sperm whale will guide you," he says. "Her name is Oooeea, and she is the only conduit between our two worlds. She carried your poor papa to his rescue in Nautika. She carried the two of us to the surface after you were born. Now she will carry you home."

"But where? This is all so fantastical! Where will I find this whale? And when I reach my motherland, how will she know me?"

"By this." From the workbench he takes the strange water pitcher and, handing it to his daughter, says, "This is the Gargoulette of Nautika."

Labiaxa touches the handle, and the earthenware vessel again begins to glow with its otherworldly light. The clay turns translucent. The hamsa waves on its flank and the hips of the moon goddess begin to sway. Then she sees the source of its animating fire, three phosphorescent jellyfish floating inside the pitcher.

"Lunar medusae," says her father. The floor trembles and the three glowing creatures bob like moons reflected on a bay. "Long exiled from their home, whenever the Gargoulette is touched by the sea—or by a daughter of the sea—the three medusae burn with longing."

Aricos beholds Labiaxa with melancholy, burning it seems with his own phosphorescent longing.

"Merely step into the surf and raise high the Gargoulette," he explains. "The medusae will summon Oooeea to your aid. And the sperm whale will convey you to Nautika. But take good care of this talisman, for it shall also be your calling card at the court of the Queen."

NINE

The next time I consulted the Helvner it was 8:38 p.m. I knew the pool closed at 9:00 so I surfaced, toweled off, and headed back to my room.

Through the wall I could hear the weather report going full throttle. The Nautikon seemed to be alone for once, and for that I was pretty grateful. I stripped off my swim trunks, showered, and changed into the slacks and Harry Truman shirt, which were now more or less dry except for some dampness in the lower fathoms of the pockets.

Suddenly I became aware of my stomach. The swimming-pool hunger and the regular hunger had combined to form a superhunger that conveyed me back to the dining area, where I ordered a jumbo plate of scrambled eggs. I could see the waitress waging an internal debate in her brain. It was dinnertime: eggs would be a special request. She would be justified in telling me to go to hell. Instead she snapped up my menu and turned on her heels. The action was so swift, so aggrieved that her spun-poly skirt actually flew up.

The eggs arrived via busboy, a depressing object lesson in the dangers of early athletic success. On the sliding scale of brawn to paunch, he was slipping inexorably paunchward. I looked inside his bland jock eyes, but I could tell that his mind was elsewhere. It sat in a dark room, watching his body score a junior-varsity touchdown on a projector screen. His mind watched, counting the record yardage that ticked by behind him. The busboy was too stupid to know he was a failure, which I guess is better than being too smart to know you'll never succeed.

I dispatched the scrambled eggs in mere minutes. I was downing my fourth ice water and awaiting a fifth, which didn't seem to be forthcoming. As for the Nautikon, he was nowhere to be seen, so I stood to get the attention of the waitress. She relayed my message to the busboy, who brought my check as slowly as humanly possible. I tipped too much, as usual, and walked to the hotel bar to kill time.

And—what do you know—there was my new friend. He sat alone on a very tall stool at a very tall table. His very tall tumbler was already drained down to the ice. The sucking sound I heard was the Nautikon trying to pick up stuff on his tabletop with a bendy straw. I watched him suck until his bluish face turned burgundy, but for all his effort, he only managed to raise a sugar packet a few inches off the table. Their lung capacity is not great. When the packet dropped, I heard him curse softly to himself.

I sat at the bar with my back to him. The bartender was a woman of about fifty. She was some kind of goth or Wiccan, with black hair, black fingernails, and a pale neck festooned with clunky runic jewelry.

"What can I get you?" she asked.

I raised one finger to stop time for a second while I took a few notes in my binder. And then, just when I was ready to place my order, I heard a voice behind me:

"Hey, man."

It was the voice of the Nautikon. As the only other man in the bar, I could easily deduce that he was talking to me. The Wiccan bartender raised her eyebrows. I did nothing. Then he started shouting:

"I said hey!"

I ordered a beer.

"What's *wrong* with you?" he said.

The fade on the back of my neck, still somewhat neat from Jean's last-ever haircut, was standing on end. If I'd been a porcupine, I would have shot the hairs out like quills and scurried into the underbrush. But I'm not a porcupine. I'm soft and defenseless. The Nautikon stood close behind me.

"Didn't I see you in Colorado . . . ?" He had to think for a moment. "In Colorado Springs?" he said. "Kinda weird we just *happen*—just *happen* to have the same travel itinerary."

I spun back on my barstool to face him, hoisting my pint glass as a gesture of détente. I was smiling, but to tell the truth the corners of my mouth were only being held up by the terror in my eyes.

"Yeah," I said, not knowing what else to say.

"What's that supposed to mean?" he asked.

"It's just an observation."

"You know what I think?" he said. I started drinking my beer, something I make a policy of never doing, for reasons that will soon become clear. The entire pint went down in one gulp, and my head instantly turned weird. "Do you know what I think?" His words came out slurry and cold, like something extruded from a soft-serve machine.

"No—"

"I think somebody sent you here is what I think. And I intend to find out who. What is it with you people? Do you think we're all oblivious, or do you think we're going to cut and run the minute you do your suicide bomber song and dance?" He was pointing at me with the bendy straw. "You try any of that cute Lockerbie shit in my jurisdiction, and—*pow!*" He jabbed at me with the straw. A single dot of pink stained my shirtfront.

The bartender set down a follow-up beer. The wooden *thunk* made me jump. I thanked her through the corner of my mouth, and by the time I turned back around, the Nautikon had advanced to within inches of my face. My field of vision was all Nautikon, his broad chest so close I could almost hug the guy, which under the circumstances would have probably sent the wrong signal.

"You mind if I—?" Inexplicably his tone had turned chummy. He gestured at the empty stool next to mine. My hands were all over my pint glass, all over the bar. The Nautikon was sitting beside me! Beside Jim! I bounded from fear to disappointment to awe and back again, stones in a raging white water of emotions. At any moment I might slip and—and what?

"Can I tell you—can I tell you what tonight is, buddy?" He extracted a ten from his pocket (terrestrial cash!). "Another Screw," he told the bartender. "And this time, hurt me a little." He gave a sour snort that was supposed to represent laughter. It was the kind of utterance designed to mock the whole institution of mirth. "Tonight"—he stared at my throat—"is my *goddamn* wedding anniversary."

Congratulating him felt like the wrong thing to do.

"That's wonderful," I said, lifting my beer and drinking again. "I understand that's a cause for great rejoicing among your people."

He looked confused, then scowled. "The bitch is dead!" He kicked the bar so hard you could hear the bottles tinkle together on the other side.

His cocktail arrived not a moment too soon. The Wiccan muttered some kind of incantation, then she smiled at me. I remember thinking that she had good teeth for somebody in her cultural subset.

The Nautikon still had the bendy straw from his previous drink. He combined it with his new straw to form a compound straw with massive sucking potential. The pink fluid disappeared in a single pull. He never took his eyes off my throat. By then I was really, really scared.

"The bitch," he repeated, now smiling. He leaned even closer to my face, and at this proximity his complexion was truly intense. From his chin to his hairline there wasn't a single pore or patch of stubble. And from this vantage point I could plainly see the white scars of his man-gills peeking out over the collar of his knit shirt.

By now the beer was flooding my spatial and temporal lobes, so the next few scenes flipped by in a series of still images, like flash cards. In the first one he slapped another bill on the bar. In the next I saw him weave across the room, bouncing from table to table. Then I was looking into my second, or third, beer. Then the second or third beer was empty. And in the final scene I heard a loud *ping* and saw the Nautikon standing in the elevator. He glared at me across the lobby. The doors closed, and I found myself alone with the Wiccan.

"Friend of yours?"

"Yeah," I said, not meeting her eyes. "He's supposed to be."

By the time I got back to my room, it was late. I could hear my neighbor whistling his ancient melody, his pitch severely compromised by alcohol. I heard a sound like a zipper, I heard the noise of a metal screw-top pirouetting on a desk and the *tick-tock* of liquid being stirred in a beaker. Alka-Seltzer, I surmised. Or something.

Three beers and the Nautikon's bizarre verbal assault had taken their toll. It wasn't long before I'd fallen fast asleep with one ear pressed against the wall. The dream I had that night was more complicated than I can explain in human language, but suffice it to say I was swimming with Steller's sea cow.

At one point she turned to me and said: "Jim, the personal *is* political!" This was the sea cow, talking to me. I said, "I know." Next thing I remember, she gave me a hug. The situation was borderline sexual until, with her whiskery muzzle right up in my ear, she shouted:

"*Ping!*"

I said, "Ping?"

She said, "Yes, *ping*."

"Ping?" I said.

"Yes, Jim, *ping* is the sound of the elevator. The Nautikon is getting away."

I jumped up, totally wide awake now, and ran out into the hallway, clutching my book bag under one arm and my wet swim trunks under the other. When I reached the elevator, it was already on a downward trajectory in the shaft. So I took the stairs, four at a time. At the ground floor I had to remind myself to remain calm. I inhaled with purpose. Don't startle him, Jim.

I slipped out of the stairwell and hid inside a pay-phone alcove. The bar was closed for the night. The clerk's shiny bell sat conspicuously on the front desk. The lobby was quiet and dim.

Then I detected motion by the source of the Lazy River. A brown dome of hair bobbed above the rocky outcropping. I crept on all fours to a spot behind the bar to get a closer look. The Nautikon knelt in front of the green box—I recognized it as the one he'd taken from the trunk earlier that day. He held a length of rubber tubing and a plastic jug filled with some kind of milky fluid. It looked like milk. Then he shifted onto his stomach, grunting as he fitted one end of the tube inside a crevice. He looked over his shoulder. The eyes were crazy with brown intent. He tipped the jug and funneled the liquid into the tube.

Even from behind the bar the odor was intense. Pointed, vengeful. His eyes narrowed, the mouth smirked. He looked like a bully with a chemistry set.

A few seconds later he was dusting off his khaki knees and packing everything in the green box. It was then that I noticed he was wearing yellow rubber gloves. I let him get as far as the stairs before I left my hidey-hole and summoned the elevator. On the fifth floor the hallway was weirdly quiet, quietly weird. As soon as I passed room 517, I knew I'd made a critical error in judgment. The Nautikon's door hung open a crack. Every light was on.

———

The houseboat *Endurance* is on loan to me. This is thanks to a friend of my mother's, a man I always knew as Uncle Keith. He's gay, but he's also a billionaire, and he was generous enough to let me use the boat for the duration of my trial. Uncle Keith isn't a blood relative; he was one of my father's fraternity brothers, and after Dad's heart attack Keith gave us a lot of support, both collateral and moral. Now he lives in a sprawling lodge in Alaska, where he does something with oil pipelines and money. The *Endurance* he usually reserves for entertaining D.C. lobbyists and such, but when he heard about my troubles, Uncle Keith made a few calls. He got me sprung from the military holding cell (wherever that was) and arranged for house arrest. Every time the ankle bracelet starts to chafe, I think of Uncle Keith and try to remain grateful.

They arrested me in Prospector's Bend, parked outside the video store, head in hands, hands palpating my head. A highway patrolman rapped on my passenger-side window with a pair of handcuffs. I started to get out of the car, but there was another officer on my side pointing a revolver at me. I rolled down the window and said: "Oh, my god. Is everybody okay?" I knew they weren't. And I knew I wasn't either.

"What do you care?" He yanked open my door. "Son, I'm arresting you on suspicion of attempted murder and—" something else procedural. Over the roar of fear and denial in my skull, I couldn't quite hear the rest of the sentence.

I spent a urine-scented night in the Summit County lockup. Unless you count the "lunar reformatory" scenario Jean and I tried that one time, I'd never been in custody before, so I was pretty shocked by how unhygienic it was. Some time before sunrise I woke up on my feet, two men in Windbreakers on either side of me. I was wearing shackles. Actual shackles. And walking down a cinder-block hallway.

The sliding door of a van opened before me like a stargate to mystery. But not the cool kind of mystery, the other kind. The Windbreakers helped me inside, where I sat on a bench in the cargo bay and waited for something else to happen. The next two months would be dominated by this feeling, always waiting for the next thing.

The van didn't have any windows, but they blindfolded me anyway. I sat there in a state of eyeless expectation for an hour or more. Finally I worked up the nerve to say: "Don't I get to call somebody?" But my voice came out in a reduced state, like it was leaking out of my ears.

"What?" said one of my handlers. "What did he fucking say?"

I didn't repeat the question.

Finally the van pitched to one side as a heavy body climbed in beside me. I could hear him breathing, and I smelled something like chest ointment. Eucalyptus and WD-40. The door slid shut, and then even the ambient light that had filtered through my blindfold was gone. I thought perversely of Jean. How was I going to explain this one? I pictured us in the kitchenette. I was pleading my case while she Purelled her hands and forearms and didn't look at me. As if that scene would ever take place in a million years. Imagine the kid after the fireworks stand explodes thinking how pissed off his boss is going to be. That was my state of mind. I was way beyond the domestic sphere of complications. I just didn't know it yet.

Then came the bright hypodermic stab that put me to sleep.

I remember, or picture myself remembering, waking up to the twin agonies of migraine and cabin pressure. Mother was throwing pottery into the air, and it stuck there between the stars. I smelled the ointment, and a man's voice said, "Jesus, hit him again." The blindfold was all sweat. I felt another needle in my arm. Saw Jean laughing at the stars. Then wheels skidded as they hit a tarmac. I smelled rain and my throat was dry.

Another van, or possibly the same one, carried me for many miles on unimproved roads. The ointment man sat beside me, farting. I felt something prod my groin area and laughter came from the front seat. The laughter didn't sound American, but that's all I can say about it. I heard a garage door grumble and then off came the blindfold. I was now awake enough to be fully terrified. I had wet myself at least once.

The holding cell wasn't like you'd picture it, if you've bothered trying to picture where we bottle up our wraiths these days. It wasn't some cinder-block latrine with a steel-grated window looking out onto a brick wall, or a bamboo cage in a dry lake bed. It was more like a conference room. There was baseboard heat. In addition to my reasonably comfortable cot, I got a table and a chair. Everything was bolted to the floor, but it was clean and new. On one wall they'd mounted a speaker, and that's how I communicated with my captors.

I even had a real window. It looked out onto a courtyard with a single old tree. I have a very limited grasp of botany, but this didn't look like any tree in the state of Colorado. It had fingery leaves like magnified pine needles and a fat trunk that looked like a tangle of calf muscles. In the moonlight the fleshy folds in the trunk appeared to open and close. I smelled sap and sex, and recognized these as pheromones. I knew the tree was trying to tell me something, but the language of the nose is subtle and hard to translate.

At that juncture I didn't know I was in the hands of the CIA or Homeland Security or whatever federal permutation they ended up being. I didn't hear the words *enemy combatant* until months later. But I'd read about renditions. And I thought no way were Colorado cops smart enough to pull that stuff off. This was a secret police scenario.

It was a covert matter, and I could think of only one reason for all the high-level secrecy. I knew about the Nautikon. I was most certainly the only civilian to identify him. The only civilian qualified to identify him. But maybe the Feds were tracking him too. It would definitely be in their interest. Here he was bringing a message of estro-wisdom to the brutish realm of the air drinker—and that's not a welcome message, especially with the present administration. This was all speculation, of course. Nobody told me directly: Jim Rath, you're under arrest for aiding and abetting an emissary from a lost aquatic species in his mission to reform humanity according to matrilineal law. Nobody came out and said that.

Most people in my situation would have been thinking about Abu Ghraib or Guantánamo. But my first thought after they locked the door was of a picture I'd seen several months before in the Colorado Springs *Gazette*. This was of a middle-aged man who'd been arrested in Baghdad. The guy resonated with me because he was a curator. He'd been working at one of those museums that got ransacked after the invasion. In the picture he wore two neckties, one around his neck and another around his eyes. His mustache was of the beefy dictator variety. You could see he was wearing plastic handcuffs, like he wasn't even important enough to get real ones. He was sitting on a bench, and the bottom three buttons of his dress shirt had popped so you could see his hairy belly bulging over his lap. The soldier standing next to him pointed a rifle at the ground. His face was blurred out.

I remember thinking, That poor guy. It's over for him. He doesn't have a mother anymore or a wife or friends or hobbies. He'll never knock off work in the middle of the afternoon again to see a movie. He won't read Ursula K. Le Guin novels aloud in bed until his wife tells him to can it. He'll never buy his mom tickets to the Maya Deren film festival to lure her out for a visit. He won't spend the next two weekends making resin molds for an invisible submarine. His Wonder Woman action figure will never pilot that submarine to rescue the Plodex Marrina from her undersea coffin. He'll never microwave another burrito or think about how a technical mishap might shower him with radiation, granting him the innate qualities of a burrito: thrift, convenience, and tastiness. This poor guy will never get to do any of that stuff.

I was subjected to a few interrogation sessions, although none of the questions made any sense. The voices came through the speaker all scratchy and scrambled, like they were crows with the power of human speech. The crows asked me for the "source of my lie," whatever that means. They wanted to know the last time I'd been to London. Was I part of a cell? Did "Jeannette" participate in the planning? They said we know about the operations center and the maps. They told me we've seized foreign military materiel that was on my person prior to the incident. How many weeks had I spent in Saudi Arabia? They didn't ask me anything about the Council of Twelve or Queen Ô or even the Nautikon, but I knew what the subtext was. These people never ask you a direct question.

Several days passed. I flipped through my mental Rolodex, looking for an ally on the outside, an acquaintance who might have the power to rescue me. There was Jean, but after my arrest and rendition to a secret prison, she was definitely off the list. There was Corey, but he was a hotel desk clerk. There was Queen Ô of Nautika, but She'd been killed in a volcanic eruption thousands of years ago. Then I thought of Uncle Keith. He was in petroleum. He had lobbyists on retainer. He watched the Washington Nationals in box seats with Dick Durbin. If Mother could get in touch with Keith, this whole matter might be straightened out. But another week passed and there was no word from anyone. I began to lose hope, which I now realize was a pointless virtue anyway. I was screwed.

This was actually happening. A situation weirder than anything that transpired in a comic book, and it was happening in real time on a material plane of being. So I decided that, to retain my sanity, I would have to replace this reality with a different, equally unreal circumstance that was more to my liking.

A month after Jean and I were married, Colorado Springs was bombarded by a massive blizzard. We made a final desperate voyage to the supermarket for microwave burritos and coffee beans before the heavy stuff started to fall. By the next morning the city was buried under two feet of snow. For days we were trapped inside the condo watching nature specials and huddling under blankets on the sofa.

To maintain our sanity we made up a story. We were two survivors of Shackleton's doomed voyage to the Antarctic. Left behind on barren Elephant Island while Shackleton sailed for help, we built a makeshift shelter from the wreckage of our boat (the condo) and survived by eating penguins (burritos). We made love like a shipwrecked Adam and Eve, constantly, as if it were up to us to populate our island refuge.

The outside world of Colorado Springs, the bookmobile and Stor-Mor, the Hilton pool and the Hot Mart, they all ceased to exist, eclipsed by our cozy snowbound fantasy. I could have played this role for weeks, forever. I loved Jean so much that I wanted it to be me and her alone, even if that meant living in a world of self-delusion and make-believe shipwrecks.

Unfortunately Jean did not share my enthusiasm for the fantastic. After three days on Elephant Island, she hurled a penguin at the icebound timbers of our lean-to and screamed into the endless polar night.

"Enough of this shit!"

I tried to stop her as she raced for the door.

"No!" I said. "We don't know what's out there!"

It was like that moment when your best friend on earth stops being a kid anymore and you're left playing with action figures all summer by yourself. I'd been abandoned to my realm of make-believe. It wasn't the first time, or the last. Jean flung open the door, and we both looked out onto the parking lot, freshly plowed and salted. The sun was shining on the Corolla. The streets were clear.

There's a lesson in this. As I sat there in that secret prison for countless weeks, I figured out what it was. Like Jean, I was trapped in somebody else's fantasy, and that's a grim place to be. This was somebody else's twisted role-playing game, where an unemployed comic enthusiast could be an enemy of the state and it was okay to put him in a secret prison with crows yelling at him over a PA system. The lesson is it's okay to live in a fantasy world of your own making, but you never, ever want to live in someone else's. Especially if they have guns.

I decided to replace this forced fantasy with one of my own. I wasn't a prisoner; I was the nascent Galactus, who having emerged from the Cosmic Egg in the second Big Bang, now lay in the incubation chamber of his starship waiting for life to form in the universe so that he could emerge and consume its newborn worlds! This fantasy was working for me. But then, randomly, a guy in a ski mask came in and shouted at me about my mercury levels. I said, "Maybe it's the enamel model paint," and he punched me.

After that I tried counting sunsets but gave up at fifty-nine or sixty. One morning a nurse in a ski mask walked in and gave me another injection.

This time I didn't wake up until I was being carried onto the houseboat. To the neighbors I must have looked like a drunk being dragged home by some very big friends. There was a digital calendar on the kitchen counter. February 4. I'd been in my secret prison for more than five months.

The next morning I was given cereal and grapefruit juice. They showed me how to operate the TV. My Harry Truman shirt was draped across the sofa, cleaned and pressed. Uncle Keith had come through.

Some nights I think I'd rather be renditioned to Poland or wherever. Rather be back in that locked conference room. The marina is quiet tonight, but last night there was a dinner party on the little yacht next door. You could smell mesquite, and the strains of Jimmy Buffett wafted over the water to my deck chair. This made it hard to relax, and believe me I needed my rest. This morning was a doozy in front of the Snowman. My lawyer told me the hearings are going well, but he says that every day, the Fat Man, squeezing my elbow and giving me a look of conviction. His smile is false, but at least it's a smile.

"Hang tough, son," he says as they escort me down the steps

and into the van. But I can see it in the Snowman's eyes. He wants to get me. He's got reasons to get me that I'll never understand.

The Fat Man tells me that "Diaz" is attending his own hearings. Whatever the Nautikon is saying about me can't be good. I wish they would let me sit in, but whenever I ask, the lawyer just laughs. I just want to see him, I say. I won't talk. This is the wrong court to try him in, I explain. It's way out of his jurisdiction. He belongs in front of the Council of Twelve. Let Queen Ô decide his fate. Mother of Us All, Mother of Mothers. The crime is treason, but it's not against us. Oaken Bucket is just a smokescreen. Even I can see that. And I'm just a jerk.

Meanwhile I'm trying hard to avoid the news. I don't watch the plasma TV Uncle Keith has installed belowdecks. But we pass a newsstand on the way to the hearings, and there he is on the cover of a morning tabloid. He's ducking into a dark sedan or drinking a soda on the Capitol steps. Even without reading the articles it's impossible not to notice the shell game the Nautikon is playing with the truth. He has been misrepresenting himself. Or he's been instructed to misrepresent himself, for the public good, whatever that might be these days. The captions all call him Agent Les Diaz, like the clerk called him in Denver, like my lawyer does. What a lame alias.

But let's get back to room 517 at the Denver Radisson. Like I said, the Nautikon's door hung open a crack. I peered inside. Every light was on, but the bed was neatly made and his luggage was nowhere to be seen. As I tiptoed into the room, the panic climbed from the arches of my feet and drove its sour tentacles into my bowels. I felt the urge to crap. And then:

ZZAAAAHHHH! KUNK!

The last things I saw were two brown eyes and a green box. Then I was on the floor, my nose badly rug-burned. My left eye was showing nothing but purple fizz, but in my right I could see the toe of a man's shoe. It nudged my forehead, and then I guess I blacked out again. The Mediterranean Sea glittered before me. And the sperm whale called my name . . . once, twice . . .

I sat up, trying to listen for the Nautikon's footsteps, but my ears were ringing too loudly. There was no question about it, he must have used some kind of sonic stun pistol. That could be the only explanation. Somehow I managed to get to my knees, and then to my feet. I must have pressed the elevator call button sixty or seventy times before it came. The light inside the elevator car blared in my brain—directly inside my brain!

When the doors finally opened on the garage level, the ringing in my ears had settled into harmless background noise. "Music Box Dancer" was playing on the elevator, I remember that. Somewhere in the near distance I could hear an engine turn over.

I wasn't too late, but if I wanted to catch the Nautikon I had to act fast. I fell against my driver's-side door, fumbling with the key, remembering too late that my car was parked right next to his. Through the windshield I saw his startled eyes. He threw the Ford into reverse and backed out, clipping my pelvis with his side mirror.

The Ford bounded up toward the exit so fiercely that its rear bumper scraped on the rumble strips. For some reason I thought about corduroy. In my rearview mirror I could see that the arm on the gate was down. He seemed to be having trouble finding his parking ticket. His brake lights throbbed red in anger. I threw the

Corolla into reverse, swung the car around. He offered the ticket to the hungry machine. It swallowed. By the time I pulled up behind him, the candy-striped arm was rising in salute.

As for *my* parking ticket, it was right where it should have been, under the sun visor. It was just a matter of inserting it in the slot and the chase could continue. But when I lowered the window, a stiff breeze poured into the garage. The ticket slipped away and fluttered under the Corolla. I unbuckled my seat belt and threw open the door, but I was too close to the ticket booth to get out, so I had to climb through the passenger door.

I watched the Nautikon hang a right and disappear in the direction of the interstate. Finally I found the ticket pasted to a blot of motor oil. I fed it into the machine and stomped on the accelerator. By then the Nautikon must have been a mile away. But where? Where? Denver was dark. I had no choice but to follow my instincts.

Even though Jean says I don't have any. She says I live in a diving bell where the real world can't get in and I can't get out. But I do have sensitivities to the motives of others. Buried, misinterpreted—but sensitivities nonetheless. I knew for instance that Jean would eventually leave me. True, I misjudged how soon that would take place, but I knew it would happen. And, yes, I *did* actually look up from my comic books for a second to see that she had needs. I looked up, Jean. And then you were gone.

And maybe I'd misjudged the Nautikon. Even dolphins are known to kill for pleasure. I just had to follow him, keep my eye on him, and take whatever measures were necessary to restore him to the sanctity of his mission and remind him of the righteousness of his cause.

I turned right on Tremont Street, made another squealing

right, clung to his bumper through twists and turns until we landed on a freeway. A few miles later we slipped onto I-70 west. I sensed the Nautikon's trajectory like we were both driving the same vehicle but in parallel realities. Our feet manipulated synchronized pedals, our hands gripped two tangents of the same Hegelian steering wheel. After a mile of hard driving, there he was, just ahead of a glazier's truck with a massive pane strapped to one side. I fell in behind the truck hoping a giant sheet of glass would not dislodge and slice me in half. And also kind of hoping it might.

The next sign we passed read: PISTON RIDGE 74 MI. Onward and upward to the land of the Oaken Bucket.

TEN

Rep. Frost: It says here that Colorado State Patrol observed you leaving the ███████ Radisson at 2:45 a.m. at what is described as a high rate of speed.

Diaz: Congressman, with respect, that was all cleared up with the CSP at the scene. And I'll tell you what I told Officer ███████ on the shoulder of I-70. I was an agent of the Department on assignment in the greater Denver area doing classified work. I explained that I was in pursuit of a suspicious party, and that this was a strictly federal matter. The best way he could aid my investigation was to keep his head down until such time as we called in local backup.

Officer ███████ was compliant. He understood the sensitive nature of what was going on. But I guess for protocol purposes I agreed to take a Breathalyzer. Everything came out more or less pristine, and I thanked him for his assistance. It can't be easy for these guys when Homeland starts stepping on local toes. Frankly it's a real pissing tournament out there. But ▮▮▮▮▮, he's a decent guy. I don't question his motives for a second.

Rep. Frost: I'm not especially interested in his motives. I keep reading from the police report, and it tells me your driving was erratic and your blood alcohol registered in excess of .08 percent. This alone would have been grounds for Department censure—not to mention a DUI. Am I wrong about this?

Diaz: No and yes. That was all addressed in the internal Department report. And the unreliability of the CSP apparatus was shown to be a mitigating factor. The charges, as reflected in my file, were summarily dropped. As far as what you call my erratic driving—

Rep. Frost: I'm just reading from what's in front of me, son.

Diaz:—all I can say is that this was what I'd classify as a high-speed-pursuit-type scenario. Whether I was doing the pursuing or the vice was versa is immaterial. My actions that night were not inconsistent with departmental procedure under said circumstances. But, Congressman, I wish you'd allow me to rewind another twelve hours so the committee can grasp the macrobandwidth of the time line here.

Rep. Frost: Whatever you need to do. We just want the complete rundown.

Diaz: Good. This is noon the day before. I got to the ▮▮▮▮▮ Radisson, parked in the underground garage, and checked in. They gave me a corner room on the top floor with a view of the Rockies. The hotel is in like a rehabbed warehouse district, with lots of brew pubs. You can get cowboy clothes made in Italy and a manicure for your dog. I had some paperwork to chew through that night, so I stayed in and ordered room service. If you're ever in Denver, please don't miss the Rocky Burger at the ███████ Radisson. Sounds weird with the jalapeños, but damn.

Next morning I hit the ground early. Like I said, this particular hotel has some creative water features. In the solarium area there's what they call a Lazy River, where they pump water nice and slow through this cement culvert and hand out inner tubes so you can just, well, float. Hell of a relaxing feature, but if the wrong people got access, I don't even want to—

Rep. Frost: Yes. Well, it seems the wrong people *did* get access. We're talking about the site of the initial incident, correct?

Diaz: Interesting thing about this process, Congressman, is it's not static. We have to learn as we go. Adapt. This Lazy River was off the map for me. I'd never seen anything like it. So I spent all morning checking out the unorthodox filter system. And that's when I noticed that creep—um—the subject of this inquiry. Mr. Rath. Tell the truth, he virtually fell on top of me, literally.

I'm below the surface collecting some humint and I feel this splash and a hairy leg across my back. I could've puked, even though I don't think that's physiologically possible underwater. So I surface and there he is barely keeping his head above water, which I can't blame him with that big head of his. Huge forehead, like I said earlier. Well, in person it's just unreal.

I thought to myself, Jesus, these Islamofascist extremists don't know when to quit. The guy followed me all the way from Colorado Springs, and now he wants to play Marco Polo in Denver?

Rep. Frost: Not to get bogged down in footnotes, but here's where I have to ask you—and I offer my apologies if this is a delicate matter—about a young lady, name of June Fresto. One of the victims in the Denver incident. Is it true the two of you were seen fraternizing that selfsame day at the ▮▮▮▮▮ Radisson?

Diaz: Fraternizing is a strong word, Congressman. Strong word. I met my share of ladies on the road. I won't lie. Remember, I was a widower on the rebound, not just an operative of the DHS. I'm human, sir. I get lonely, as I'm sure the Congressman does too.

Rep. Frost: I'd like to meet the man who hasn't known loneliness.

Diaz: But yes, Mrs. Fresto and I made each other's acquaintance prior to the incident in question. I wouldn't say we quote unquote befriended each other. But she could see I was traveling solo, and she did me the kindness of inviting me to lunch. Rocky Burger number two. Couldn't get enough.

It was in the hotel restaurant where I noticed Rath's behavior growing more irregular. He was clearly singling out Mrs. Fresto because of my passing association with her. If I'd known I was endangering anyone's life, I never would've, you know, interacted. At lunch that day I observed him at a nearby table with his three-ring binder. He appeared to be taking more notes. Mrs. Fresto had a little boy who was, as you say, sadly involved in the Denver incident. I was entertaining him with a little bar trick I knew. You take a drink and gargle it like mouthwash, but at the same time you sing.

Rep. Frost: Sounds like fun.

Diaz: The kid liked it. I gargle-sang some Bob Marley for him—
"Jamming." It's a positive song with a message. I believe deeply in
the power of optimism, provided it's the cautious variety. I only
hope I lifted the boy's spirits a little bit before the terrible episode
that was to befall him the next morning. Poor kid, and with no father
figure in his life. I hope you pardon me speaking ill of the afflicted
party, but his mother was no model of womanly virtue either. I imagine I wasn't the first single gentleman she'd turned to for comfort.
And I'm not blaming the victim here, as you suggested the other day.
This isn't another "Blame America First" thing. It's just a simple
statement of fact.

After lunch I had work to do. I ran some tests, and everything
checked out for the most part. I admit in retrospect there were some
oversights. I might have been more diligent, but we're ascertaining
as we go with this terrorism thing. It's what we refer to in the
Department as a curve of learning.

It had been a long day. And I'm a man who believes work is its
own reward, but a cold one is good too. So I parked it at the bar and
ordered a Comfortable Screw. Not an hour later there's Rath again.
By this juncture, I've about had it. I feel like I'm trying to shake a
wood tick off my pecker, you know? Sorry, but that's how I felt. Plus
I'm starting to understand that he's got ulterior motives, ones that
aren't apparent on the surface.

Rep. Frost: Was this when you first suspected you were dealing with
a foreign operative of some sort?

Diaz: I'd had my inklings from the get-go. My inner gyroscope was spinning in that direction. Forget night-vision goggles—the gyro-scope of intuition is an agent's best recon device. Like I've always said, if it walks like a duck, even one percent like a duck, then we have to presume we're dealing with some form of waterfowl. And, Congressman, it's duck season.

In other words, he'd passed my threshold of suspicion, and I decided it was high time I confronted him.

He made some evasive comments, even said something about my wife, which I don't know how he'd be privy to that information. That really got my hackles in an upright position. I can see the bar-tender lady is already prejudiced against me, and I don't want to drag Department business out in the open. Our directive is to keep it covert. So I make the determination that it's best I leave the scene. As in check out of the hotel altogether, and pronto. If he tails me again, it's on for real.

I go back to my suite to pack. Rath—did I mention this?—Rath has somehow booked the room adjacent to mine. So if I press my ear to the wall, I can hear him dicking around in there. He's got the Weather Channel on real low. Five-day forecast and the lake levels—I can hear all that. Then it goes quiet, and the next thing I hear is the guy snoring. That's my cue to vacate.

I would've left directly but there was one more test I still needed to run. And I decided to knock it out in a hurry right then. We've got a one-stop battery of tests that evaluates pH, turbidity, total and fecal coliform, total organic carbon, ultraviolet absorption, free and total chlorine residual, and heterotrophic plate count. It's called the PHT-COCUA-CHPC.

You take a water sample and drop it on a blotter grid. If all the squares turn blue, you're golden; anything turns red, it's go time. We can detect down to three parts per million, anything from sheep shit to cyanide. I ran the PHT-COCUA-CHPC, and the blotter grid came out looking like a pretty blue patchwork quilt, which is to say the Lazy River was safe.

Rep. Frost: How do you explain the discrepancy between your test result and the samples taken at the crime scene the following day?

Diaz: Could be a number of factors, Congressman. Lye, which is what I understand the agent was, isn't detected by the PHT-COCUA-CHPC. That's another whole battery of tests that DHS won't foot the bill for. Talk to your bean counters. Then there's the time factor. A window of x number of minutes between my finishing up at the Lazy River and my subsequent encounter with Mr. Rath. I judged this to be sufficient time for him to dose the water with lye after I completed the test, and then haul ass back upstairs to my room.

Rep. Frost: Though you testify that he was sleeping.

Diaz: We're dealing with an enemy that does not play by the conventional rules. That's all I can say. I get back to my room, takes me three, four minutes by elevator. I go to the can, get my shaving kit, make the bed, rehang my wet towels, and box up the test equipment. That takes maybe ten minutes, plenty of time for Rath to slip downstairs and do his terrorism in the river.

I was standing there in the bathroom, and all of a sudden I feel this presence in the doorway. Sometimes I wonder if I'm especially attuned to negative presences. I peek around the corner of the bathroom and see Rath poking his big fat forehead inside my room. I'd made the mistake of leaving the door open a crack—

Rep. Frost: Yes. And what happened next?

Diaz: One interesting aspect of my room is I had a perfect vista of the capitol dome. Knowing what I know, seeing what I've seen, a sight like this sets off alarm bells. Did you know that dome is twenty-four-karat gold? From the aerial view it's just like one big jihad bull's-eye, like a giant Kick Me sign. An extremist could make a potent symbolic statement there with a single pipe bomb. One more thing while we're on the subject: Were you aware that at Coors Field the twentieth row in the upper deck is painted purple? That's to designate that it's precisely one mile above sea level. There's another symbolic target.

We talk a lot of hot air about first line of defense and about protecting lives, Congressman, but really what they're after? It's our symbols.

Rep. Frost: Sure, son, the symbols. Mr. Rath testified that you used some kind of sonic weapon to disable him. Are you going to tell me this too was Department protocol?

Diaz: It wasn't sonic. And it wasn't a weapon per se. I Tasered him. I'm of the considered opinion that if you're going to cock it, you better fire it, and you better not talk about it too much. You have to bear in mind the situation I was confronting at that juncture. And in retrospect I wish I'd done more than Taser the guy. We might have averted Oaken Bucket two days later. But they don't let field inspectors carry anymore. Anyway, I checked Rath's vitals and everything seemed fine, so I left him there on the floor and went down to my car. But I barely turn the key in the ignition when who do I see at my passenger window? Rath, back from the dead. I mean this guy's cojones were bigger than Barbara Bush's earrings.

I tried to make a quick exit, but the ticket—I couldn't find the parking ticket. It's my usual practice to slide it under the sun visor; that way you always know where it is at all times. But American cars these days, frankly, the craftsmanship isn't there anymore. The metal visor armatures—and I know this for a fact—are manufactured in Malaysia, where who knows if they even have parking garages. Well, the ticket must've slipped out. I looked everywhere and finally found it under the seat.

By then Rath was riding my bumper, but he still had to clear the ticket booth too. That bought me some time, so I gunned it to the expressway. After a few miles I started to relax. I thought, Okay, I'm free and clear. Then I consulted my rearview, and there was that beat-up old rice burner two cars back.

That's when I saw the flashing lights. I pulled over to the right, and when I did, Rath passed by me real slow, like he was ogling me. His interior dome light was on the whole way. It was a spooky image, I tell you. I dealt with the state trooper, and as soon as I was back on the road, there he was again, pulling out of a weigh station behind me.

Did you know what *corolla* stands for in botanical language? It's part of a flower, the crown or something. My wife's father drove one too. The car, not the flower.

Rep. Frost: Yes, you do raise a critical issue, one that I've only recently seen as germane. This is a personal detour, and you might call it a fishing expedition, but if this inquiry is about optimizing our agency performance in the field, it's critical that we know our agents.

Diaz: Not sure what you're driving at, Congressman, but fire away.

Rep. Frost: Agent Diaz, I know the subject of your wife must be painful, but I'm wondering if you could describe for us the circumstances of her . . . What I mean to say is, could you tell us how she . . . ?

Diaz: Died? Yeah. She drowned. Any more questions?

Rep. Frost: This was in the summer of 2005?

Diaz: That's correct. Late summer.

Rep. Frost: I'm going to have to ask you to give me the bullet points of this tragic episode.

Diaz: I don't see how this pertains, but hell, these are your hearings, Congressman. We were in Myrtle Beach on vacation. That town has the highest concentration of world-class golf courses on the planet, or any other planet that I know of, and I was determined to play as many as I could in a week. It was a Saturday about 11:00 a.m. I was on the tenth hole, which is like a 354-yard par four. It doglegs right around these cypresses or oaks or something. I remember thinking I could make it in two, but if I wasn't careful it might slip off into the bunkers and land in the river.

Rep. Frost: What are you using on the second shot, a five?

Diaz: Six-iron.

Rep. Frost: Smart thinking.

Diaz: Thanks. But I knew if I wanted to nail this baby, I needed to keep my inner gyroscope level, so I'd stopped for some refreshment and a strategy session with my caddie. Nice local girl. When all of a sudden this state trooper came humping across the sandpit in his aviators.

I was still with TTIC, doing lab work. Nothing so sensitive I needed to be on call 24–7, so I never carried a pager. But in my line of work you prepare for the worst—there's always the danger you'll get interrupted in the middle of a hole. So I thought, Heck, I guess it's back to work.

Well, this wasn't official business.

Me and the caddie, we were comparing tans when the cop walked up. Cop said: "You Agent Diaz?" I set down my Cuba libre on the rear of the cart and showed him my badge. The caddie perked up like she'd never seen a federal badge before.

"I got some troubling news," he said. Big redneck.

"Look, Officer—I get two weeks a year—"

Says: "Your wife's name Janet Diaz, sir?"

It was like time stopped. I didn't nod. I didn't have to.

Janet was an Ohio girl with limited experience of the ocean. She didn't know the first thing about undertow. Apparently she went out for her morning swim and got out too far, and well—when the riptide comes, you can't fight it. Marines down at Parris Island get sucked out to sea all the time. Big strapping boys all pumped up for Basra, but in that riptide they go down like marshmallow Peeps in a FryDaddy.

Speaking of golf courses, there's another serious gap in our defenses. You could put anthrax in the sandpits. You could spike the sprinkler system with DDT, inflict a heck of a lot of havoc. Somebody should look into that.

But Janet, she was my whole life. My everything. My princess. Her loss was a hurtle, Congressman, I'm telling you. I'm still not completely healed, and we're coming up on two years now.

Rep. Frost: I'm truly sorry for your loss, son. But I bring this up because in your HR file at the Department it states that after the death of Janet Diaz, that's when you put in for the transfer to WATERT. Am I correct? Did you not also seek psychiatric treatment at that time?

Diaz: It was recommended that I see a grief counselor for at least a month and a half. That's Department protocol. I don't place much stock in headshrinking, but I played ball, did my six weeks on the couch. Took some R & R. And when I was all better, they rubber-stamped my transfer to WATERT. Best thing that ever happened to me. Going out to eyeball some actual hard targets, getting your boots dirty—for an agent that's what you call therapy. The open road helped me clear my head and get beyond Janet's, you know, passing. But to answer your question, her death did turn me against the forces that are out to jeopardize our water. No question I was on a mission.

Rep. Frost: But your wife's death was ruled accidental. Are you say-ing this was a criminal act? Are you linking the drowning to some kind of terrorism?

Diaz: I'm not linking anything to anything. All I'm saying is, What is it going to take? Would you prefer to wait until—all due respect, Congressman—but would you want to wait until somebody plants a pipe bomb on a waterslide? All those kids blown up during their funnest hour. Then will you wake up and do something to protect the inalienable right of every American to recreate in our public waters without the imminent threat of attack?

Rep. Frost: I think I speak for the whole subcommittee when I say nobody desires a pipe bomb or any explosive on or near a waterslide. But I can see this is a convenient time for us to address another sensitive topic: the Psychological Fitness Report authored by the DHS forensic psychologist, Dr. Ronald Schacht, in September 2005, not long before your transfer to WATERT and not long after your wife's passing.

I'm reading aloud here, and I hope you'll bear with me because I'm sure you've read this a dozen times before.

"In the opinion of the psych board all Agent Diaz's pending assignments or transfers should be closely vetted. On mental status examination including cognitive assessment he performs less than optimally. From our first session (09/09/05) subject displayed heightened anxiety and spoke of periods of depression. In subsequent interviews (09/15/05; 09/19/05) the object of these anxieties had grown more particular. Unprompted, subject stated ambivalent feelings toward large bodies of water. He spoke of enjoying water sports but had compulsive worries about water safety (relating no doubt to the manner of his wife's death). On one occasion, when presented with a glass of ordinary tap water, subject became irritable, addressing the water with abusive language as if it were an adversary. Subject complained of 'foreign elements' in the water and began to make nonsense sounds until the glass was removed."

I could keep reading if you want, but the gist of it is that after this assessment was filed, your transfer to WATERT was downgraded from a management spot to what Dick Dodd refers to in his testimony as "pool patrol."

Diaz: I don't know what you want me to say. I've read that report. Who hasn't? Everyone inside the Department knows they were doing a mental on me. All I can tell you is, What is it going to take? Do you want a dose of polonium—do you want a teaspoon of polonium 210 in your Jacuzzi, Congressman? You do have a Jacuzzi bath, don't you, Congressman? I mean, is that what it's going to take? Huh? Would that be a loud enough wake-up call for you?

Rep. Frost: [*coughs*] After Denver your next destination was the town of Piston Ridge, Colorado, where the second incident took place. My understanding is this isn't much more than a little ghost town way up in the Rockies. Kind of an out-of-the-way place for Homeland, didn't you think?

Diaz: Congressman, I never question the asset list. You have to understand I'm just ticking off the sites, doing my job. Piston Ridge might be just a wide spot in a narrow road, but right up the mountain is the oldest water park in the Rockies, which as you know is called ███████████. I suppose DHS deemed this a valuable enough asset to warrant our scrutiny. You want to talk symbolism, this place is one fat juicy slice of Americana. Those Muslim fascists would cream in their dishdashas if they could explode an antitank mine inside their dining facility. Can't you just see it on Al Jazeera now: girls in bikinis all covered in blood and soot, and then cut to kids dancing in the streets of Kabul. To me that's a disturbing image.

Rep. Frost: We've all seen this water park on the news. But I'm wondering if you could paint us a picture of your impressions, in your own words.

Diaz: Okay. Piston Ridge is up past Breckenridge, with all the ski resorts. You get off the interstate and take this two-lane that winds all over the mountains. It's like Tora Bora out there. Caves and hollows and arroyos and such. I mean, they could be hiding anywhere.

You get off the paved road and finally there's this little green sign. THIS WAY TO ███████████. Then you follow this logging road maybe four miles up until you come to a hairpin turn. On the left is a video store and an auto parts shop; on the right it's like the whole Rocky Mountains spread out below you. It's majestic, but scary too. All those hidey-holes.

At the auto parts shop I hung a left, which is to say uphill. And just when I thought I'd run out of mountain I saw the Prospector, who is this old statue guy about twenty-five feet tall holding a pan filled with gold nuggets that spell out ███████████.

There's a little two-story motel. They set me up in a corner suite on the top floor with a California king and no TV. I get up to my room, and let me tell you I am beat. But I can't sleep. It's Rath. I close my eyes and all I see is that creepy forehead in the dome light. So I get out of bed and open the curtains.

It's early in the morning, I judge it to be about 6:30 or something. The sun must be coming up, but that's all happening behind the mountain. Only a little bit of orange is creeping in through the tree line, just enough light for me to survey the grounds. ███████████ isn't much to look at relative to today's water parks, but it's got the basics.

There's one big creek that cuts right down the middle. And off of that shoot all these—what's the opposite of a tributary?—well, little streams that fill up the different rides. One feeds into this pond that's got wooden ducks for kids to cruise around in. It's called the Duck Pond or something. At that hour all the ducks are corralled together in one corner under a tarp. But there's one and his head is sticking out. I can see that big blue duck eye staring at me through the window. I know rationally that it's just paint and ply-wood, but it seems to me at that moment like a harbinger. I believe in that sort of thing, Congressman. I think that duck was giving me a warning.

Next to the Duck Pond is what they call the Water Wheel. Which is exactly what it sounds like, except it's more like a Ferris wheel that dips into the water at the bottom. Just above the Water Wheel you get to Flatiron Falls. There's a big sign that says: DANGER! FLATIRON FALLS! 200 FEET! or some nonsense. But in reality it's more like fifteen feet, max. Maybe twenty yards above that you get to the Oaken Bucket, but I guess I don't have to describe that to you.

Rep. Frost: Yes. I'd say everyone with CNN is familiar with the Oaken Bucket by now. But just for the record, I wish you'd describe it for the subcommittee.

Diaz: Basically it's a big bucket with an oak veneer, maybe eight foot in diameter, five foot high, with seating inside for four. Not really roomy enough, in my opinion. It's mounted on these rails but they're under the water so the illusion is you're hurtling down a white-water creek in a crazy, out-of-control bucket. The good part comes when you get to the edge of Flatiron Falls. The bucket leans out maybe fif-teen, twenty degrees, and then rights itself just in the nick of time.

After that you go through this mine shaft and when you come out it's like *wham,* you land in this big pool.

But of course none of this is happening when I get there. The place is dead quiet. I look all around and there's just one Indian guy with a push broom out on the patio. Or maybe he was Pakistani.

Rep. Frost: Again, we're told that you made the acquaintance of the victims shortly prior to the incident. Tell me, Agent Diaz, exactly how well did you come to know Brenda Mills, Jenny Mills, and Keesha Stephens, and what were the circumstances?

Diaz: Well, Congressman, it sounds like you knew those girls better than I did. We were strictly on a first-name basis. I feel like it's part of my cover to blend in with the guests. We're directed to do so, in fact. You see, I was utilizing tradecraft, or clandestine methodologies, to gather a lot of this vulnerability data, while still trying to, in a sense, fade into the fabric of pedestrian life. The lay public, and even our elected officials for that matter, are often stymied by this, but it's the nature of clandestine work that it's not going to be transparent, unless by transparent you mean invisible.

In other words, yes, we interacted on a social basis the night before the incident. Brenda and Keesha were roommates from, I think, Colorado State, and Jenny was Brenda's little sister. They were just out there to blow off a little steam before classes started. So I helped them in that regard, in the steam part.

But let's be clear. I mourn these girls' deaths along with the rest of America, but the bottom line is, if that incident hadn't transpired on the Oaken Bucket, you and I wouldn't be sitting here today having this conversation. Loss of American life is always an unfortunate outcome, but we've also got to acknowledge the positives. We've finally got a public dialogue going about water terrorism. And any way you julienne it, that's constructive.

Rep. Frost: Of course you know those girls didn't actually die. Nobody died.

Diaz: Yes. I know that.

ELEVEN

I have word from Jean. Not direct word. Indirect word. Which might as well be no word at all.

Two days ago Uncle Keith was nice enough to send over a cell phone for my personal use. So what if my conversations are being monitored? The Fat Man, my attorney, told me as much. But I don't care. It's mid-March; I've been floating here in this leisure gulag for a month and a half with no line to the outside world. I haven't spoken to or heard from my wife for nearly seven months, and I have grave concerns for her emotional safety. And her personal well-being. Surely there must be death threats, or worse. So I've been placing calls—probably too many calls—to Jean's co-workers.

Last night I was scrolling through the telephonic directory of extensions at my wife's work when someone actually picked up.

Josh has always been frank with me, maybe more than I deserved, so when he answered the phone I was filled with as much dread as excitement.

"She doesn't like you anymore," he said, probing to the core of the issue before I could even pose the question properly. "Mainly because you won't shut up about the Little Mermaid. And also because you're a terrorist."

"Where is she, Josh? I'm worried."

"Jesus, man, I shouldn't even be having this conversation. Probably being taped."

"I'm worried about her, Josh."

"Look, if you're going to worry, dude, worry about yourself. Worry about what you're doing for the rest of your life, whatever's left of it. That's what Jean's worrying about."

"She's worried about me?"

"No. Her life. *Her* life."

"Sure, Josh—but where is she? With that cabinetmaker?"

"Who? Look, she's staying with friends. Somebody who'll take care of her. That's all I'm allowed to say. But she wants you to stop calling the office, and if she has to get a restraining order—Hey, Curtis—Yeah, I'll be off soon as I wrap it up with Unabomber Junior."

The pressure to hang up was intense. It made the receiver feel heavy against my cheek, like some superdense galactic matter. But I wouldn't give up that easy. I needed more. After a few seconds Josh said:

"So, Jim. What are you going to do, call here fifteen times a day, or let Jean move on? Haven't you done enough damage?"

"It hasn't been fifteen times. I keep phone records, you know!"

"Sure you do. Look, man, I gotta run. Just grab the elevator,

Curt—I'll meet you there in a sec. Do yourself a favor, Jim, and take my advice."

I was ready for it, open to it: the advice. I wanted to hear it. Then, mysteriously, the line went dead. When I speed-dialed Josh again seconds later, I got the voice mail.

Then the call-waiting beeped. The noise went straight through my bloodstream like a charged wire. I clicked over too quickly, without looking at the caller ID. For the first four syllables I thought it was Jean herself. It wasn't; not even close.

My mother was saying this wasn't her baby. Her Jim would never do this. But if I did do something I regretted, if I was angry about something, I should tell her. She knew things hadn't been easy with Jean. She blamed herself for neglecting my emotional growth. Tell her the truth, she said: Were they torturing me?

Something was off with her timbre. Her voice was tinny, like a microprocessor pretending to care. Like the wake-up service in the hotel. She was asking suspicious questions. Every awkward pause was filled with an electronic hum. Was this my real mother, or some advanced government simulacrum? Either way she didn't even say hi.

I refused to respond, except to grunt as a way of marking the desired end point of each of her trailing reluctant momlike sentences. When she'd run out of questions to ask, she said she loved me. And that's when I knew it was her. Those are words no synthetic voice clone can ever mimic. I love you, baby.

"All mammals have tear glands, whether they weep or not."

This piece of zoological wisdom we learn from Elaine Morgan, author of *The Aquatic Ape* among other titles. But out of all the land mammals only elephants and humans cry actual tears motivated by anguish. I guess we've both got our reasons to cry, elephants and us. My mother, for her part, was an exemplary bawler. She wept when she drank rosé, she wept on holidays, and she cried her eyes out watching TV ads for suicide hotlines.

After my talk with Josh, I sat on the deck trying to weep. But nothing came out, even though I worked at it for close to an hour, exerting so much internal force on my tear ducts that I gave myself a headache. I've been assured by my lawyer that a serious cry would expel Jean from my system; without the purgative sob I'm doomed to retain the impression of her memory under the surface of my face forever. But nothing came out, so I closed my eyes on the bay and returned to the Colorado interstate of memory, where I was still tailing the Nautikon into the Rocky Mountains.

I drove through the early-morning darkness, uncertain but resolute. Interstate 70 climbed steadily into the mountains. I was light-headed, whacked-out, and still a little buzzed from the three beers in Denver, but turning back now was not an option. There was nothing to go back to. My life was onward and upward, his taillights three car lengths ahead, luring me to some soft destiny.

Just west of Denver I saw the Mother Cabrini Shrine in the distance, its big white Christ glowing like a night-light on top of one of the hills. If you married a Roman Catholic like I did, you'd know that Saint Frances Xavier Cabrini is the patron saint of immigrants. I felt her guiding presence. She blessed the Nautikon with safe passage. So much for blessings.

Next came the brown historical marker for Buffalo Bill's Grave. I cracked my driver's-side window and took a deep breath.

You could actually smell the herd of buffalo, all warm and loafy in the distance. It wasn't long before I could see the white frosted hackles of the Front Range directly ahead. The moonlight collapsed the distance to make it seem like the mountains were sitting right there on the end of my hood.

The Nautikon took a single pee break, at a rest area designed to look like a corporate retreat center. You could see the colorful humps of Winnebagos and hear their generators humming. I pulled in beside a big one. Through the side curtain I could see the silhouette of a couple playing cards while their nasty pachyderm sump-pumped the contents of its waste tank into the loose summer soil.

The Ford was parked several spots down. I waited until I thought the Nautikon was in the men's room, then I crept over to the vending machine kiosk. The rest area had one thing to recommend it, a considerable stock of Paycheck bars. I fed eight dollars into the slot and was rewarded with a whole night's worth of nutrition. Actually I only got seven bars. I must have keyed in the wrong code (4D instead of 4B), because the machine gave me one baggie of edible pectin worms. I tossed them in the backseat, where they remain to this day in a secret CIA impound lot, unless they've been entered into evidence.

We got under way again. I remember a tanker truck rumbling past. The driver tipped a cigarette out his cracked window. It skittered toward me on the road, spraying up a little fanfare of sparks whenever it struck the blacktop. We entered a long tunnel, the screaming orange-lit bore swallowing our cars like a wormhole to destiny. On the other side the interstate had been carved out of solid rock. A stepped wall rose on my right, bristling with pines. I remember thinking I was in a model train set in a child's dark basement. But not mine, not my basement. I never had a basement.

I was tired, but I drew sustenance from the familiar taillight pattern on the road ahead. Every time the Nautikon hit the brakes, which was often enough on this winding road, my heart issued a corresponding throb of exigency.

When we cleared the Eisenhower Tunnel and passed the sign for Summit County, my dashboard clock registered 4:15 a.m. COLORADO'S PLAYGROUND, said the big green sign. Several more miles passed before the Ford exited onto a steep rural route going south. I followed carefully behind, eventually killing my headlamps to fly by the glow of the parking lights. The two-lane did its best to confound my expectations, winding and wiggling with sadistic asphalt glee. There were times when I felt like I was steering a car on TV, just steering and steering with no reference to reality. On the few occasions when I thought I'd lost him, my forehead went cold and wet. The mountainside soared up on my left; on my right was the Lite-Brite display of towns and ski resorts. Every single one of those lights, I told myself, represented a cell of humanity, a family, or a business. Something I ought to cherish. Something I should want. But when I pictured my own light, the light of the town house as viewed from the high satellite of nostalgia, it looked cold and empty. Every light was on, but Jean wasn't home and I wasn't either.

Another half hour passed before the Ford braked abruptly. He cut a gravelly left onto an even crappier rural road. I followed uphill for a few more miles until the road leveled out. Together we rounded a tight bend and I saw a video-rental shop and auto-supply store combo shuttered for the night. The Ford took a hesitant left onto an old logging road. Trailing him any farther would have been seriously pushing my luck, so I pulled over in the auto-supply parking lot to catch some sleep. It was about 5:00 a.m. The Nautikon couldn't go anywhere from here but up. And if he came back down, I'd be waiting for him.

I woke up a couple hours later to a rapping on my driver's-side window. The knuckles were knuckly in the extreme and scored with axle grease. The man was missing one index finger, his face old and empty of expression, but he looked friendly enough.

I rolled down the window and rubbed my forehead.

"You been here all night?" the man asked.

"No." He looked at the heap of candy wrappers on the seat beside me. "Just a couple hours," I said.

"There's a motel up the mountain." The man pointed with his right hand, but without an index finger the gesture seemed incomplete. "More like a water-park-type place. It's got ducks you can ride in, but the rooms are reasonable priced. Looks like you could use some shut-eye."

It was a eureka moment for me. That explained my Nautikon's strange trajectory. He was like a human divining rod, seeking some mythical mountaintop water park where he could continue his arcane experiments.

"Just up there?" I felt self-conscious about my own index finger, so I pointed with my pinkie, but this didn't feel right either. We both looked up the dirt road that ran beside the auto-supply store, the same road the Ford had taken hours ago.

"Can't miss it. Look for the giant prospector." He slapped the side of my car.

The giant prospector is molded from concrete and rebar and stands about thirty feet high. He's your stereotypical forty-niner in a droopy calfskin hat and dungarees, with a grizzled beard and wild eyes that scan the valley below. In his outstretched hands he's carrying a pan filled with gold nuggets. They're actually yellow lightbulbs and they spell out the name of the amusement park: PROSPECTOR'S BEND. At the back of the statue an iron-rung ladder leads to a small door in the seat of his pants.

The parking lot was nearly deserted. I took a spot beside a mini SUV with Colorado plates and most of the Greek alphabet decaled on the hatchback window. The backseat was littered with mail-order clothing catalogs and frozen yogurt cups. On the way to the motel office I passed the white Ford. Its hood was cool to the touch. I looked up at the motel, a two-story box made to resemble a mountain lodge. Most of the brown paint had peeled off the fake timbers, and an array of satellite dishes waddled in the high wind on the rooftop.

Above the motel the sky was a waxy blue. Little swabs of cloud stuff moved swift and high overhead. The weather suggested all kinds of change and inevitabilities. I sneaked up the exterior stairwell and pressed my ear against each of the doors on the second floor. The rooms were dead quiet until I got to room 19. From inside I heard perky morning TV and a hair dryer. A girl's voice was singing "I wanna sex you up."

Two doors down I came to room 22, a corner suite. A window faced the breezeway, but the curtain was drawn tight. I concentrated and thought I could hear the Weather Channel prognosticating from somewhere within. Then I heard the familiar booming voice, chanting along with the forecast.

Downstairs in the front office I found a pamphlet that provided the history of the place. Prospector's Bend was built in 1969 during that weird revival of Gold Rush nostalgia. The site really was a prospecting town back in its day, and when the park first opened kids could still try their hand at panning for gold. But by 1972 all you could expect to get was pyrite and pull tabs, so the owners started adding water rides to keep the customers coming.

The oldest attraction is called the Duck Pond, built in 1973 (coincidentally the same year Marvel Comics premiered *Howard the Duck*). The Darn Tootin' Straight Shootin' Water Chute arrived a year later, followed by a pond stocked with actual trout and a Ferris-type wheel shaped like a waterwheel. The existing swimming pool was rechristened the Waterin' Hole. Then in 1976 they debuted the now infamous Oaken Bucket. You've all seen this one on the news, so I won't bore you with the specs.

In the 1990s local college kids made Prospector's Bend a shrine of hipster kitsch. Along with their insincere mustaches and T-shirts promoting little league teams they never played for, every Colorado coed's irony training included a pilgrimage to Prospector's Bend. At spring break they'd converge here to get their faux-bois jollies, get ironically wasted, and ironically have sex. This wasn't in the pamphlet; that part I learned by observation.

"You just here to read, or do you need a room?" The woman behind the desk was talking to me. "This ain't a library, you know."

The counter came up to her bosom, and her bosom rested on the counter. She was wearing a bonnet.

"Give me room 21," I said.

"Pretty particular, ain't you?" said the desk clerk. "You been here before?"

"Nope. Just my lucky number."

"You don't look so lucky."

She gave me a skeptical look, or maybe it was just the way her face was made. Her features were drawn with worry lines. Alarming red hair poked out from under the bonnet like fire under an Easter basket. And her mouth was the kind that never stopped moving, even when it wasn't saying anything.

"How many nights?"

I showed her the number one with my hand.

"You got to pay in advance," she said.

Room 21 was several shades of brown, including deep chocolate wainscoting and a shower curtain that covered the whole spectrum of tan. The single bed was humped up on one side, and when I sat down the springs complained openly. The wallpaper behind the headboard was worn in the outline of a headboard, suggesting countless nights of coed amorousness. I was becoming a real archaeologist of hotel decor.

When I opened the curtains, they hissed on the traverse rod like spilled rice. The sun was coming up behind the mountain, so that the whole mass of geology appeared to be on fire. This was my first glimpse of the Oaken Bucket, concealed under its nighttime tarp. The twin tracks gleamed under the water. Flatiron Falls emptied endlessly into the Waterin' Hole. I lay on the bed and listened to the raging cataract, and it wasn't long before I was totally conked out.

What woke me up was the crazy noise of girls having fun. My sorority neighbors bounced down the breezeway past my room, three pairs of flip-flops slapping against six neatly pumiced heels. There was laughter and singing and playful shrieking. I lay still with my eyes closed thinking about Jean. I thought about her responsible hemp sandals, and her voice hollering at me from the bathroom: "What's wrong with you? Why can't you get your own razor?"

It was well after noon when I got up and went to the window, and what I saw wiped Jean completely off the surface of my mind. There was the Nautikon. He wasn't wearing a shirt, just the Jams and a pair of Tevas with calf-length athletic socks. He stood on the patio speaking to a custodian in a gray jumpsuit, their heads close together. The Nautikon gave him one of those elaborate soulful handshakes and jangled a ring of keys. Then he found a free deck chair close to the Waterin' Hole, cranked it into the horizontal position, and lay down. I watched him smooth his hair and gaze over his chin to admire his own sculpted chest. My heart had been battered and chipped by his crass behavior, but it was not yet broken. Nothing could buff the luster of myth off his marble body. What I beheld before me was still a Nautikon, and I could not allow myself to forget that core truth. A few seconds later out came the girls.

You know their names; everybody does. The famous Mills Sisters, Brenda and Jenny, and their friend Keesha Stephens. The Mills girls had apparently performed some kind of mix and match with their bikinis. Brenda wore a yellow top with safety orange bottoms; her sister wore the converse combination: orange top, yellow briefs. With their big eyes and lemon-colored ponytails, they cut alarming figures, like a warning of oncoming fun. Keesha's appearance was more understated. I think she might be of West Indian descent. Her kinky short-cropped hair framed a sweet, reliable face. In their resting position her eyelids were droopy, but when she laughed the eyes exploded at you like blue flowers. I liked Keesha from the moment I saw her.

The girls grabbed three lounge chairs at the opposite end of the patio and started applying sunscreen with great vigor. The teamwork was amazing, and I wasn't the only one enjoying the view. The Nautikon sat up.

From Elaine Morgan we learn that "sexual selection . . . sometimes operates to a point where it cannot be said to be conducive to the comfort or convenience of the individual animal." Think of the peacock, or certain male porn actors, or the proboscis monkey with its huge lusty nose. The Mills girls too were afflicted by the Darwinian sex burden.

I'm dancing around the subject probably because the breast issue is a big one for me. Jean said that being raised by a single mother had turned me into "a boob guy." I disagree, but I can't disagree very strongly. I remember the night when the Mars Rover *Opportunity* was having all that trouble broadcasting back to earth. It was late January 2004, and Jean and I had been together for a little more than six months. We lay naked on the futon worrying, like the rest of the country, about how NASA would fix the signal.

I playfully mentioned the idea that womankind is the earthly receptor of galactic knowledge. You know, just kidding around. I was only thinking out loud when I said that all information in the universe passes through the Great Cervix of Epistemology. I said: "Think about it, Jean; maybe if we could tune all the earth's females to the Great Cervix of Epistemology, we'd know everything we wanted to know about Mars and everything else in the universe."

I was just joking, of course, kind of. And I'm pretty sure she laughed, at first. I do remember she pulled on her pajama bottoms and said something about keeping her "receptor covered."

At this point the mood in the bedroom was still mostly positive. But then I went too far.

"Or maybe"—I propped myself up on one elbow and looked her in the eye—"maybe it's the breasts that act as receptors. Maybe every bosom on earth is tuned to the frequency of some All-Knowing Space Breast. Like how when a baby enters a room all the women start lactating." I was too excited now. My ideas were outpacing my reason and my tact. I knelt on the mattress.

"Christ, Jim," she said, hiding her face underneath the blanket. "Do you have any idea what a sociopath you are?"

I didn't stop to answer this question. "If we could just find the frequency," I said, and here's where I really took things beyond the accepted threshold of marital bedroom banter.

I peeled back the blanket, took her left breast in my hand, and turned it, ever so gently, like you would tune a radio. I think I made a beeping sound, a sonar sound, which was probably a mistake. Jean is what they call a statuesque woman. She has about seven inches on me and maybe twenty pounds. Her bosom is not to be beeped.

"Can you feel it, Jean?" I said, still beeping softly. "Can you detect some kind of signal coming in?" I was half-joking and half-not joking. And trust me, the whole thing made a lot more sense at the time.

Before I knew it she was on my chest, pinning my shoulders under her knees, but not in a romantic way. I could see her breasts heaving above me, and for the first time they looked really threatening. She reached back and took my left nipple between thumb and index finger, twisting until I gasped and nearly lost consciousness. Then she stripped the blanket off the bed and walked to the couch. Though she accepted my proposal of marriage a few months later, I think this was a harbinger of negative feelings to come.

So maybe you can see why I'm reluctant to dwell too much on the now-famous chests of the Mills girls. But empirically speaking, they are stacked. The Nautikon was keenly aware of this fact as well. I heard the screech of a deck chair being dragged across the patio and watched him take a seat beside Jenny. He was looking at her breasts, I was looking at him. Then it hit me. Of course this guy's a breast man; he comes from a matrilineal society. The breast would probably be like an object of devotion, an emblem of social, political, and economic power, like the presidential seal.

I spent the afternoon writing in my room, occasionally checking out the window to see what the Nautikon was up to. The bedside radio was on a twenty-four-hour news station. I wanted everything to seem normal. It *was* normal, of course, perfectly normal; but sometimes people can get the wrong impression.

I was sitting there at the foot of the bed immersed in a state of utter normalcy when the radio began to speak to me. As a teletype chattered in the background, I heard the words *Denver, Lazy River,* and *Single Mom.*

We each exist on a separate bandwidth. I honestly believe that. But sometimes those bandwidths get crossed. The radio had gotten tuned to the frequency of my individual experience, it was addressing my own peculiar circumstances, and it was freaking me out. Walk into a pet store, a turtle speaks your name; that's how I felt.

I stood up and pushed aside the Conestoga curtains. The Nautikon lay facedown on his chaise longue.

The reporter spoke in fake grave reporterly tones about the alleged victims, June Fresto of Albuquerque and her son. Second-degree burns over eighty percent of their bodies, the man said, irreversible blindness a distinct possibility for the boy. By the time they pulled June Fresto out of the River, said the radio, the acidic compound in the water had eaten through the straps of her swimsuit. The Denver police were still treating it like an accident. They weren't ruling out a bad batch of chlorine. There was no talk of foul play or terrorism.

"June," said my mental Nautikon. "Give the rug rat a little time-out. Let him watch *Dora the Explorer*. Cut loose, girrrrl!"

He crouched behind the rocks at the source of the Lazy River. Probing the crevice with his rubber tube, he turned to me—the insignificant little me who occupies my mind—a finger laid across his lips. *Shhhh*.

Meanwhile the radio had traveled on to someone else's bandwidth. The next item was about a Fort Collins woman who had been married to five anesthesiologists simultaneously. Somewhere an anesthesiologist was listening to this story. He was thinking about his wife and wearing an expression much like my own. Wide eyes, downturned mouth. Crushed astonishment.

I shut the curtains and stared into nothing, the blank geometry of my room. The rubber tubing snaked into my consciousness like a conspiracy. It flooded the ventricles of my brain with a most caustic fluid—suspicion. Everything the Nautikon had done to disappoint me, every small act of betrayal, burned suddenly like hydrochloric acid.

But come on, Jim! I actually slapped myself. Don't be ridiculous. The Nautikon had nothing to do with this! Why would he hurt a defenseless woman, especially after all the loud, energetic love he'd shown her? I expelled the milky fluid of suspicion from my mind. If I lost faith in the Nautikon, my whole project would be meaningless. I would be single, adrift, homeless . . . for what? For nothing. I couldn't afford to doubt him.

But after that day, something changed. If doubt does germinate from seeds, my husks were splitting. The green tendril was reaching through the dark soil to find the sun. There was something wrong with the Nautikon. I knew it. I just didn't know that I knew it.

At about four o'clock he parted company with the girls and started making the rounds of the amusement rides, lugging his green box up the hillside. He took samples from the Waterin' Hole and the Duck Pond. For several minutes he disappeared inside a brown hutch at the base of the Water Wheel. The wheel turned on and off and every time it did the lights dimmed in my room.

By 6:00 p.m. I was starving. The Old Prospector's Kettle Cabin serves up items like the Grizzly Dog (a beef frank wearing a bearish coat of chili) and the Forty-Niner Sirloin (actual weight: sixteen ounces). When I entered the nonsmoking area, the waitress was serving side salads to Keesha and the Mills sisters. She turned toward me and I saw that she was the same woman who'd checked me in at the front desk earlier that morning—or was she? Same fiery hair, same bonnet, same top-heavy build and worry-wrought face. But something was different.

I seated myself and waited.

"You don't get a day off, do you?" I said, when she finally came to my table. I was trying to make conversation by saying something to her.

"What?" She set down a laminated menu. It was a bifold layout and stood about a foot and a half tall. I had to move it aside to see her face.

"They've got you working the front desk too, huh?" I said.

"No."

It wasn't turning out to be much of a conversation, so I changed tacks.

"I just want eggs. Can you do that at dinner?"

"Huh-uh."

I studied the menu as the waitress unsheathed a drinking straw and pulled a tightly swaddled bundle of flatware from her apron pocket. There must have been a hundred choices for dinner. I picked the third thing I saw under "Vittles." The Golden Yardbird. It came with something called Nuggets and a choice of dipping sauces.

"I'll take this."

"Comes with Nuggets," she said. I acted surprised to hear this.

The waitress turned on her heels and headed for the kitchen. I watched her ruffled skirt sway from side to side, watched her bump a rolling cart out of her path with her hip before she pushed through the swinging doors. Inside I heard the *click-clack* of ramekins; a deep fryer chuckled in the distance. The sound of laughter caught my attention. I turned toward the girls' table and saw teeth spread from one pretty face to the next. They were all smiles, all except Keesha, who was blushing. She swatted Brenda or Jenny with the giant menu. Then she caught my eye and I heard a throat being cleared. The laughter stopped. The girls were drinking a pink fluid from Mason jars. A pitcher stood in the middle of the table half full of the same lively substance.

My food arrived with suspicious speed. The Golden Yardbird and the Nuggets were served in a small skillet with a stack of ten or fifteen napkins.

"Can I get some more napkins?" I said with a smile. It was a joke.

"That was my sister," said the waitress.

"What?"

"That you saw this morning."

"Oh," I said.

"Did you want something to drink or was water okay?"

I looked over at the girls' table. The waitress followed my gaze with pinpoint accuracy.

"That's the house special. The Mine Shaft. You can get a Golden Shaft, which is ginger ale, or what they're having."

I must have hesitated a second too long, because the waitress decided for me.

"You'll like that one," she said. "The Pink Mine Shaft."

"Actually, I was just thinking if you had iced tea—" She slipped her order pad back in the apron pocket and walked away, only to return seconds later with a Mason jar.

"Pink Shaft," she said, setting it before me. "Now have you got everything you need?"

I built an iceberg lettuce dam to keep the chicken sandwich sequestered in one quadrant of the skillet. Then I proceeded to eat every last Nugget, carefully rationing the dipping sauces so that I wouldn't be forced to suffer a dry mouthful. When I was done I ran my tongue inside the rims of the ramekins until they were clean. The waitress watched me do this, and I could tell she was flattered. I turned my attention to the Mason jar and sucked deeply. After two drafts the straw drew nothing but air. The waitress brought me another one without my even asking.

I drank this too, watching the fluid recede and the cylinders of ice emerge like rocks under an ebbing pink tide. I thought about what I was doing here. My mission felt valuable. I had a purpose. And Jean could go to hell if she didn't understand that.

I must have been lost in this strand of thinking for some time, because when the waitress dropped a fresh napkin on the table I realized I'd been slurping. Everyone says slurping is rude, but only the superwealthy can afford not to do it. The rest of us would never leave anything behind at the bottom of a glass.

"What the Jesus?"

I turned my head in the direction of the voice and saw the Nautikon. How long he'd been sitting at the girls' table I don't know.

"What the Christ?" he shouted.

"What's wrong?" said Brenda and/or Jenny.

"I can't fucking believe," said the Nautikon.

The blood rushed to my head, or maybe away from it, I'm not sure. Either way, I felt funny. The Pink Shaft was working its insidious magic.

"See this guy?" The Nautikon was pointing me out to the girls, talking loud enough so everyone could hear. "He's a freaking stalker, to put it mildly."

The Mills sisters burst out laughing, but to her credit Keesha looked concerned.

"This guy followed me all the way from Colorado Springs. He was in Denver too. Everywhere I go, there he is." He was looking right at me now, gesturing toward my table with his Mason jar.

"Maybe he likes you," said Brenda/Jenny. "Maybe he's got a thing for cops."

Cops?

"I'm not a cop," said the Nautikon. Yeah, I thought; not even close. "And no, this isn't a gay thing. I know what this guy's up to. And I think he ought to know I'm onto him." He drank deeply, leveling his eyes on the edge of the jar like it was the scope of a rifle. I was his target. "Take your jihad somewhere else, little man!"

My jihad? The girls laughed, I blushed, the Nautikon turned his back to me and refilled his Mason jar from the pitcher. *"Uno más!"* He signaled the waitress. "This one's on me, girls. And tomorrow—tomorrow I'm taking you three hotties for a ride on the Oaken Bucket!"

He hoisted his freshly filled jar. "To the Oaken Bucket!" He pounded it.

"To the Oaken Bucket!" They pounded theirs.

You could see it through the restaurant window. In its little pool at the tip-top of the mountain, the Bucket looked so volatile in the moonlight.

When she delivered their second pitcher, the waitress swung by my table and dropped off the check. I was fortunate enough to have exact change, so I pinned it under the golf tee puzzle game and left the dining room. The Nautikon sucked through his teeth when I passed him. His skin had never looked bluer.

This was going badly. I knew it now. I'd tried to insinuate myself into the Nautikon's life, but all he did was rebuke me and disappoint me with his macho, boozing antics. I needed to focus my energies on something positive. All I wanted to do was teach this guy a lesson. You don't come here as an emissary from a great dying race and waste your time picking up sorority girls. If there was only something I could do to snap him back to his senses. Maybe Nautika herself could tell me what to do. I went to my room and changed into my swimming trunks.

I was still a little buzzed when I lowered myself into the Waterin' Hole. Through the lens of my scuba mask I could see the gaseous turbulence where the creek emptied itself into the pool. The water was full of little green filaments and gusts of brown algae. So was my mind, so was my conscience. I craved the comforts of *ooeee* like never before, and *ooeee* obliged, coming on like a stalking manta, slow and rubbery and enveloping. I soon found myself hovering in a mental state of otherworldliness above a vast undersea city of milky glass spires. I saw the coral red ribbing of a colossal dome. And just ahead of me a barnacle-bellied whale and a bare-chested young woman swam toward the city's enormous gate.

TWELVE

First we behold the sea, the limpid open waters of the Mediterranean. Deep below its surface swims a mighty sperm whale, in length six times the arm span of a grown man. The gentle titan races forward, her broad tail fanning the fathoms and the wise bulb of her head streaming with bubbles. Astride the whale, on a litter of supple green leather, sits Labiaxa, daughter of Aricos. She has stripped to a goatskin skirt and a pair of sandals tightly lashed to her supple calves. Reflected in her unbelieving eyes we see an astonishing sight: a colossal openwork dome of red rises from the white sand of the seabed. It glitters within like a cageful of enchanted birds.

This—at last—is the city of Nautika! Labiaxa's glorious but ill-fated destiny—it rushes toward her, draws her in.

Now, as Labiaxa sits on her litter of green leather, flying athwart the long spine of the sperm whale Oooeea, she feels as if she is breathing for the first time. She drinks greedily from the cold waters, feels them pass over her gills. The nutrient sea enters her bloodstream, her brain, rousing in her a long-latent consciousness. She is aware as never before, free as never before, like a woman trapped inside her own ovaries, now loosed upon the world! She is free! Free! But so terribly afraid.

When first she stepped into the surf at the foot of the Sican cliffs, there passed a chilling interval of doubt. She stood with her head below the surface, long black hair streaming about her like the tremulous feelers of a doomed insect. These gills, she thought, how do they work? *Do* they work? She touched them, pried at their scabrous edges with her fingertips, and felt naught but horny old scars.

She held her breath till her lungs burned and a violent humming filled her skull. Clawing her way to the surface, she sucked at the air and wept, steeled her nerves and then descended again. And again the panic assaulted her body—like an animal trapped in her lungs. She raced up to expel it into the air.

For several minutes she treaded water, feeling the late-morning sun warm the damp whorls of her hair. When she slipped under for the third time, Labiaxa decided this would be it. Fail now, and she would have to return to her father's home in shame. Opening her eyes to the briny sting, she chose a point in the distance where refracted rays of sunlight met in a crystalline blue nexus. Seconds passed. A full minute. Two. Her diaphragm jerked, her lips struggled to part, and the humming in her head escalated to a scream. But she dug her feet into the sand and refused to let go.

By and by the screaming in her brain softened to a dulcet fluting: *oooee . . . oooee . . . oooeee . . .* The panic subsided and her lungs ceased their struggle.

She might have drifted off to sleep, so dull and languid went the throb of her heart. She felt the crescent folds of her throat, those dead vestiges, soften and split. The sea spilled down her windpipe, triggering the faintest urge to gag. Then that too passed and Labiaxa was at last realizing her anatomical destiny. She was breathing underwater!

The Gargoulette burned in her grasp. She opened her eyes again, raised it, and waited . . . *oooee . . . oooee . . . oooeeeeee . . .*

The journey, though in hours quite brief, has seemed interminable to Labiaxa. Now, with the city at last before her, she grips the green arms of her litter and thinks of her mother, pictures that indistinct blue haze behind which she has hidden her whole life.

Suddenly she hears a voice, but it does not register in her ears. The words pierce the very hollows of her mind. The sperm whale Oooeea speaks. Low, mothering, hers is a strange tongue to be sure, a dreamlike harmony of hieroglyphs and sighs. But to Labiaxa's astonishment, she understands every word.

Raise high the Gargoulette of Nautika! commands the whale.

Before them stands a tremendous gate carved from black basalt. Labiaxa does as she is instructed. The three lunar medusae, perhaps recognizing their home, burn more brightly than ever. With a blast of trumpets, the gate swings open. The fanfare strikes her air-drinker ears like the groans of feminine ecstasy. Perhaps it is her own.

As they penetrate the strange city, Oooeea narrates in her telepathic mind-tongue. The gate, she explains, is called the Sperm's Portal, so named because it is massive enough to welcome a visitor of baleen proportions. It is the only opening through which the uninitiated may enter Nautika.

The water, though remarkably clear, obscures anything at a distance of more than a few furlongs, so that as Labiaxa presses forward the city reveals itself in stages, like the leaves of an illuminated codex. Inside the gate their path is blocked by an army of aquatic warriors. A cavalry of women—perhaps hundreds of them—mounted on sleek and stately dolphins!

Behold, says Oooeea, *the six hundred-strong Prophylaxes of Peace. Pity them as we pass, dear Princess.*

Arrayed in a fearsome phalanx just inside the dome, each soldier is outfitted for imminent combat. Her fists bristle with spears of blood-red glass and her shoulder is slung with a slender glass rifle. A red breastplate protects her blue musculature. Under each helmet Labiaxa can see a face furrowed with concern and sadness.

Warriors! thinks Labiaxa. *But how can that be? Father told me war was forbidden in Nautika!*

Yes, very astute, my Princess, says the whale, answering her thoughts. *These six hundred live outside the Code of Nautika. They alone may know the primitive pain your air-drinker brethren call "murder"—the Nautikon tongue has no word for this aberration. But after their horrific deed is done, they are sworn to self-immolation. This, you see, is why the Prophylaxes are so desperately sad.*

Oooeea gives a signal and the dolorous army parts. Labiaxa and her huge escort pass between their ranks to enter a lush garden of sea foliage. She is afraid—afraid and perhaps aroused—but the sperm whale calms her at once with a mothering mind-tone.

You are safe here, Princess, she says, drawing to a halt. *But here is where I must leave you. I beg you dismount. The rest of your journey must perforce be your own.*

With hesitation Labiaxa loosens her leather straps and slides down the animal's flank to the sandy floor. She stands in a bower of ferns that tower on huge stalks, like swaying palms or, she thinks, like supplicating hands. Clinging to the fronds of these stately trees is some deep-sea species of rhododendron. The vines coil all around her, touching her waist and brushing her lips with lusty pink flowers. They bow and scrape before their other-worldly guest.

Oooeea turns one baleful eye to her charge, issues a single piercing farewell, and in a confetti of bubbles exits through the Sperm's Portal. Labiaxa watches the whale soar over the vast dome. Then she is alone in this strange land, mired in the unknown as surely as she is immersed in the sea. On all sides, the strange botany of the deep. Above, the dome and the infinite fathoms. At her feet, shifting sand. She is alone.

But not for long. Out of the foliage stroll a pair of Nautikon women. In appearance they are precisely as her father described them. Their skin is all over a chalky blue, bluer even than her own and infinitely smoother. Their strong legs end in broad webbed feet. The tops of their heads are bare. Indeed when the loose vestments of pearlescent cloth part, she sees that even their most intimate features are hairless. The eyes that meet her own are large, wide-set—and now huge with astonishment.

At the sight of Labiaxa, and her Gargoulette of Nautika, they scurry back into the briar of rhododendron from whence they have come.

Wait! Labiaxa shouts out in the echo chamber of her mind. *I am—I must—!*

But the Nautikons are gone.

She springs after them into the greenery but is suddenly hurled back into the arms of a fern tree. A violent concussion has ripped through the garden. Then comes another—and yet another. Labiaxa is thrown to the sand, tasting grit and blood. She leaps again, just as the seabed falls away beneath her. With a thud, a great fissure splits the garden path, disgorging the roots of several fern trees. A fusillade of sulfur gas escapes from the crevice and Labiaxa feels intense heat. Swimming up and away from the conflagration, she paddles over the tree line to find herself floating above a bustling marketplace.

On a broad plain of white sand are arranged dozens of monger stalls, each piled with merchandise. Cages of medusae hang at intervals on long cables, casting over everything a tremulous golden glow. Sea cows roam unyoked among the vendors.

At one stall succulent sea vegetables glisten in reedy baskets. At another a man sells tunics and scarves sewn from that alluring pearly fabric. Nearby a stooped man hawks flatware fashioned from seashells. Old tomes bound in green leather are displayed in long crates. Bright gongs wink in the medusa-light like small suns—*three Eea apiece! Five Eea for two!*

But no one is buying. The tremor has thrown the market into disarray. Nautikons, male and female, dart about like fish around an egret's suddenly stabbing beak. Labiaxa can see where the cruel fissure has torn the marketplace asunder. A glass chariot with mechanical flippers for wheels lies on its side, its bounty of sea urchins spilled across the sand. One stall has collapsed entirely into the widening crack. Here and there steam belches up torrid storms of sand and clay.

Suddenly a fist of magma erupts, hissing, from the fissure,

gutting a sea cow. Her suckling calves keen and roll helplessly about their mother's ruptured body. Labiaxa thinks she hears laughter, cruel manly laughter echoing up from the earth below.

Earth, her father had warned her, is a man. And water a woman. When Earth-Man yields to his long-suppressed andro-rage, Water-Woman has much cause to fear.

But even amid the buckling stone and death cries, Labiaxa can feel the eyes of the market goers fall upon her. The Nautikons gaze with fear at her long raven hair and her thighs draped in rough leather. Then, as they catch sight of the Gargoulette glowing at her side, each one stiffens and bows before their alien visitor.

She hears them whisper: *Who is this Princess?*

She bears the Gargoulette of Nautika, and yet, she appears so . . . monstrous.

Could she be the oracled one? The Mother of . . .

The Final . . . !

But no! It is impossible!

Labiaxa presses on, half-swimming, half-leaping through the water. When she passes the flatware merchant, trying now to right his overturned cart, he looks at her with profound anxiety. His thoughts reach her in tangles. A question trembles on his lower lip, but he dares not give it voice.

Who is . . . ? But no . . . must not ask! Must not . . . even . . . think to ask! The Code of Nautika forbids me to question a . . . a Princess! The punishment . . . castration!

In his expression she sees something of her father—his help-lessness, his predestined grief—and once more the cold seed of doubt begins to germinate.

The sea shudders around her! Volcanic fires boil the sand like grains in a pot! Labiaxa is thrown painfully against a barrow of spiny whelks. For a brief instant, her lungs regress. They suck and convulse for air. Air! they seem to cry. Air! Bring back the old dry world! Bring back Papa!

Then a tiny webbed hand touches her shoulder.

Princess! Princess!

A girl child, naked and pure, embraces her from behind, pressing her lips against one of Labiaxa's gills in a clumsy childish kiss. In a rush Labiaxa's faith is restored. It floods her starving lungs. She inhales and imagines that she has tasted it—knows she has tasted it: the hormone-infused waters of Nautika that her father called "estro-wisdom."

Estro-wisdom, he'd explained, is the elixir of femininity that suffuses Nautika. It gives strength to her women and reason to her men. The more Labiaxa drinks of it, the more familiar grows this uncanny city. She feels like a wanderer at last returned to her native land. Now even the thundering earth cannot shake her feeling of peace and, yes, arrival.

Settling the girl atop a bale of sea grass, she implores her: *What happens next, child? Where do I go?*

But the girl's mind is strangely empty. Wordlessly, thoughtlessly even, she points. Labiaxa bestows a kiss upon the child's finned brow and swims toward a darkened alley at the far end of the market.

Beyond the light of the medusa lanterns, she must feel her way through near total darkness. The alley tapers to a narrow trail, and suddenly she stands in a gloomy forest of fern trees. Under the soles of her sandals she feels the crunch of frail shells. The glow of her Gargoulette shows a path paved with oily mussels. It splays off this way and that, a puzzle tree of forking trails, a dark hand of indecision. There are no straight lines in this dim wood, no right angles, no clear options. Each trail curves as if by caprice to meet its invisible destiny.

She clings to a broad avenue until, as she passes one unremarkable footpath, the Gargoulette begins to glow with great urgency. Taking this as a sign, she follows the little path into the gloom. She winds left, veers right, seems to come full circle. Once she loses the trail altogether and must crawl on all fours to find it again amid the rhododendron. At last, she rounds a corner where the path ends abruptly at a massive white wall.

Labiaxa reaches out to touch it: glass. The wall pulsates with a soft but insistent inner light. It curves in either direction for many furlongs before disappearing into the dark. Gazing up, she sees how high it soars, almost to the fretwork of the dome itself, where it blooms into a glowing blue bulb. This is no mere wall—it is the foundation of a tower, a tower of incalculable circumference!

She follows it to the left for what must be hundreds of strokes until at last she finds herself in a vast oval courtyard. Around her loom a dozen more towers, identical to the one she has circumnavigated. They cast a ghost-white glow over the central lawn. At her feet lies a carpet of red and blue, some dizzying flora that quivers with a trillion particolored cilia. Drifting down to the ground, she wriggles her sandaled toes in the enchanted seabed.

Ha! It tickles! It stings! She laughs, winces.

Standing on her hands to get a better look, she feels the charge of pain and pleasure course up her arms. She presses her face closer to the tentacled nap and receives a strong jolt on her nose!

Careful, Princess! The voice is that of a twittering soubrette. It seems to bubble up from the region of the brain that regulates goose bumps and fits of giggling. *The Lawn of the Anemones is stimulating underfoot,* says the voice, *but on your nose—lo, it can smart like a medusa's kiss!*

Righting herself, Labiaxa comes face-to-face with the most lovely example of Nautikon womanhood she has yet encountered. Her slight stature and bashful eyes tell Labiaxa that she is an adolescent of the species. Yet she is clearly a person of status. Swaddled in pearl-cloth, her hairless body studded with red gemstones, she bears in her left hand a luminous Gargoulette of her own. As the girl draws near, Labiaxa's medusae throb excitedly in welcome.

The Nautikon bows deeply before her, and Labiaxa, not knowing what decorum requires, repeats the gesture. The woman laughs again, so awkwardly that it puts Labiaxa at ease. She smiles.

You needn't bow before me, shouts the Nautikon, returning the smile. *I know who you are! You are the Mother of the One True Man. You were shown to me in the mirror of Oooee! I knew you would come . . . the others would not believe me, but I insisted . . . yes, she will come unto us anon! The Queen has promised us a Final Mother to birth the One True Man, and now . . . and now . . . !*

On and on the girl chatters, Labiaxa understanding almost nothing. The girl holds out both hands to draw Labiaxa to her breast, but when Labiaxa hesitates, the chattering stops. The Nautikon bows again, sputtering apologies.

I'm sorry . . . to touch you . . . it was a grave impertinence! . . . She lowers her wide-set eyes. Her blue complexion purples. *I humbly beg your forgiveness . . . O Princess Labiaxa . . . !*

Labiaxa gasps, her gills aflutter.

How, she thinks, *how could this stranger know my name?*

But the Nautikon has read her thoughts.

How could I fail to know your name? Is it an offense to mind-speak it?

THE UNKNOWN KNOWNS

The woman bows still lower, fairly scraping the tentacled ground with her cranial fin. As for her own name, she says, the Princess may call her Oôo. And though she is the youngest of the Council of Twelve, she is a confidante of the Queen . . . perhaps, though she does not wish to boast, Her closest adviser. Of all the Twelve, Oôo alone has prophesied the time of Labiaxa's arrival. Though no one believed her.

Oh, but now they will have to believe me . . . !

The woman prattles on excitedly. Her eyes flash. Labiaxa is reminded of the girls at school in their gossipy clutches.

You appeared before me in the mirror of Oooee . . . I knew your arrival would be soon . . . and now . . . Mother of the One True Man! You have come . . . and now the prophesy may be fulfilled . . . your own man child shall carry estro-wisdom to the world of air . . . to the sacred water place atop the holy mountain . . . and there shall be three maidens to test Him . . . water and blood to purge Him of His demons . . . and the True Man in His infinite wisdom . . . He will rise above His own base urges to save mankind from itself!

Holy mountain? Blood? Mother? says Labiaxa. *But I am no child's mother! What is all this nonsense?*

Forgive me . . . I have said too much! I always say too much! I bid you welcome, Princess! The Nautikon gestures broadly. *Welcome to our Zone of Estro-Wisdom and Governance!*

Labiaxa looks away from her adolescent hostess to survey the towers. Twelve are of equal stature, identical in majesty and light. But one tower, at the apogee of the elliptical courtyard, looms larger than the rest. The glass is more lustrous. The light is more vivid. And high above its companions, at the very capital of this grand spire, perch not one but two coruscating blue domes. Inside this grandest of towers Labiaxa can see a pantomime of fig-

187

ures haloed by the pale internal glow—hundreds of them, turning spirals and falling in clusters. They rain down and, as if magnified by the thickening glass at the base, appear to grow larger as they fall.

Labiaxa follows them with her eyes until they reach the lowest part of the tower. There the glass is of a wholly different character. Supple, gelatinous, it ripples and throbs like matter suspended between its liquid and solid states. Now and again openings appear in this pliant wall—huge arcades and small portholes no bigger than a child—and out of these openings Nautikon children spill onto the Lawn of the Anemones. They mass confusedly about the foundation of the tower and then, as more children pour out behind them, fly off into the water like bees from a hive.

Oôo's eyes glitter on the sides of her proud head like twin pearls.

You seem alarmed, dear Princess! But why? This is your city, she mind-speaks. *These . . . these are your children who pour forth from the lofty Ôva. The Spires of the Twelve are your birthright. As is all of Nautika. Princess, if I may—*

But suddenly there is another massive explosion. A rift tears across the Lawn of the Anemones, and black coils of stone big as cypresses reach out in all directions. A single aching red finger touches a nearby tower. Labiaxa watches in horror as the glass crazes and crackles. The water is riven by an earsplitting shriek. But the tower refuses to fall.

Oôo screams. She stoops close to Labiaxa, grasping her goatskin skirt like a child.

Papa was right, Labiaxa mind-whispers, forgetting that her companion can hear her every dreadful thought. *A terrible fate shall soon befall this miraculous city. Nothing can stop the rage of Earth-Man. He will bury Nautika forever.*

What? says Oôo, looking up beseechingly into Labiaxa's eyes. *Bury us . . . forever?*

Labiaxa's mouth draws tight across her face. She feels pity, but for whom? For Oôo? For Nautika? For herself?

I am afraid this is true, she says. *My father is a very wise man. This very morning he warned me of—* But here Labiaxa pauses. How can she tell this woman that her civilization is about to meet its fiery end?

Yes, it is of Aricos you speak! Father of the Mother of the One True Man. His wisdom is legendary! But please, go on, Princess. I beg you.

By day's end, the mountain we call Etna will cast its innards upon the sea and bury your fair city—our fair city—for eternity!

Oôo extends her trembling arms toward Labiaxa. Unexpectedly she begins to speak aloud. Labiaxa hears the Nautikon tongue voiced for the first time. The words extrude from a pool of pure vowels. They come in a torrent, in a trill, like a flute played by constant wind.

"Ooooeeeaeeeoooooooooaaaaaaa . . ."

At first all Labiaxa hears is a long lament. But gradually the wail subdivides into words, coalesces into sentences. To her astonishment she understands everything the Nautikon says.

"Please, Princess—I beg of you, follow me! Do you understand? Yes? Of course you do! I would mind-speak, but this trembling . . . these portents . . . my mind is a jumble of . . . And this matter, your arrival, is more urgent than I thought. You must . . . you must speak with the Queen now—"

Another clap of volcanic thunder. A bright fissure races up the side of a distant minaret.

"—before it is too late!"

Oôo fans out her flippered hands. She draws taut the webbing under her arms, seizes Labiaxa by the hand, and together they sprint across the lawn toward the highest tower. Through a throng of naked young Nautikons, Oôo drags her messianic charge. Though the city quakes and burns, these children of the sea coo and smile. They dance and laugh. They reach out to embrace Labiaxa, but Oôo shoves them roughly aside until they reach the base of the tower. An opening appears before them, and Oôo ushers Labiaxa inside.

The spire, she sees now, has no floors, no parapets or stairs, no features that Labiaxa can discern. Only those smooth cylindrical walls that taper to a vanishing point many fathoms above. At intervals that point dilates to reveal a disk of blue radiance that cascades down the tower.

The Nautikon children frolic more thickly here. They appear on all sides, stroke her hair, nuzzle her breasts. Soon Labiaxa loses Oôo in the writhing blue mass. A child lands astride her shoulders and she can feel the girl's naked sex on the back of her neck. Another wraps its arms around a thigh, like a toddler who has at last found his mother in a crowd.

Finally a hand seizes Labiaxa by the elbow. Oôo darts upward, and the children fall away from them, giggling and cooing. Over the riot of children's voices, she can hear Oôo sputtering on about singing spermata and mirrored halls, the fleshly straits called the Royal Vulvorum and the legion fingers of the great and awesome Ôva . . .

As they climb higher inside the tower, the crowd grows thin and—though this must be a trick of the mind—the children appear to grow younger. Some sort of reverse ontogeny is taking place in this magic spire. One moment Labiaxa is surrounded by adolescents; a few paces upward and she sees only toddlers, thumb-sucking and babbling; farther still and she dodges a swirl of falling infants, knees drawn and gurgling.

The hand that clutches hers has grown smaller as well. She looks up at Oôo but sees that she is holding the hand of a small girl, no more than three or four years of age. Releasing the child's hand, Labiaxa looks frantically for her guide.

"Oôo! Oôo!"

"Silly!" the little girl shouts. "Silly, silly Princess! I'm right here!"

"Oôo?"

"I leave go down or maybe I'm a baby too!" She laughs. "Baby-baby too-too! Baby-baby too!"

"Oôo! What is happening to you? What is this place?"

In reply Oôo jabs her little index finger toward the dilating blue disk far overhead.

"Mama house!" she says. "Princess Mama-Baby! You go Mama house!"

Then, after giving Labiaxa a quick kiss on the brow, the diminished Oôo somersaults down into the cascade of children. She is gone.

You go Mama house!

Labiaxa looks at her own hands, at her full breasts, her downy sex, her knees and feet. She remains a woman. But as she continues upward, the transformation she undergoes is perhaps more profound. Her muscles grow stronger. The walls of her heart thicken. Her womb expands in direct proportion to her widening mind. And even as the tower rumbles around her, she feels peace and purpose. All is still unknown to her, but it feels known, and that is enough.

You go Mama house!

She swims. Labiaxa's flesh quickens with nerves that have never before been touched. The water caresses her throat. It effervesces inside her every cell. At the core of her being she bristles with a thousand anemones of pure sensation. She groans. She shivers. Her tongue goes cold in her mouth. Just half a furlong farther, Labiaxa tells herself, and she will surely climax!

You go Mama house!

She swims. Her gills contract. The very breath is stolen from her breast. The blue light inside the tower fades to gray. She swims, and blood-red sparks spiral around the dying sun of her mind. She swims as if she were ascending an endless cataract. She swims, spiraling upward, upward, until the estro-wisdom pours so thickly into her gills that she swoons, convulses, and at long last, climaxes.

THIRTEEN

Rep. Frost: I want to pick up where we left off yesterday with the subject of the victims in the so-called Oaken Bucket incident. You are on record as saying you socialized with the Mills girls and Miss Stephens. What were the parameters of your interaction?

Agent Diaz: Suntanning, dinner.

Rep. Frost: Did you know these girls before, before your arrival at the ███████████ theme park?

Diaz: Absolutely not. And look, if you're trying to insinuate—

Rep. Frost: Nobody's insinuating. The House of Representatives isn't a forum for insinuation. Now please describe your initial encounter with the victims.

Diaz: Gladly. It was the day I arrived. I'd spent the morning vetting the custodial staff, asking my usual bullet-point questions. Management was cooperative in terms of keys and schematics and whatnot. The sisters who run that place have a genuine concern for the homeland. They were sensitive to the needs of my investigation, although it was difficult at times to tell them apart.

I'd been driving all night so, man, was I bushed. I found a chaise what-do-you-call-it on the patio and put my dogs up. The weather was unseasonably warm, I'm told, for that altitude, even in August. No sooner do I close my eyes when I hear the aforementioned young ladies enter the premises. Miss Mills number one—that would be I think Brenda—she was in a situation with her folding patio chair. Because of my expertise with my dad's pool business, I'm intimately familiar with every make of collapsible furniture. So I offered my assistance, nothing more.

Then it was later that evening that I ran across them again in the, uh, dining area.

Rep. Frost: So you had dinner with them?

Diaz: In a manner of speaking. I got a basket of what they call Nuggets. Everything on the menu is done in a Gold Rush motif, consistent with the overall conceit of the facility. So I got Nuggets, and these girls—they were college girls, as I said, there to blow off steam. So they were maybe having some beverages.

Rep. Frost: Were you, Agent Diaz, partaking?

Diaz: In the beverages? Yes, in moderation. It was a house specialty called the Pink Mine Shaft, which come to think of it, is a suggestive name. I was off duty, so I helped them polish off a pitcher. You have to understand our directive at WATERT. It's to blend in with the populace to whatever extent is deemed safe. I deemed the Pink Mine Shaft to be within the parameters of safe.

But circumstances quickly exceeded those parameters. I looked over and who's sitting nearby but him—Mr. Rath. I mean the nerve, not to mention the unprofessionalism, considering the covert nature of his own operation. It was kind of, from a peer professional angle, kind of unreal. If the 9/11 guys had been this bold, we would have nabbed them in a heartbeat.

Rep. Frost: And yet no one, as you say, nabbed Mr. Rath.

Diaz: Well, yes, there's that element of irony again. An element of irony that led to the endangerment of innocent life. The Patriot Act doesn't give us authority to just detain American citizens because they share your taste in hotels. Maybe you'll take that into consideration when the act comes up for review. With Rath I was still in a watch-and-observe mode.

Rep. Frost: Did you at that time inform any of your superiors back in Maryland about the Rath situation?

Diaz: What situation? We weren't at this juncture in any situation. I placed a quick call to my AB informing him that there was this suspicious character and I had him under observation. I was discouraged from taking any action at that time. And I'm sure the AB can corroborate on this.

I did however put the perpetrator, put Mr. Rath, on notice that I was in possession of his number. I let him know in no uncertain terms that he had been identified as an enemy combatant and that I would deal with him harshly should the need arise.

Rep. Frost: You yelled at the suspect.

Diaz: Is that what Rath told you? Little ▆▆▆▆▆ bastard. You can't trust these people to tell the white toast truth! The truth is that all they do is hate, 24–7, and freedom isn't the only thing they hate. They hate the truth too. I most certainly did not yell. Absolutely not.

I simply gave our boy the heads-up that his cover was blown. There wouldn't be any jihad perpetrated on my watch. I'd run out the kite string on tolerating this guy's behavior, and he'd punched every single ticket on being an irresponsible member of the world community. I simply notified Jim Rath that the string had been run and the tickets punched. His number was up.

After dinner, I retired to the patio. It was a cool night and totally clear. You could see all the way up the mountain past the rides and the waterfalls. Beyond that it was just stars and stars. I wished I knew some constellations because they were everywhere.

We took a pitcher of Pink Shafts out to a patio table and just, you know, absorbed the ambience of being in the mountains, with the altitude and the Gold Rush scenery. Then along comes the suspicious party dressed in his bathing trunks like he's Jacques goddamn Cousteau looking for the *Andrea Doria*. He's got a scuba mask around his neck and a snorkel. I thought, What the heck is this? Well, the girls got a good laugh out of him, hairy little monkey with his diving gear. I maintained a professional demeanor because I alone could sense the threat that he posed, despite his comical, you know, appurtenances. And I tried to act professional, but what I did next I'm not proud of. If you're going to convict me of anything—

Rep. Frost: Nobody's here to convict a federal agent of anything. We stand by the efforts of the men and women who serve on the front lines. Period.

Diaz: Yeah, I guess you'd have to. But if you wanted to blacken my file with any misconduct, here's your chance. Rath gets in the pool, what they call the Waterin' Hole. He's got a notebook, one of those waterproof kinds like they use on *Nova* programs about eels. Damn, I'm thinking, for a terrorist he sure is a weirdo. He doesn't fit any profile I'm aware of. I mean, who recruited this guy? That's the question I want this committee to answer. Jim Rath makes Jose Padilla look like the freaking Jackal.

So he gets in the pool and all you can see from where we're sitting is the strands of whatever he's got for hair floating in the water above his head. The intake of the snorkel's just barely breaching the surface. And he's just, I don't know, standing there—not even swimming—just standing there. I swear a half hour goes by and Rath hasn't budged.

I might blame the altitude and maybe the drinks for what I did, but mostly it was my own lack of sensitivity. I'm working on that. Anyway, the girls were getting a good laugh out of this guy, started calling him Aquaman, which was admittedly pretty funny under the circumstances. I mean, he was no Aquaman. So I said, Check this out, and I tiptoed over to the edge of the Waterin' Hole. I looked in and I could see Rath's eyes were closed behind the scuba mask, almost like he was asleep. I shushed the girls. Then ever so gently, ever so quietly, I placed one thumb over the snorkel hole.

I felt the tube jerk away, but I held it fast. I saw his eyes shoot open and those long arms of his start thrashing around. Then he's clawing at his scuba mask. The girls run over and they're like, Come on, Les, that's not funny. Let him go, let him go! You know: girls. But you could tell they were loving it.

All of a sudden he blasts up out of the water and he's gasping for air and his arms are slapping the water, and I think, I'll be darned, this guy can't even swim.

I'm wearing socks with my Teva sandals—and this is an interesting footnote, but I have poor circulation, so even when I'm in flip-flops, as I was that night, I prefer to wear tube socks. It's an unconventional look, but I believe in the principle of whatever works. Well, Rath is splashing around so much my socks get totally soaked.

Finally Keesha jumps in. Turns out she was a lifeguard or something. She gets Rath in the tow hold and drags him over to the edge. Got him laid out on the patio, and the poor guy, he's gasping like a guppy on a hot plate. Keesha has to administer some mouth-to-mouth, which was frankly pretty gross to watch. He certainly didn't deserve any first aid, especially of the sexy young lady variety.

Rep. Frost: This is the first time the committee is hearing this part of the story. Did you inform any of your superiors back at WATERT of this incident?

Diaz: We're talking about a delicate situation. Frankly I didn't know how to relay what happened, and not just because I had mixed feelings about my own actions. I was concerned—believe it or not—for Mr. Rath's own reputation. You start making accusations of any kind with Homeland, they stick. And this was before the incident, you've got to understand, so naturally I felt different about the guy. Now I don't care who knows, but at the time I had to consider Rath's feelings.

To put this in as plain of terms as possible—and again I have to apologize to the congressladies for the coarseness of my language, but Mr. Rath, he—while Miss Stephens was administering the mouth-to-mouth—Mr. Rath appeared to attain orgasm.

Rep. Frost: He what?

Diaz: He spooged in his swimming trunks.

FOURTEEN

I was having difficulty sleeping. Maybe it was the residual Pink Mine Shaft gumming up my circadian rhythms. Or perhaps it was all the redundant tan decor in my Prospector's Bend motel room. (Tan is a surprisingly provocative color; I've seen studies.) More likely it was the leftover shame that had spackled the creases of my eyelids and stopped them from closing properly.

I'd suffered another run-in with the Nautikon, and this one was way worse than the Lazy River episode. Without getting into the boring details, I'll say only that he pranked me at the expense of my research. I was having a fruitful session of *oooee*. Truly astonishing things were being revealed to me—undersea gardens, an earthquake in a subaquatic market, milk-glass towers touched by fists of magma, reverse ontogeny—until the Nautikon cut off my psychic flow. He knew what I was doing. He knew I was getting closer to his secret. And for some reason he found this threatening. Which is a personal bummer to me because my intentions regarding him and his culture have always been positive.

Not that it matters, but he also made a laughingstock out of me in front of the Mills sisters. Who cares, right? It's not like I feel some untapped need to impress a pair of bosomy sorority girls with pastel brains. They were in on the joke, goading him on. The whole patio was charged with some kind of antiestro-wisdom, andro-jerkdom.

But if the Mills sisters tested my faith in womankind, Keesha Stephens restored it—with a kiss. She saved my life, mouth to mouth, but there's no real reason to retread that miserable experience, either my life or the saving of it. Let me say one thing: no matter who gets intubated or demoted or gitmoed or house-arrested or plutoed by the end of this stupid story, I want the record to show that Ms. Stephens was and always will be an unimpeachable and completely awesome person.

The bedside LED showed 3:40 a.m. I lay on the mattress replaying the previous day on the retractable white screen of my mind. As the minutes wore on, sleep became a more and more remote possibility, a rabbit you'd been chasing across a vast field until it finally occurred to you that you didn't even like rabbits, and that catching a rabbit would mean exactly nothing to you. So I stopped running and watched the cottontail of sleep vanish under the far hedge.

By then I had a serious headache. The pain started in my pineal gland, the most primitive site in the brain. It was an atavistic kind of torment that seemed to harken back to those dim days before we slipped into the sea, when rapacious humanoid predators roamed the savannas, driving humanity to seek shelter in the fecund tidal pools of North Africa. Way back, way back before history, that's where my headache came from.

It wasn't a cold night, so I'd left the casement window cranked open. The breeze coming down the mountainside sent undulations through the curtains so that the pattern of Conestoga wagons appeared to be in transit. I could hear Flatiron Falls crash endlessly into the Waterin' Hole and thought of Labiaxa rushing up the cataract of estro-wisdom toward her audience with the Queen. Then I thought about what I'd left in my refrigerator back in Colorado Springs. I wondered if Jean had returned to clean out anything that might spoil, the ground beef for instance. Maybe she'd brought someone along to help, someone to run interference in case she crossed paths with her lunatic ex-husband. The cabinetmaker, or Josh from the office. And after they'd dumped the moldering tortilla pie and clumpy milk down the Disposall, they would sully our marital sofa bed with their lovemaking. Then I remembered that *Nova* was on TV that night. On the ceiling of the motel room I conjured up the hurtful movie of Jean and the rugby-playing cabinetmaker, knees pressed together under the afghan, draining glasses of pinot noir and watching dung beetles roll up their little shit balls. I couldn't sleep. I couldn't sleep.

I couldn't sleep. And in the storehouse of my insomniac mind, betrayal piled on top of betrayal. I looked up through the depths of the Waterin' Hole and saw the Nautikon's mocking face. His thumb stuck in the end of my snorkel. His smile, distorted by the water, looked fanged. His eyes glinted with caprice. The air, I thought, was poison to him. It was turning this innocent, this idol, into a cyclops, a total jerkwad.

I'm ashamed to admit it now, but I wasn't thinking only of

Nautika. I was thinking about myself too. If being let down by ordinary mortals is hard, the disappointment of an advanced oceanic being who starts acting like a frat boy is a pain without precedent.

Jean never really believed in God. She didn't have the supernatural bent for belief. But I know she was a big Jesus fan. She liked the sandals and the sermons, the whole messianic packaging. She liked the way He introduced a change in divine policy to a stubborn world with a gentle, lamblike smile, while the divine CEO, His father, sat upstairs threatening mass layoffs. Jean was in the field of organizational planning, and Jesus, He was her ultimate middle manager. So she clung to the concept of Christ without much in the way of belief.

Substitute the Nautikon for Jesus, and you get a sense of my own disintegrating situation. As I lay there in the dark, my faith was going to hell, while my *attachment* to said faith grew more and more intractable. Plus I couldn't sleep.

I couldn't sleep, so I got up and looked out the window. I knew from my most recent session of *ooeee* that the True Man must be tested by three maidens. I knew he would be led to the virtuous path by the one called Jim (i.e., me). We already stood atop the holy mountain, He and I. Before us lay water and blood.

I saw the Oaken Bucket out there under its tarp, the moonlit water lapping at its sides. It looked like the applecart of wanton fun—and who wouldn't want to upset that applecart? That's when it hit me. That was when I got the idea: hatched my evil plan, plotted my purported misdeed, initiated the alleged disservice to my nation that earned me a tracking device on my ankle and a guy with a headset watching my every move while I grow older day in and day out on the deck of a houseboat. The germ of the scheme came to me in a flash of inspiration as I stood there in the motel-room window. I would do something bad with the Oaken Bucket. Something so shocking that it would remind the Nautikon of his true mission. Remind him that he was sent here to save a dangerous world from itself. I would do something bad. Something shocking.

If he thought this was all a personal joyride, a vacation from cultural extinction, I was prepared to remind him otherwise! Vengeance was in my eye. I saw it in the half mirror of the window, then watched the vengeance travel down to my legs, murky electricity. My hands felt restless, restless and evil. I left room 21 and let my cruel purpose guide me, let it propel my bare feet to the very precipice of mischief.

I stood on the patio. The moon and the water were enjoying each other's company as I began to climb the mountain. The flagstones were cold enough to numb the balls of my feet. Soon I found myself sniffing around the Oaken Bucket. At the back of the ride I discovered a low shed stuccoed to look like a boulder. The midget door was padlocked, but a sustained tug with one foot braced against the frame did the job. When I ducked inside I heard scampering, the scampering of paws. I had only a vague idea of what I was going to do. It was dark. My hands prowled the floor and walls. I felt sweaty pipes, the round glass face of a meter, a stopcock wadded with spiderwebs. Behind me the Oaken Bucket rocked gently on its rails and I could hear the wooden staves groan.

They weren't exactly speaking to me, the staves. No, that's what a crazy person would say relating the genesis of his crime. The ax or the howitzer or the piano wire spoke to me, told me to do it: *Do it! Kill her now! Do it!* The seabirds told you to sever the cable and send the whole gondola of Italian tourists hurtling into the fjord. But the "talking dog" alibi has always seemed like a lame excuse to me. If a dog tells you to bind an old man with duct tape and pull out his molars with a pair of pliers, I don't know, that strikes me as kind of dubious. You wouldn't listen to a talking dog under ordinary circumstances, so why would you listen to a dog that was telling you to do something illegal? You'd have to be criminally insane to take orders from a dog. So the groaning staves of the Oaken Bucket, they might have made some suggestions, might have offered their point of view, but I didn't take them seriously. I don't listen to staves, and I never have.

Inside the boulder-shaped shed I came across a toolbox. I dragged it out into the sodium light and found a locking wrench with mean jaws. I looked at the wrench; I looked at the wheels of the Oaken Bucket resting underwater on their gleaming rails, and I made a mental connection, like a syllogism or something.

I remembered the Nautikon toasting the girls back in the restaurant: "Tomorrow I'm taking you three hotties for a ride on the Oaken Bucket!" I remembered his arrogance, his cruelty. My plan took form and stiffened with the starch of hatred.

I gazed down at the motel. His corner room was dark. The Helvner told me that the hour was 4:30 a.m. Soon it would be light. If I wanted to act, I would have to do it now. I picked up the locking wrench and stepped into the hip-deep water, gripping the rim of the Bucket for balance. The two right wheels were attached to the axles with single bolts.

I followed the path of the rails with my eyes. The Bucket would exit the pool and drop about twenty meters at a sixty-degree angle. It would level out before taking the first hairpin curve. Two small waterfalls would come next, then another hairpin turn to the left, before the Bucket crossed the top of Flatiron Falls. There I knew from observation that the Bucket leaned hard to the right, giving passengers the sensation that they were slipping over the edge of the raging cataract. Just in the nick of time the Bucket righted itself and plunged shrieking into the mine shaft. From there it was a straight shot down to the safe harbor of the Waterin' Hole and the motel patio.

But not if I had my way.

I'm not mechanically inclined, but I had a theory. If I loosened the right-hand pair of wheels, the Bucket might not be able to recover from the tilting passage across Flatiron Falls. It would lean out . . . out . . . out . . . and more out until it met oblivion. Tumble end over end in the bleak summer air some fifteen feet to the shallow pool below. Not far enough to hurt anybody, I reasoned, only enough to scare them. And my theory proved to be surprisingly sound, all except for that last part.

I squatted down in the water and fitted the wrench over one of the hubs, just gauging the size of it. I adjusted the width of the grip by twisting the peg at the end of the handle. I repositioned the wrench on the hub and squeezed, feeling with satisfaction as the jaws bit the steel nut. Then I stood up to get some leverage.

But that, I'm happy to report, was where I stopped. The evil seemed to drain out of my hands like briny green seawater from a ballast tank. I loosened my grip on the wrench and stared into the dark pool, at the aborted inevitability of my would-be crime. At the alternate future that was but a wrench turn away. My reflection scared me—that poison Narcissus, the negative me who only seconds earlier was the only me. He scared me. I scared me. I could still feel his presence, my presence, the wake of his careless laughter throbbing across the water.

The Feds didn't believe me when I told them this; neither did the press or even the Fat Man, my lawyer; you won't believe me either, but I couldn't go through with it. I did not loosen the wheels on the Oaken Bucket. I wasn't the one who upset the applecart. I couldn't hurt anyone. Not Jim.

Why did I wimp out? Two words: Keesha Stephens. In my muscle memory I could still feel her soft life-giving lips pressed against mine. My mouth still burned with the urgency and concern of her breath, with the piney taste of liquor.

I let go of the wrench.

"Hey, buddy! You okay?"

The hairs of alarm stood up on my nape, and I turned to see the maintenance man, a flashlight swinging at his side. The guy's question seemed sensible enough. Was I, in fact, okay? I didn't know how to answer this. I did have a vague sense that I was totally busted if I didn't think fast. The tiny fragment of my brain that wasn't being flooded with panic hormones or self-loathing hatched a plan: remove the Helvner . . . let it drop to the bottom of the pool . . .

"Yo, you shouldn't be in there, man!"

. . . try to act normal . . . breathe . . . look like a regular person doing something.

"It's just," I said, affecting shame. "This is embarrassing—but I think I dropped my watch. I was out here taking a walk. It's a nice night." I indicated the moon. He acknowledged it. "And my watch must've slipped off. It's waterproof."

He shone his flashlight on the pool, but the oily surface gave back only his own rubbery beam. I squatted and picked up the Helvner.

"Ah! Got it!"

"That a Helvner?" he said, training the light on my dripping timepiece. "Let me see that."

I handed him the Helvner. What I didn't need now was a protracted chat about wristwatches. What if he noticed the wrench? What if he spotted the busted padlock or the toolbox that still lay open on the path? All the evidence pointed to me being a bad person. I *was* a bad person, or almost.

"Saudi navy, right?" said the maintenance man. He certainly knew a lot about watches. "You got to be on a list to get one of these, yeah?"

"My uncle knows a guy," I explained. The more I talked the more nervous I got, the more complicated the cover-up and the situation I had to cover up. "He was an admiral or something. He expedited the process."

I hopped out of the pool and tried to angle past him.

"I always did want a watch like this," he said.

"Keep it," I said, or heard myself say.

"What?" I nudged the door to the shed with my foot. It swung shut without the maintenance guy taking notice. "You shitting me?" he said.

I wasn't. "No. I'm not shitting you," I said. But dear god, I wish I'd been shitting him.

"You're shitting me."

"No. I'm not shitting you in the least. Take the watch."

"Yeah, you are." Jesus, when was this going to end? "You're straight-up shitting me."

"Look, I wouldn't shit you," I said. "Keep the watch." He slipped it on and a lump formed in my throat that you could probably see from the outside.

"Thanks, man. Hey—what's your name anyway? I'm Roland."

He extended his hand. The hand that was attached to the wrist that was wearing my watch. My mouth—the mouth that was allegedly attached to my brain—hung open, but no name came out. What *was* my name?

"Diaz," I said at last, remembering the stupid alias the hotel clerk in Denver had used for the Nautikon. "Les Diaz."

It was a pleasure to meet me, Les Diaz. He shook my hand and the watchband caught in the sodium light. Just when I thought he was ready to let go, when I thought the handshake had reached the outer limit of sociability, Roland gripped me even tighter and started shaking again. We shook hands for what seemed like hours. I took advantage of the awkward interlude to get one last farewell glimpse at the face of the Helvner. The time was 4:47 a.m.

As I scuttled back down the path toward the motel, I felt that I had jettisoned a vital part of my life. In an attempt to lose some deadweight, I'd ditched the parachute. Losing the watch felt like losing Jean all over again. Or to be more specific, it felt like the completion of a long phase of loss that began with Jean's good-bye note and ended with the passing of the Helvner. I was morphing into a new Jim, entering the third act of my life. I had no idea the curtain would come down here, on my uncle's houseboat on the Chesapeake with a bracelet strapped to my leg. In retrospect, it's almost like I'd traded a custom Saudi Arabian timepiece for an ankle-mounted tracking device. It was a symbolic exchange and it was totally depressing.

"Good night, Les Diaz!" The maintenance guy was calling to me from the top of the mountain. "I'll never forget this!" he said.

My heart was beating at an astounding rate. I broke into a run. I couldn't control my trajectory. There was no way I could go back to my room. I was a rat or a rhesus monkey, a lab animal that had just been released after years of experimentation, an animal with unacknowledged intellect and emotions who had given his pancreas and his teeth to test glow-in-the-dark taffy or lip balm that tastes like steak. At least I had my life, I thought, though I wasn't entirely convinced of this either. I circled the motel two or three times before coming to a halt in the parking lot. There I noticed the little door in the seat of the Old Prospector statue. I needed to collect my thoughts. Needed solitude. I approached the pants of the colossus, climbed the three or four iron rungs, and tried the knob.

Inside was bright. I could see the bank of bulbs that backlit the gold lettering in the prospector's pan, the ones that spelled out PROSPECTOR'S BEND. A second ladder took me into the torso of the big man. The electric light was hot on my face, and I realized I must be level with his heart. I touched the inside of the man's rib cage and felt the hatch marks of raw fiberglass. The arms flared out on either side of me, two tunnels stuffed with pink batting or insulation. I heard something rooting around in his left biceps. Maybe it was a rat or a vole.

I climbed on, shrugging my shoulders to squeeze in through the narrow passage of the throat. On the other side I found the cranial cavity, a small, roughly oval room with a ledge where the hairy chin jutted out. Opposite this, above the brim of his floppy calfskin hat, was a low rectangular window. If I perched on the chin ledge, I could look out over the roof of the motel, clear up to the top of the mountain, to the starlight above Summit County.

The Oaken Bucket was in plain sight, but the maintenance man, Roland, was long gone, presumably showing off his cool new watch to the desk clerk or her weird twin sister. A breeze picked up, cascading down the mountain. The slope was dotted with firs, and they responded to the wind in a dark undulation that began at the top and worked its way down to the patio like a green bird ruffling its feathers.

I observed all these details through the walls of the Old Prospector's skull, like I was looking through his pie-size fiberglass eyes. The panic subsided while I considered my unique vantage point. I thought to myself, How would an old forty-niner, awoken after 150-odd years, see this twisted-up world of mine? Maybe he would have some homespun, grandfatherly advice. How would he judge the Nautikon? I wondered. How would he see Jean? How would he see the crime that I'd almost committed on his own mountain?

But the Old Prospector only saw what he'd always seen: gold. His eyes were like sieves that sorted every substance into two categories: gold or not-gold. He saw the world in nuggets and flakes and granules. If it wasn't gold, it didn't need to exist.

It's not so weird, the Old Prospector's solid-gold worldview. Everyone's world is like that. Because the world is actually the museum of your world. Your own personal museum of everybody and everything that's organized into dioramas that suit your own expectations. If you walk through the Old Prospector's museum, you see gold leaf on the walls and gold plate in the water fountains. A gold elevator and golden-haired patrons to ride in it, each one wearing a little gold visitor's pin clipped to her gold lapel.

If you're a Nautikon, all you see is loss and ruins, a British Museum of aquatic plunder and failure. Mothers live in a museum of sharp corners and electrical outlets and bullies. Children live in a museum of mothers. The president lives in a museum of terror. Jihadists live in a museum of outrage. And if you're Jean, the museum of the world is all about the Holy, Catholic, and Apostolic Church and about what a dope your husband is. It's organized like the Stations of the Cross, with Jim Rath starring as one of the other guys who got crucified that day, but for totally unmemorable reasons.

I was startled out of the Old Prospector's head space by the sight of a dark figure emerging from the mouth of the Mine Shaft. The man scrambled up the loose scree to the lip of Flat-iron Falls, where he crouched in the shadows. I saw his head dart from side to side, looking. Then he was on the move again. As he sprinted across the flagstones to the Duck Pond, I recognized him. It was the Nautikon.

Seconds later he zigzagged the rest of the way up the mountain, from the Water Wheel to a clump of firs, and finally to the Oaken Bucket. He stooped by the boulder-shaped shed with his hands on his knees, like he was trying to catch his breath. I leaned in closer to the narrow window and saw that he was snooping around inside the shed on all fours, his backside to me. Then he stood and scratched his head. I heard the gentlest splash and watched the Nautikon wade into the pool toward the base of the Oaken Bucket. He dropped out of sight for several minutes, then I saw him straighten up. The locking wrench was in his hands and his head was darting from side to side again. Next he was on the walkway, pushing the toolbox back inside the boulder. He shut the door, rubbed his hands together, and sped back down the mountain, following the same spazzy trajectory he'd taken on the way up.

Minutes later the light came on in room 22. Then it went off, and once again Prospector's Bend was as quiet as the ghost town it should have been.

I woke up fully dressed under the oily motel blanket. The clock radio told me that the morning had transpired without me. Music was playing on the patio below. The girls sang along with some grim tune about everyday people and the power of love.

I ate my late breakfast alone in the dining area. Scrambled eggs and a bottomless cup of coffee. Then I walked to the patio to review the site of last night's weirdness, returning to the scene of the crime I'd failed to commit. The Mills sisters and Keesha were at their table swaying their pretty heads to the sounds of a jambox. I had just settled into my chaise longue when the bellow of the Nautikon split the serene afternoon in two.

"Woooo-hoooo!" He was shouting from his balcony. "It's Oaken Bucket time, ladies! And you can't deny it!"

The girls responded in kind, all but Keesha. I buried my face in my three-ring binder and made some sketches of Nautika's Zone of Estro-Wisdom and Governance. The milky glass spires. The spectral Nautikon embryos. I heard someone uncap a bottle of beer.

"Looks like we got company, girls," said the Nautikon, now standing at their table. Obviously he was talking about me, but I refused to rise to the bait.

"Come on," said Keesha. "Leave the guy alone."

"Sure thing. Anything for you, my sweet Caribbean queen. Matter of fact, let's be neighborly. Maybe we should invite your little lover-boy along for the ride." The Mills sisters laughed. Keesha did not.

"I think it would be nice if we asked him," she said. I looked up to see her smiling at me. "I mean, he's all alone here."

Silence. Then: "Somebody's got a boyfriend!" The Nautikon delivered this line singsong-style, like he was in a middle-school lunchroom.

"All right, G." He turned to address me. "What do you say, ready for a white-knuckle hell ride? Or are you too chicken to ride the Bucket?"

They were the first civilized words he'd ever spoken to me, but I couldn't help feeling that there was some threatening subtext. I closed the three-ring binder and slipped it into my satchel.

"Yeah," I said, looking at Keesha. "I'll ride the Bucket." My hands went to work on the zipper of the satchel. I zipped and unzipped. I buckled. I unbuckled. Then I slung the bag across my shoulder and crossed the patio to join the party.

We started up the flagstone path, the Nautikon leading the way followed by the sisters. I was far enough back to be about eye level with their ankles. He was wearing Tevas with tube socks, an unusual combo. And suspicious too: he must have been concealing his flippered feet. The sisters had on matching leather sandals. A friendship bracelet made a slow rotation around Brenda's ankle. Keesha walked beside me, her feet bare.

"What are you doing here all by yourself?" she asked.

I thought for a minute.

"I used to come here when I was a kid," I said, making it up as I went along. "Guess I'm just sentimental."

"That's sweet." She touched my shoulder and the kiss came back to me, the lips of memory on my lips of flesh. "Keesha," she said, indicating herself.

"Jim," I said, indicating me. "Thanks for what you—the thing you did yesterday."

"Oh, that. Happens all the time where I work."

"Where's that?"

"I'm a swim teacher at a geriatrics center."

"Want to hear a cool fact? I heard humans would age forty percent slower if we lived underwater."

"That's fascinating." I'd recited this same statistic to Jean once, but she didn't call it fascinating.

"Yeah. I know a lot of that kind of stuff. Anyway, thanks for letting me live. Seemed like your mouth is really well formed for that sort of task."

I'm not sure where I was going with this, but Keesha just laughed nervously. Her eyes exploded at me like blue flowers, and my diaphragm did something weird.

Suddenly I heard a splash and saw the Nautikon standing up to his knees in the shoals of the Duck Pond.

"Fuck!" he said, leaping back onto the flagstones. "My fucking socks!"

I saw him rip off his tube socks and wring them out. The water painted fingers of dark blue on the dry stone. With some difficulty, he tugged them back onto his feet and stood up. "Fuck! I've got to go back and change socks. You guys better just go on without me. I'll go next time. Fucking socks!"

"What do you mean?" said Jenny, or maybe it was her sister. "Just lose the socks. You don't need socks on the Bucket."

"No." He seemed genuinely bummed, boyish. "I've got this thing with my circulation. Have to keep the feet covered at all times or they, you know, seize up."

Without another word he started back down the mountain

toward the motel. When he passed me, I could hear his feet go *squish, squish, squish, squish.* Just then I remembered the tube socks I'd bought at the Radisson gift shop in Denver. They'd come in a bargain two-pack, but I'd only worn one pair. I reached into my shoulder bag.

"Here," I said. "They came in a two-pack."

I wish I could describe the fury in his eyes. The brown irises flashed gold in the hard Colorado light. His blue face reddened, which made it look kind of purple. He shook his head and hissed like a moray eel.

"Problem solved," said Keesha, giving me a congratulatory look. I held out the pair of socks. They were still bound together with the little plastic coupler. The Nautikon didn't move.

"What's wrong?" said one of the Mills sisters. "Take the stupid socks."

"Yeah, take the socks, Les," said the other Mills sister. "Take the socks."

The Nautikon snatched them from me, cursing under his breath. He shot me a glance and I looked away, up the mountain.

When we reached the Oaken Bucket, the maintenance man was there to greet us. He had traded the gray jumpsuit for a yellow knit shirt with a name tag that said ROLAND.

"Mr. Diaz!" he said, flashing me a smile. The Nautikon looked confused.

"Hey, G," said the Nautikon to Roland. Roland looked at the Nautikon. The Nautikon looked at me. I looked at Roland, completing the circuit of suspicious glares. It was a tense moment.

"Got the time?" I asked, hoping to break the tension.

"Two fifteen, on the dot!" said Roland. He extended one fist. I processed this gesture quickly: I was expected to hammer his fist gently with my own. I did so and Roland flashed me a smile. I saw with some satisfaction that his canine teeth were capped with gold. We were friends.

Roland helped the Mills girls into the Bucket, pulling the straps across their ample chests. He took his time with the belt-tensioning mechanism. After he was done seating the girls, he rubbed his forehead. I could see he was making a mental calculation.

"Okay, folks. We got to draw straws here. The Oaken Bucket seats four. Which means one of you's got to stay behind."

"I will." Keesha and I volunteered more or less simultaneously. We giggled. She slapped my arm.

"Come on, Kee." This was the Mills girls, also simultaneous. "I'm sure your boyfriend doesn't mind. Jump in."

The Nautikon's face lit up, the filament of inspiration burning in his skull. He gestured with the damp tube socks. "Hey, girls," he said. "No need to argue. It's cool. I don't need to go this time. You two jump in." He draped one arm around my shoulder and started shoving me toward the Bucket. I resisted.

"No way, Lester," said one of the Mills girls. "This was your idea, dude. You get in this Bucket this instant, young man!" We all looked at him. His expression was not that of humble magnanimity, or even annoyance. He looked terrified. But after a few deep breaths, he complied.

"I'm staying here with Jim," said Keesha. Roland shot me a questioning look, then he swung the door shut and slapped the side of the Bucket.

"Let's roll!" he said, stepping behind the console to flip a pair of switches. Somewhere inside the fake boulder a motor began to chug and grunt, building up momentum and attitude. The staves started creaking again. "Let's roll," they said. "Let's roll." Roland gave the Bucket a good shove with his boot, and it started the suspenseful creep out of the holding pool. It lurched forward, and the goose-bump music of shrieking girls accompanied its fateful descent.

At the first hairpin turn I heard a loud metallic snap. The Nautikon gave out some kind of aquatic war cry as the Bucket crashed down a staircase of small waterfalls. At the second hairpin turn came a second snap, but softer this time, more miserable and resigned. With Flatiron Falls dead ahead, the laughter of the Mills girls was baffled by the shouting cataract. White froth sprayed up all around the Bucket, then the water parted for one horrific long clear slo-mo instant to reveal to me the Nautikon's mortified face. He was gripping one of the Mills girls by the arm. His mouth hung open but nothing came out.

It wasn't the cabinetmaker. Did I mention that? Jean never hooked up with the cabinetmaker. It was Josh, from her office. But that was a rebound situation. Now she's alone and, from what I can tell, living back in our old town house. How do I know all this privileged information? Corey the night clerk called me the other evening when I got back from the hearings. No idea how he got my number. Jean wants to sell the condo, he said, and she needs your permission. I can't see why. The place is in her name. She paid for it, or her mother did.

Roland elbowed me in the arm and winked. "This is the good part," he said.

The Oaken Bucket leaned out over the edge of Flatiron Falls, and even through the white nonsense of water I could hear a pair of bone-chilling metallic thunks. *Thunk*. And: *Thunk*. The Bucket tipped farther out and then it just . . . hung there. Roland, close beside me, chuckled. This was the good part. Oh, was it ever. I caught one last glimpse of the Nautikon's wide brown eyes before the Bucket upended and flipped over the cliff.

Then came a slide show of terror. A frozen plume of water. The Oaken Bucket upside down in the water. The Oaken Bucket right-side up in the water. Two yellow ponytails flinging hair water in the summer air. The top of the Nautikon's head, lustrous and bald in the sun. I knew he'd been wearing a wig. I knew it. Keesha screamed. So did Roland. So did I.

When the Bucket came to rest on the bottom of the pool, the three passengers were up to their chests in water. The Nautikon was leaning back, eyes closed. If you didn't know better, you might have thought he was enjoying himself, soaking up the sun, taking pleasure in a Rocky Mountain summer's day with a pair of all-American blondes. Then you saw the blood. A cloud of pink erupted inside the Bucket, like hibiscus tea in a big broken cup. One of the all-American blondes, Jenny Mills, was clawing wildly at her sister Brenda's seat belt. Brenda's head was bent to one side at an unnatural angle.

Roland covered his eyes with his hands and I saw the face of the Helvner. It was 2:19 p.m.

FIFTEEN

Rep. Frost: This was at approximately 2:20 p.m., correct?

Diaz: I believe so.

Rep. Frost: Go on.

Diaz: The first thing I heard was a noise in my ears. It wasn't like a ringing. It was like the noise a balloon makes when you stretch the little nozzle end and let the air out. It felt like somebody'd stuck a balloon nozzle directly inside my left ear canal.

In my right ear I heard shrieking. Just the longest, most freaked-out scream you've ever heard in your life. My left eye was swollen shut, but I could open my right one enough to see Jenny grabbing her sister, trying to, I don't know, unbuckle her seat belt, I guess.

Then I saw the blood next to me in the water coming over to touch me. You'd think all that water would have, I don't know, diluted it or washed it away, but there was too much of it. I couldn't get away, I was strapped in and my arm felt broken.

The Bucket had come to a resting position on the bottom of the pond. One side was caved in, so we were up to our shoulders in water. Jenny was screaming and Brenda wouldn't move. I sat up a little and saw that her head—her head was at a weird angle. And then I saw where the blood was coming from. Part of her scalp had kind of popped open.

I must have blacked out again, because the next thing I knew I was wrapped in one of those foily thermal blankets on the walkway. Somebody said I was in shock. Down the hill I could see where they'd backed an ambulance up to the Waterin' Hole. I don't know how they got it on the patio, but there they were loading a gurney into the back. I could see Brenda's feet sticking out one end. She had this South American friendship bracelet on one ankle. The next thing I remember is being in the hospital and the light hurt my eyes and some doctor was sewing up my shoulder.

I remember thinking, This is a prime illustration of what I've been talking about all along. Which is that while our public attention drifts from matters of terrorism to the social agenda and health care, a huge blind spot is opening up right directly behind us. That blind spot is the water. Enemy combatants and extremists and fascist ideologues and undocumented workers, they're all pouring in through the water. And we're doing nothing—we aren't doing two ██ to close the gap. Not even one single ██. I mean, ██.

Congressman, we had a chance to stop Jim Rath from hurting those girls. We could have stopped him from putting that young lady in a wheelchair and sticking tubes inside her for the rest of her life. We let Brenda Mills down. We let her sister down. We let me down.

Rath gave us ample opportunity to nab him. Maybe he even wanted to be nabbed. But we were too stupid or too scared to look in the water. We missed our chance when he funneled corrosive compound into that Denver river thing. That was a shot right over the bow and we were, like, too busy playing shuffleboard to notice.

But you want the good news, Congressman? The good news is we have another chance. There's more Raths to disable. More water-based terrorists to render inoperable. There are Raths out there we can't even imagine. Our job is to imagine them and shut them down, one by one. All we need to do is think the unthinkable and then prevent it from happening.

Rep. Frost: That's the good news?

Diaz: To quote a personal hero of mine, it's the unknown unknowns that are going to come back and bite us. It's all those scraps of intel that we can't confirm and we don't know. All those evil schemes that reside outside the perimeter of our Western mind-set. They're like some kind of scary fish with a thousand teeth and a fluorescent thing hanging in front of its face like you see on nature specials. What kind of lure do you use to catch them? Where do you drop your net? You don't know, because you never even dreamed a fish that ugly could ever exist.

Am I making myself clear? We live in a world of surprise. That's the real weapon of terrorism. Surprise. And explosions too. But mostly it's surprise. So how do we prep for the unexpected?

Think big. We need to recalibrate ourselves as a society, like Harry Truman did at the outset of the Cold War. But Truman? He was lucky. He had World War II to kick history in the back pocket. His enemy? It was a bunch of drunk guys banging their loafers on the table. And plus he knew where the bastards lived. Harry could've bombed them back to the Stone Age any time he wanted.

Us? We got 9/11. In the scheme of historical flash points it wasn't exactly Iwo Jima. And for enemies, we got the worst. A bunch of slippery cowards with Ivy League degrees and a big wad of oil money.

Rep. Frost: Wait—who are we talking about again? Our guys or theirs?

Diaz: Theirs. Jesus.

Rep. Frost: Just asking.

Diaz: The upshot is we need to recalibrate our whole society to deal with this asymmetrical bullcrap. How do we do it? Easy. We've got to project ourselves forward. Put ourselves in the worst-case scenario and then think backward from that hypothetical spot to where we're standing right now. How would you arrange yourself and the government so that you have sensitized the people in the country to know the urgency and magnitude of an event before it happens? That's the task.

Rep. Frost: Are we talking about a time machine?

Diaz: Time machines don't exist, Congressman. And if they did, don't you think that'd be classified? And even if it was classified, the enemy could just travel to the future when everything's declassified, read the file on the time machine, and travel back through time to use it against us. That's the trouble with the elected official: they don't stop to think these things through. No offense.

This isn't about time travel, Congressman. It's simply about using your inner gyroscope to lead you into the future unknown and then back to the present-day known to alter that known in such a way as to prevent said unknown. I mean, you want to be at different ends of the temporal rubber band, simultaneously. That's the only way to bring justice to the enemy before you have to bring the enemy to justice. Get it?

Rep. Frost: Well, I guess I get it. As an elected official, you'll excuse my limited capacity to think such matters through, but I'd like to put it to you in a way you possibly haven't considered. The problem to my mind, Agent Diaz, is that when you get these hypothetical threat scenarios fixed in your head, what you're grappling with isn't "unknown unknowns," it's "unknown *knowns*."

Diaz: Beg your pardon, sir?

Rep. Frost: I'm just thinking out loud here, but in your parlance, the "unknown knowns" would be the facts you can't confirm that you know, but you're damn sure you know them. You might call it faith. Or fantasies. Or delusions.

If we take it on faith that the world contains these unimaginable threats, then the unimaginable threat becomes our guiding principle. Our inner gyroscope, if I might borrow a phrase. As a consequence, we begin to make foreign policy based on bugaboos, myths, make-believe. Son, you don't go to war because there's a bump under the bed. And I'm not saying that's what we did, or might do. Or that people like yourself aren't acting in the national interest.

Diaz: Fair enough, sir. You're entitled to use my logic against me. That's an American right, enshrined—if not in the Constitution, then in the spirit of it. But—

Rep. Frost: I'm not using anybody's logic. You yourself have pointed out that elected officials aren't smart enough for that level of discourse. I'm just acknowledging that it takes imagination to lead, but you can't let your imagination do the leading. There are consequences to imagination.

Diaz: All I know is there's bad stuff out there that we can't even begin to know, and it's not going away just because we don't believe it exists. We have to pursue the unknown with certainty or it's going to jump up and bite us. This is a new age, Congressman. Absolute proof can't be a precondition for action.

I mean, nobody could have foreseen them using airplanes, right? What else can we not foresee? What can they do to our water that we haven't thought of, that we can't even begin to think of? Before you let the public dip one single toe in the national Jacuzzi, you've got to think ahead to the unknown unknown scenario where the jihadists dump in a jug of lye or loosen the wheels on the bucket, and you bring the hammer down hard on whoever might do that before they can even think of doing it.

The absence of evidence, somebody once said, is not evidence of absence. The only way to fight this thing is to alter behavior. To force people who believe in freedom to redress that balance between freedom and security. Maintain the freedom, but modify it with an eye toward security. If we don't, the terrorists win. Full stop.

Rep. Frost: If we could leave the realm of the unknown for a moment. [*laughter*] Oaken Bucket—now that you've had time to reflect, are there any tactical or operational lessons that you've learned from this episode, as an analyst?

Diaz: I swore an oath of frankness, so let me be frank. Part of me is glad. Part of me is okay in my conscience about the Oaken Bucket incident. Why? Because how else were we going to sit up and take notice, as a nation, to the vulnerability of our recreational waters?

Does it pain me that people suffered? Sure. I suffered too. Not like Brenda Mills, but I took my lumps. I got stitches and a dislocated shoulder—looked like something out of the Baghdad morgue. But part of me's grateful for the pain. Because now we've got a national dialogue going.

You elected officials, you're so goddamn smug. You can sit there and debate what gets earmarked for this or that, whose barrel gets the pork, but we don't have that luxury. We're on the front lines on this water issue. It's a war. And what we did at Prospector's Bend was just the first shot—

Rep. Frost: I believe the agent has misspoken. This isn't a "we" scenario. The quote unquote "shot" here was fired by Jim Rath, and by him alone, as the preponderance of evidence indicates. That phase of the investigation is complete, son, and it's time we moved on.

Diaz: Sure, Congressman. Let's just move on. Until the next incident, or the next. What's it going to take for you to stop moving on? A dirty bomb in your Jacuzzi bath up there in Chevy Chase? Or how about a bucket of industrial solvent in the congressional lap pool? Or a capsule of Ebola in your wasabi mashed potatoes over in the House commissary?

Rep. Frost: I'm not entirely comfortable with the direction this dialogue is taking here.

Diaz: No? I don't get paid to make you comfortable, Congressman. Quite the opposite.

How about your wife? You'll be pretty surprised to see what the water can do to your wife. Have you ever seen a drowned wife, sir? Do you even know what a drowned wife looks like?

SIXTEEN

My mother came to visit me today. Uncle Keith must have given her the key, but I don't know how she got past the security detail. When I heard her voice I locked myself in the bathroom. This time was better than the phone call; she went away after half an hour and hardly even cried.

Keith has a nice houseboat, but it's more boat than house. It's cramped. Everything looks expensive, the paint job is subtle, and the carpet is soft like a bed of expensive moss. But all the furnishings are scaled down, almost like you're in the floating domain of some lavish billionaire gnome. The galley kitchen has a miniature fridge that makes miniature ice cubes. The microwave is barely large enough for a single burrito.

The walls of the living room are covered with downsize prints of American masterworks. I recognize Bellows's boxers and

Winslow Homer's children. The sofa suite is a shrunken version of those massive pit groups you see on talk shows. The plasma TV, though not large, is given prominence of place, partly blocking the mural window that looks out onto the deck and the bay.

The pink bathroom has a cute little scalloped sink, a standing shower with gold hardware and trial-size soaps. The rim of the toilet is of a circumference slightly too small for human buttocks. You have to shift a lot, and sometimes your legs fall asleep before you're done.

I could hear my mother moving in the kitchenette.

"Jim," she called, but cautiously.

She knew I was there; a mother can sense these things. Plus I'm under arrest, so where else would I be? I heard her looking through the cupboards and the fridge. That was the first thing she did. Once she'd confirmed that I wasn't on a hunger strike (she shook the near empty cereal box), her cries became more emboldened.

"Jim," she said. "Jim."

It was my name. The name she had given me. Spoken by the first person ever to speak it.

When they pulled June Fresto out of the Lazy River, she was clinging to her little boy, his red legs punting her bare stomach. They showed me the pictures when I was in my secret prison, to break me down. (But to what?)

In the photos mother and child are both burning, but they hold each other tight, one flesh blistering the other. The boy's mouth is open at her ear. She presses her head close to his, leans to one side like she doesn't want to spill his screaming, like she can hear his pain away, swallow it down into her own nervous system so that he'll stop burning.

"If you're hurting, I want to help you." My mother was talking in her reasonable voice now, small and large as she moved from room to room. "Jim, it's Mother. Mother is here."

She too wanted to hear me hurt, so she could hold the sound, pluck it out, a thorn, only a splinter. But some barbs are buried so deep even a mother can't tweezer them out. I stood in the shower stall and toyed with the omnidirectional massage head, trying to do something absentminded. But my mind was right there, exactly in the middle of everything as it was happening.

After a while I thought, This is ridiculous, I can't hide in the shower forever. So I sat on the toilet. By then she'd reached the bathroom door. Her knuckles on the laminate, one knock, then a pause. I turned on the tap and the pink basin started to fill, an ear. She started knocking in earnest.

"It doesn't matter, Jim."

I heard a single bulbous knuckle, rheumatoid, and then something sharper, the cast silver ring she wore on her wedding band finger. She was knocking backward, her palm facing in: the customary knock of caution. She was afraid of me. I turned off the tap and let one hand dangle in the water.

"Whatever you've done," she said. "Or haven't done. To a mother it never matters."

Her voice was muffled, and I realized that she had pressed her face to the door, the closest she could get to whispering in my ear.

"I love you," she said. "Even if they never let me see you again, Jim, I love you."

Hearing your own mother say those words, it was enough to make anyone throw himself over the railing. On the short list of things to say to make a guy kill himself, "I love you" has to be right at the top. I pressed my face to the small porthole window that looked out over the bay. I was resisting the idea of my own reverse ontogeny. Resisting the easy way out. Open the door; hug your mother; kill yourself; stay here; wait; make them wait; unwrap a cake of trial-size soap; kill yourself; don't. I saw the gray water and offered my brain to it, opened the door to my skull and let it come rushing in. I wanted an elevated consciousness, a mind I could set afloat on the rising tide. I had to keep a level head or I really might do myself in.

I had a realization. Of course, I thought, perched there on the dwarf's toilet. That explains why they let my mother come to see me. It's all part of their game. I'm not naïve. I know full well why the authorities and the Snowman and everybody else were all so willing to let me stay on the *Endurance* during the hearings. House arrest is an unusual concession for a high-value prisoner like myself, and houseboat arrest—that's even rarer. But my uncle had no trouble arranging it.

Why? It's simple: they want me to drown myself. They're hyperaware of my ambivalent relationship with water, so they parked me in front of it hoping I'd dive in.

You're thinking, Wouldn't it be easier to lock me up forever, make an example out of me? They could drag me out of solitary confinement every five years for probation hearings, give Morley Safer an exclusive interview. Squeeze all the PR they could out of me, like they did Peltier or Padilla.

The trouble is there are doubts about my conviction. Doubts have been cast. Some rich civil libertarian is calling it a monkey trial. The Fat Man whispers to me about dissident voices. They're saying the real bad guy is the Nautikon. They're saying he was the one who dumped lye in the Lazy River, saying he loosened the wheels on the Oaken Bucket.

I'm not an unrealistic person. After all, I saw the Nautikon meddling with the Bucket the night before the incident. I know he didn't want to ride that morning. In retrospect even I can see that wet socks were a pretty lame excuse. When you add it all up, there's plenty of evidence that he did the bad things they want me to be guilty of.

And once I start traveling on this painful line of inquiry, it's like I'm on a sliding board covered with bees. Even though it stings, it's hard to stop. If he did it, *why* would he do it? Again the Fat Man supplies an answer. It was some kind of wake-up call. And that makes sense. The Nautikon wanted to spark a public debate on Nautika—initiate a national dialogue about his native land.

But evidence, as I told Jean a long time ago, can't be a precondition for knowing something is true. Even if I admit that the Nautikon did something bad, even if I acknowledge that he screwed up his one chance to bring estro-wisdom to the warlike humanoids of the surface world, my faith in the enduring power of Nautika will not be shaken.

But I don't have to worry about the Nautikon getting blamed for this. There are way too many shades of gray in that story and within those shades even more shades, grayer and less gray. And nobody wants subtlety at a time like this. I mean, what's easier to explain to the American people, that some rogue domestic terrorist (i.e., me) went nuts with spousal grief and perpetrated an isolated criminal act? Or that our collective disinterest in and ignorance about a lost aquatic civilization with an unapologetic feminist worldview has finally come back to bite us?

If I drown myself, the game's over. Any doubts about my guilt would vanish with me. Suicide would be as good as a sworn confession. Case closed. And then Nautika can go back where it was, to the volcanic purgatory it's been trapped in for centuries, go back to being some boring footnote in *Bulfinch's Mythology* that nobody ever reads, or some page in a comic book that nobody ever took seriously, or some diorama in a museum that some loser never got built.

But suicide? Please. I wouldn't give those congressional so-called investigators the satisfaction. I won't take my own life just to keep their stupid lie alive. I'm not the mastermind behind Oaken Bucket. Sure, I tried; I admit that; I didn't have the nerve—and I'll be damned if I'm going to go to my grave as somebody's scapegoat.

The bathroom window went white with my breath, but all it takes to erase human breath is a wad of toilet paper. And there it was again. There was the water. I needed to look at the water, so I looked at the water. Let the water in and keep a level head.

Unexpectedly I slipped into a deep state of *ooeee,* and it caught me way off guard. Such exo-aquatic trances are rare, usually brought on by episodes of high stress or profound misery. Whatever the cause, I let it happen; I sank into the water trance and let it saturate my mind. I heard music.

SEVENTEEN

Distant music. A mingling of male voices, now loud, now soft, as if a heavy curtain has been drawn and then draped before a vast choir.

Oôo has turned back to reclaim her womanhood, leaving Labiaxa to reach the summit of the tower alone. Her mother calls to her; a prophesy awaits. The Nautikon brood precipitates all around her, a joyous rain of wrinkled purple faces and shoulders matted with soft black hair. These are the newborns of their race; the birth canal, she reasons, must be close at hand.

Then—unexpectedly—the shaft ends! Overhead, Labiaxa sees folds of fleshy material that interleave to form a kind of inverted roof of large blue shingles. She treads water to study the soft ceiling, thinking: The end? So soon? Impossible. This cannot be my final destination. I must find a way through.

Gradually she becomes aware of a subtle change in the fleshy folds. A loosening, an expanding, like a braid of leavened dough on a sunlit windowsill. The color shifts, ever so subtly, from blue to pink to an exigent red. Finally the folds part and down pour a dozen more Nautikon infants, each shedding a meniscus of red jelly as she falls. Labiaxa presses her palms against her ears. The male chorus erupts into a crescendo. Then the folds of the fleshy roof draw closed again. Could this be what Oôo meant by the Royal Vulvorum? And that riotous music? It must be the vast choir she called the Court of the Spermata.

She waits, watching the barrier overhead. It will open again. And when it does, she will be ready. Finally, it happens, the slow organic dilation. Labiaxa squeezes past the falling brood and shoots up into the gap. Halfway through—she can see an opening on the other side, the chorus grows louder, the light, the light! But this is as far as she goes. The slick pillows of the Vulvorum constrict around her.

Trapped! Pinned, or so it seems, between conception and birth. So close to her mother, yet the more she struggles the more the sinewed portal tightens around her, denying her entry. Her legs are pressed together. Her rib cage is crushed. She expels the water from her gills with a groan. Freeing one hand, she uses it to cover first one ear then the other, trying in vain to mute the maddening music of the chorus that is now so close overhead.

She must focus, must relax. The pain will pass. Her head protrudes into the bottom of a large room. From her perspective it looks like a hollowed glass pear, with an irregular cup-shaped floor and a tapered dome for a ceiling. Halfway up the wall, arranged around the perimeter of the room, is an ornate chancel. She sees them swaying there, arm in arm, a host of robed singers with mouths agape. Above the choir, at the apex of the dome, is a stemlike passage that burns with dazzling blue light. She must reach that far passage!

But how? The mingled voices ring so loudly here that the very atoms seem to strain against the hypersonic assault. This is no mere music; it is a siege on sensation. Tactile, hot, tormenting, bright, emetic, and orgiastic. An auditory drug that triggers a circuit of pain and pleasure from her loins to the recesses of her mind. She writhes in the grip of the Vulvorum, but for all her struggling it closes still tighter around her. She surrenders.

The floor nearby, she sees, is littered with gelatinous red parcels, each one attached to the floor by a fat rope of blue flesh. Labiaxa reaches out to touch one, and it turns on its tether. A small gasping face appears through the diaphanous wrapping. She screams. An embryo! She has entered the womb, the uterus of an entire race.

Then as slowly and discreetly as it closed, the Vulvorum begins to open again. The blue constraints pinken, and Labiaxa gasps for water, claws her way to freedom. Next she is standing on the concave floor of the womb, stepping carefully around the embryonic parcels as they spiral through the opening, like marbles down an unstoppered basin.

She kicks off toward the upper reaches of the chamber, but as if by some invisible force, she is thrown back to the floor. It is the Court of the Spermata. Their voices rain down upon her like a raging cataract. She can't go on; she must go on. Pushing off again, she paddles ferociously into the noisome blast, the determined minnow that fights the riptide.

At last, and with great effort, she draws level with the chancel. On all sides the singers shimmer and sway in pearl-cloth tunics, each eyeless head open as they perform their endless canticle. Strangely, the nearer she draws to the Spermata the less violent is the force of their hypersonic hymn. The water is measurably warmer here, as if she has swum inside the belly of a great mammal. Suddenly she is becalmed, all turbulence and struggle cease. Can she recall a time when she felt more protected, more loved?

She pauses now to admire the ornately carved choir screen. Thereupon is engraved the whole long saga of Nautika. The primeval battles with rival humanoids. The enslavement. The famine in a bounteous land. The Great Estrodus that led the elders north to the ancient Berber sea. The convening of the First Council of Twelve. And finally the construction of Nautika herself. The foundries glowing in massive sandpits. A leviathan blowing hot glass to form a towering minaret with a blast of its monstrous airhole. The century of labor by trillions of intelligent polyps to produce the city's coral dome.

Labiaxa is startled out of her reverie by a spray of small fish from above. They dart and caper all around her, pale blue creatures about the size of her fist with pointed tails streaked in red. One specimen hovers close to her face and she sees that it bears on its bulbous head the mild countenance of a newborn. A few of these larval children are already sprouting twiglike appendages, little arms and legs. Beneath their pale skin she can discern the ghosted tracery of bone. These must be the fertilized eggs and the song of the Spermata their nutrient.

She watches as they settle to the floor of the womb, where each is enveloped in its own red meniscus. It happens so swiftly, this strange aquatic oogenesis. Suddenly Labiaxa is racked with remorse. These are the soon-to-be-born. Here in this choir loft of birth, they will attain estro-wisdom and the force of being. But what awaits them on the other side of the Vulvorum? Only death. Fire and death.

Pushing upward, she enters the stemlike passage at the apex of the dome, a narrow tunnel scarcely wide enough to accommodate her shoulders. She climbs and climbs for many leagues until quite suddenly the small shaft forks off in two directions, each way burning with its own blue light.

Before me lie two paths, identical in dimension and equal in ambiguity, she thinks. Which passage leads to my mother? Where do I turn?

Then she remembers Oôo's fragmentary counsel.

"Above the Court of the Spermata lies the Mirror Hall . . . this you must remember, Princess . . . it matters not which path you choose! Ô is the Mirror Queen . . . meet her in one Ôvum and she will greet you in the other as well!"

Labiaxa chooses one path and swims on, but she seems to travel in two directions at once. Her thoughts, her actions run in parallel with those of another self, her own self. She is her own twin. And through the diaphanous wall she can see the other shaft, see herself swimming, matching herself stroke for stroke.

The Mirror Hall curves left (or is it right?) before ending at another fleshy stricture about the circumference of a chariot wheel. She touches its veined surface and it opens like a valve. After hauling herself through, she stands in the most perplexing and magnificent chamber yet. The walls glisten with the hues of menstrual effluvia, red, black. But the shape of the room is unspeakable, unknowable. About its dimensions, its scope, its character, nothing rational can be said.

The walls are composed of red corbels, rounded bricks about the size of a fist. She thinks of the tempered clay building blocks of her home in Sica. But this substance, this is hardly clay. The blocks are in constant motion, sliding in and out from the contours of the walls. Closer inspection reveals that each block, in turn, is an aggregate of tiny beads that are also in a state of swarming atomism, so that each block looks like a pomegranate quickened by some dark magic. The ceaseless movement of its constituent parts lends the room a decidedly shapeless shape—no fixed height, no measurable width or volume.

Before Labiaxa's eyes it slowly but steadily remakes itself, the architecture arranging and rearranging in a display of infinite geometry.

At last, she thinks, I have attained the Sacred Ôva!

Above her head one of the protean corbels begins to glow a fevered crimson. It extrudes from the wall, a bloodied tentacle, until the tip stops inches from Labiaxa's breast. She feels it, like the heat of a brand, the radiant intensity of its estro-wisdom. The tentacle touches her just below the navel. The merest touch, a tickle, and every sinew of her body slackens. Her flesh liquefies. Her belly flashes white, and in the center of this whiteness appears an embryonic red star. The star doubles, triples, spreading outward from her loins like a drop of blood in a bowl of milk until her entire body has metastasized into a furious cloud of menses. Then, just as suddenly, she resumes her corporeal form.

Another tentacle reaches out of the shifting vault to encircle her waist. Another toys with her hair like a child, another caresses her cheeks. Two more tentacles seize her around the ankles; then two more; and two more, until her entire body is swaddled in red ribbons.

The water falls silent. Even the convulsing walls and slithering tentacles produce no sound whatsoever.

All at once the mass of tentacles appears to melt. It recombines into a giant sphere of black-red gel. And Labiaxa is no longer inside the Ôvum; the Ôvum is beside her, rolling and pulsating, a throbbing bulk more massive than a pod of sperm whales. She drifts athwart this miraculous apparition in a limitless abyss, like a satellite orbiting a moon of congealed blood. But the surface of this moon is still changing. A small seam rips across its flank, and the sphere splits open to reveal a white interior.

A seedpod, she thinks, about to germinate.

And indeed the husk peels away to reveal a hollow core. And inside, a column of blue droplets.

Ô, it says.

Mirror Queen, Holy Mother, Only Mother. Labiaxa's mother. A pillar of tears, exactly as her father described her.

Mother? she says.

Sleep, child, says the pillar of tears.

How long she has lain on the white divan, she cannot say. How long the world has been here, floating all around her, she does not know. Has she just been born? Or has she at last been transported to the realm of the dead?

A woman sits beside her. She cradles Labiaxa's head in her lap and strokes her hot brow.

"Daughter," says the Queen, letting this single buoyant word hover in the water between them. She is young, her kind face drawn with the clean mirrored lines of a noblewoman. She has Labiaxa's wide mouth, the easy slope of her jaw, the changeable eyes. And save for her crown, a white diadem alive with a hundred tentacles, she is naked.

Precisely as her father described it, the room is a changeable sphere of milky glass. On the floor Labiaxa sees the round opening, the pool where her father first spied Queen Ô. This is the very room where Papa convalesced, where he lay with the Queen, the bedchamber where Labiaxa was conceived some eighteen years ago.

"Are you comfortable, Daughter?"

Labiaxa nods.

"I suffered greatly summoning you here," says the Queen. Her inner agony registers in her eyes. They go black like buried things, fossils. "I need you to know that."

Labiaxa cradles her head deeper in her mother's lap. She knows.

"But even a mother may not defy prophesy. How much has your dear father told you?"

"Not much. Nothing."

"Of course," says the Queen. "These are matters a dry tongue cannot convey. The secrets of water elude the language of air. I will try to explain.

"After the Great Estrodus, our ancestors sought shelter beneath the sea. For aeons our surface-dwelling cousins remained on dry land where they evolved to a state of absolute barbarism. Meanwhile, Nautika flourished without war, hunger, fear, rape, terror, envy, or the struggle for power.

"But our fate, our divine purpose was not to be fulfilled beneath the sea. We went under the waves to cultivate a gentler way of living, an ancient way. We built this domed capital to preserve kindness in a sort of museum of the humane, until such time as our surface brethren were prepared to receive it back into their hearts. One day, when the world above is ready, the One

True Man will carry estro-wisdom to the air and with it restore the virtues of humanity to mankind."

The divan shudders as the room is pounded once, twice by a seismic fist.

"But Mother . . . Queen . . . surely it is too late for all that."

Ô smiles. "No. You have arrived just in time, at the preordained moment. You, daughter, are the prophesied Mother of the One True Man. Born of the Eleventh Queen of Nautika, sired by her air-drinker consort, you will this very day give birth to the last of our species, a boy child with the gills of a Nautikon, the lungs of the air drinker, and the infinite compassion of a queen. He alone will survive the Great Kataklysm.

"When mankind is ready to receive Him, the One True Man will voyage to the barbaric societies of the air. In a city at the foot of a mighty mountain range, He will enlist the aid of the air drinker called Jim, and together they shall ascend to a lost city and commence the rehumanizing of man."

"Jim?" says Labiaxa.

"But before the prophesy can be complete, before you can give birth to the One True Man, there is one more act you must perform."

"Anything, Mother. If this be prophesy, then I accept its terms."

"You must wear the crown."

"The crown?" Labiaxa gasps. "But I am of air drinker born. A monster am I, an outcast. Never could I be Queen of Nautika!"

"You underestimate yourself, Daughter," replies the Queen. "For you know not who you are. You are not Labiaxa, daughter of Aricos. You are the Mother of the One True Man, the Twelfth Queen of Nautika, the one called Â. Any other woman would have perished in the Royal Vulvorum. Any other woman would have been unborn, embryonized. But not you, Daughter; you have arrived to claim your rightful place as the Final Queen of Nautika. Your coming has been prophesied. And prophesies must be fulfilled."

Labiaxa's eyes brim with sorrow's-brine. Her voice comes remote and whispery.

"Father was right. This is the greatest gift a daughter could receive on her Arrival Day, even if her Arrival must also be her departure. But what shall I do? Without a consort of my own, how will I birth this True Man?"

"All will be clear momentarily, once the Transnautification is complete."

Queen Ô pulls Labiaxa to her feet. She touches the wall beside her and the glass turns suddenly translucent. Sprawling below is the entire city of Nautika, a marvel even in collapse. And these are indeed its final moments. Fists of magma burst through the seabed, incinerating the gardens, routing the helpless Prophylaxes on their shrieking steeds.

"Gaze upon your queendom, while you may."

Labiaxa surveys her dying city. The marketplace has already vanished under a suffocating blanket of stone. The Zone of Estro-Wisdom and Governance is aboil, its Lawn of the Anemones flooded with creeping black rock. The magnificent spires craze, scream, shatter in the heat. Soon the andro-rage of Earth-Man will find its prize, the Royal Ôvum itself, the Queen will perish, and Nautika will be no more.

When Labiaxa turns back to face her mother, her mother already holds the crown above her head.

Labiaxa bows before the Eleventh Queen of Nautika. Ô settles the squirming diadem on her daughter's head, and Labiaxa feels . . . almost nothing, just the merest shift in her mass, as if her bones have lost a portion of their weight. For a last, long moment, mother and daughter stand close together, regarding one another through sorrowful eyes as the tower trembles below. The moment is love, but the moment cannot endure.

Even now Earth-Man's fiery fingers are strangling the spire, cupping the very sphere in which they stand. The water around them grows hotter by the second.

Labiaxa screams at the flames. "No! Not yet!"

She looks again to her mother. The woman has already changed, withered. Her skin is now a shallower shade of blue. The eyes sink in their sockets. The webbing under her arms sags, and her fingers twist into rheumatic knots.

Ô gives one last maternal smile as a swollen probe of liquid stone shatters the sphere and plunges daggerlike into her back.

A second dagger pierces the wall. It draws so near to Labiaxa's face that the water boils before her eyes. Taking a step back, Labiaxa falls into the opening in the floor.

"No! Mother! Mother!"

But it is too late. Labiaxa is already elsewhere. She is already someone, or something, else. The Transnautification is complete. When she draws her next breath, the walls of the Royal Ôvum swell like bellows. Her name is Queen Â and she flexes her million tentacles of pure menses to rouse the Court of the Spermata to song. Her name is the Mirror Queen and she is eternal with estros. Her name is Only Mother and her single eye swells through the folds of her flesh to keep watch over all of Nautika. The eye weeps. The Queen groans. She convulses in pleasure and in hurting. Her manifold flesh pulses and tightens, pushing until with great effort a small plume of blood is discharged from her folds.

Queen Â watches the lonely egg descend into the Mirror Hall. Watches it float down and ever downward past the choir loft. She watches the egg pause for a moment, held in stasis by the nutrient hymn of the Spermata, until it unfurls a blue tail and lies down at the threshold of the Vulvorum.

The child will be a boy. The One True Man. The irony does not elude her. The last example of a once mighty race ruled by womankind will be . . . a man. She watches Him now with a mother's adoring eyes. His legs are drawn up, and she can see that they are somewhat stunted. But even through the walls of His fetal sac, she can tell that His back will be broad and strong.

The Vulvorum pinkens and parts. The One True Man, last true Nautikon, sheds His meniscus and spirals down into the folds. But seconds before He vanishes into the apocalyptic fire below, His boyish brown eyes peer up through the collapsing tower, seeking Queen Â—Mirror Queen, Mother of Us All, Only Mother, His mother—and she hears, as the crescendo chord of the Great Kataklysm resounds and the tower shatters around her, the final Nautikon's first thought:

I will not fail the world.

EIGHTEEN

My mother leaves and I have to do something. Have to do something so I won't do the last thing.

I step out onto the deck and dial Jean's number. For the first time she actually picks up. I'm speaking to her on the phone. Or I'm speaking through the phone in the direction of Jean, and she seems to be listening. At least I think she seems to be listening. There's too much nation between us. From the Chesapeake Bay to Colorado Springs adds up to some sixteen hundred miles of all-American interference. It sounds like I'm shouting into one end of a steam pipe with the weird vapor of telecommunications clotting and condensing in between. You can feel the pressure build and hear the *clank, clank, hiss* of expanding steel.

She says, "Hi, Jim." I hear that part. Her voice sounds resigned and maybe a little scared. Like she's talking to a criminal, not her husband. The divorce is on hold while they resolve this other matter, the federal one. Right from the outset it's the tone of her voice, the timbre of disassociation you might call it, that's hurting my feelings.

I say, "Hi, Jean."

A plane flies over and the signal starts to fade. I pull the cell phone away from my ear to watch the little chiclets of LED go pop, pop, pop.

"I'm so sorry, Jean," I say. Then I shout it again and wait for what seems like minutes. I think she says she's sorry too, but I can't be one hundred percent certain.

I say, "I love you, Jean," and it's like a magic incantation. The signal returns and for a moment I can hear everything so clearly: the room she's sitting in, our living room, the cushions of the couch huffing under her backside. I can hear the car keys jingle on the hook by the door, hear the lovelorn *ping* of our microwave oven. Burritos, I think. *Nova* plays softly in the background, Turkana Boy chipping at his hand ax, Richard Leakey's plangent voice reciting the prey of early man like evil poetry.

Jean groans, and for the first time in recent memory, I'm crying. Big tear-shaped drops, they pool up in the fissure between the cell phone and my cheek. But it's amazing how quickly the wind turns them icy and alien. All of a sudden they're someone else's tears that have landed on my cheek. Then it's someone else's cheek, someone else's life happening on the deck of a houseboat I've only seen from the height of a cliffside village, the houseboat anchored in a harbor far below. My emotional moment slips away.

I hear a tanker talking to another tanker in the far reaches of the bay, I see a pinprick of light wink and wink somewhere out in the shipping channel. The beam of the lighthouse wipes the black stucco of the bay, catching in the whitecaps. They used to spell things out for me, those whitecaps. There used to be messages written on the water, but not tonight.

The next sound I hear is the nauseating *beep* of the cell phone telling me my call has been lost.

The groan and the dial tone. Jean's last sound and then the cold pulse of a conversation ending forever. It was a code; a sentence. A farewell. *Good-bye, Jim.*

All along I'd been telling myself I wouldn't go. Jim won't say good-bye. Jim won't die for them. If they wanted Jim Rath out of the picture, they'd have to wait a long time. I'm not a suicide or a scapegoat. But when I hear Jean groan over the cell phone, it sounds like a directive, a command, or maybe just a strong suggestion: die, it says. Jean's groan is her way of saying she'll never take me back, nobody will. I'm damaged goods, and I might as well go away. That single groan makes me realize that it is in fact time to depart.

I put down the phone and look at the water.

I never really told you what Jean looks like. Seeing as this is my last chance to set the record straight about how lovely she is, I'll do it now and quickly.

She is, as I said earlier, taller than I am by at least six inches. Her build is on the magnitude of what you might call Amazonian, even though the press has been less charitable in the way they describe her. But to me her big figure is sexually unimprovable, a Platonic model of sexiness.

Like with most women, everything starts at the top of her

head and works its way down. She's got a jaw-length brown bob that conveys Catholic certainty and righteousness. It moves in counterpoint to her head. When she shakes her head no, like she did a thousand times during our brief marriage, the hair rotates at a different frequency and in an opposing direction. If you had the right equipment, you could measure its spin and number like those of an electron.

She has the most profound eyebrows ever worn on a woman's face. They're like brown rivers that converge at the bridge of her noble nose. And underneath the beds of these rivers, like old organic forms compressed by slow geological forces, lie the flashing diamonds of her eyes. The eyes themselves, they're coal-colored or brown-colored depending on the light or her shirt or the severity of her thoughts.

In the mornings her eyes would open several seconds before she was actually awake. I would lie there beside her, waiting for this magic preconscious moment, watching her lids for the faintest first quiver. When she woke up I wanted to be the first thing Jean saw, and I wanted to be the first one to see her seeing the first thing she would see, which in turn would be me. This, at the risk of sounding reductionist or stupid, was the only reason I ever did anything.

For the first few seconds after her eyes opened, she wore the expression of an Alzheimer's patient trying to recognize her own face in the mirror. Her eyes remained hazy and questioning, the eyebrows pressed down in confusion or disbelief, as if she was trying to figure out the puzzling final scene in a dream. That's how I knew that sleep showed her ugly things.

The next part to open was the mouth. Her lips formed a pink fissure straight across the lower third of her face. It made Jean's chin seem almost puppetlike, so whenever she opened it, it was quite an event. The mouth would open, she would start to speak, but then she wouldn't. That was the moment every morning when I knew she'd recognized me. The perplexed dream look would solidify into disappointment. As cruel and false as her dreams might have been, they were better than waking up to Jim Rath as a husband. I watched the resentment congeal behind her eyes as she remembered all the bad events that had passed between us the day before, the week before, the whole year. Jean was remembering the town house, remembering our parking spot with the stenciled number on the yellow curb, remembering the candy wrappers on the floor of the Corolla, the storage space, my comics, my unemployed status, Nautika, and the Hilton pool. She'd say:

"Jim, what the hell are you staring at?"

Most nights Jean slept naked, and she didn't care if I saw her when she got up to go to the bathroom. This wasn't a sexual provocation, not in our case. Her nakedness, especially in the last weeks of our marriage, was a sign of indifference. The bare flesh said she didn't care if I saw her, didn't care if I ogled her breasts or objectified her backside. I wasn't important enough, didn't matter, wasn't a sexual object, so I couldn't objectify her even if I tried. I might as well have been a tree watching her, or a crab.

She'd get out of bed and stand in the doorway, stretching first one leg, then the other. Her glorious big behind cinched in on either side as she moved, the calves turned glossy and hard. There was a slight bulging at the level of the coccyx as she reached for the ceiling. The color raced up her broad back, she shivered, and left the bedroom.

I would listen for the changing timbre of her footsteps as she moved from the deep-pile carpet of the hall to the slappy bathroom tiles. She pissed shamelessly. The toilet paper roll tumbled on the other side of the wall. Water ran in the sink. She handled the toothbrush with so much conviction that I could hear each bristle flexing in turn across the enamel of her molars. I lay there worrying about her receding gums.

The next thing I knew she would be back in the bedroom rifling through drawers. Rejected underpants piled up at her feet as she made her selection for the day, this pair expelled for being too frilly, this pair discarded for its frayed piping. She worked her legs into glossy black pants like the blades of a posthole digger. Even the bra was strapped on with ruthless efficiency. Her wide mouth twisted into a sneer as she sought the clasp between her shoulder blades, the breasts pulsing up over the cups of the bra until she repositioned her nipples. On cold mornings it was easier to see if she'd centered them properly.

When she was dressed she took one last inventory of the bedroom, taking notice of every single object but one. I sat propped against the headboard, watching her.

While I listened to her move about the kitchen, while the coffeemaker gargled and coughed, I would gradually lean forward until my head fell between my knees. In this depressing and painful yoga pose, I listened for the car keys to cackle and the town house door to close behind her with a mean suffocating sigh.

I throw one leg over the railing.

NINETEEN

Rep. Frost: I'm afraid there's been an unforeseen turn of events, Agent Diaz.

Diaz: That's what I hear.

Rep. Frost: As I think everyone knows by now, a body was retrieved from Chesapeake Bay in the early hours of the morning. It fits the description of the defendant, of Mr. Rath, and all indications are of a suicide.

I don't know what to say about this. Death is tragic. Death is a negative under any circumstances. But sometimes death is only divine justice attaining its own verdict.

Diaz: Maybe so.

Rep. Frost: Agent Diaz, it seems that this case has outlived its perpetrator, and this subcommittee outserved its purpose. But before I close up shop I'd like to give you a minute to deliver any closing statements you might wish to make.

Diaz: I just hope he's gone to a better place.

Rep. Frost: Amen to that. I guess.

Diaz: Sure. Amen.

Rep. Frost: Well, then, this hearing is adjourned.

Diaz: Adjourned, Congressman? Adjourned? All due respect, but you can't just adjourn a thing like this! Is Brenda Mills adjourned? She'll never walk again. Is my wife adjourned? She's gone. You going to adjourn her too? And Rath? Just because he's dead doesn't mean you've got the right to adjourn a man.

Rep. Frost: There isn't really much else to say, Agent.

Diaz: Oh, there's plenty more to say, Congressman. And you know it. I don't want anyone to suffer from any illusions anymore, like I used to. I want the facts laid out there. I want them held up to the light of scrutiny. I do indeed have something to say!

Rep. Frost: I'm afraid you'll have to say it somewhere else, Agent. Our time is up here.

Diaz: But you don't understand—there's something else I have to say! Something that's gone unsaid and has to be said.

Rep. Frost: I think I understand you very well, son. Look, you're under a lot of stress. We get that. I just don't want you to lose your focus and say anything that would impugn you or your department or the effort that we've all worked so hard to develop. Reflect on what you're doing before you do it. There's no reason to incriminate an innocent party when the culprit has already been apprehended.

Diaz: Oh, I know full well what I'm doing, Congressman—

Rep. Frost: I'm warning you, son. These hearings are officially—

Diaz: I know very well what I'm doing, old man. Put this in your official record: ▮▮▮▮▮▮▮▮▮.

Rep. Frost:—adjourned.

TWENTY

Everybody has their own way to describe water. But water? It can absorb any description you throw at it without ever accepting any of them. Look at the Chesapeake Bay at night: it's one big soggy thesaurus of adjectives and verbs that poets and politicians and scientists and regular people have dumped into it by the truckload: unalphabetized, unconjugated, unpunctuated.

Brackish, crystalline, emerald, white, deep, shallow, filmy, unfathomable. Swell, surge, break, blow, buffet, shiver, shine. Glisten in the moonlight.

I rub my foot for a second to get the feeling back, then sling my other leg over the railing. My neighbors are having another one of their endless chitchatty dinner parties. I hear music and close my eyes to let it touch the lobe of regret in my overfull brain.

We're beside the Lazy River in Denver. The Nautikon is singing his gargle-song to the child. But this time it's different; I'm the child. Jean is there too. She takes me by one hand. The Nautikon takes the other. I can feel the fine webbing between his fingers. Jean tousles my hair and I look up to see the two of them smiling down at me. I pull my knees up toward my chest so that they can swing me out over the water, like a monkey. It's fun. If I lean way, way back, I can even see Jean's face. She's upside down and laughing and everything is all right. I'm swinging back and forth and back and forth over the water, back and forth goes their little monkey. The Nautikon's hairpiece is slightly off-center, but that's okay too. Everything is okay. It's nice to see the moon painting the water at night. It's nice to let go and swing free over the water.

AQUATIC EVOLUTION

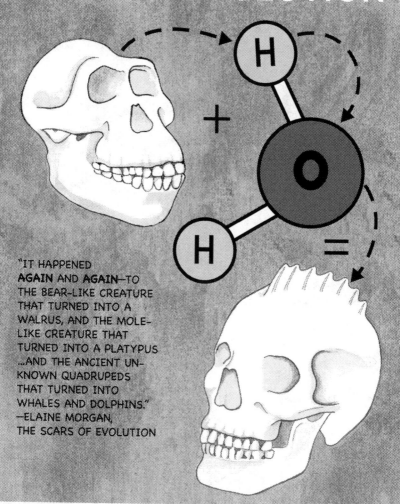

"IT HAPPENED **AGAIN** AND **AGAIN**—TO THE BEAR-LIKE CREATURE THAT TURNED INTO A WALRUS, AND THE MOLE-LIKE CREATURE THAT TURNED INTO A PLATYPUS ...AND THE ANCIENT UN-KNOWN QUADRUPEDS THAT TURNED INTO WHALES AND DOLPHINS." —ELAINE MORGAN, THE SCARS OF EVOLUTION

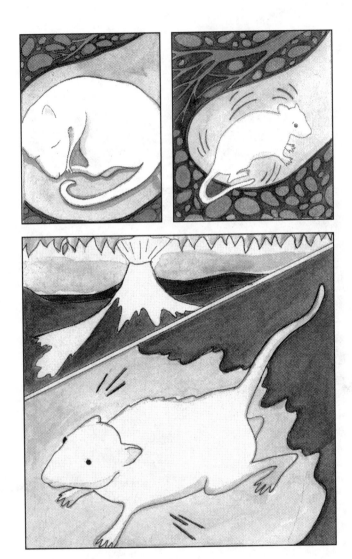

ACKNOWLEDGMENTS

Thanks to my parents, Jonathan Rotter (and his killer comics collection), Nicole Aragi, Nan Graham, Peter Carey, everyone at Hunter College, Jennifer Egan, David Rogers, the Brooklyn Public Library, and everyone who was kind enough to read this book.

Printed in the United States
By Bookmasters